the Booby Trap

Anne Browning Walker

A Pixel Entertainment Publication
www.PixelEntertainment.com

A Pixel Entertainment Publication
www.pixelentertainment.com

For Justin:
I carry your heart with me

the Booby Trap

She is too fond of books, and it has turned her brain.

—*Louisa May Alcott*

People only see what they are prepared to see.

—*Ralph Waldo Emerson*

CHAPTER ONE

Bambi had gotten used to the leers, the winks, the whistles and the surreptitious hands reached out for a feel as she went by. She suffered through the spanks, pinches, and rubs as long as they were short and not too strong. But tonight, Lou had crossed the line.

"Geez, Lou. Get your hands off my ass," she complained.

"What's the problem, sugar?" Lou asked, laughing it up with his buddies around the slick black high top table.

"I know you're feeling a little free and easy tonight since it's your birthday. But the name is Bambi. See, here it is, written right on the tag." She pointed with one long, cherry-red nail to the tag pinned to her chest. "I know you've seen it, 'cause you can barely get your eyes all the way up to my face. Keep your fingers to yourself. I'll bring you some ice water."

Lou's buddies laughed at him as she walked away, sashaying in high heels that matched her nail color and short skirt. *Damn,* her feet hurt. Thank goodness her shift was almost over. Bambi knew she wasn't meant to wander through life in six-inch pumps. She wondered how the other girls did it. It was all part of the illusion, Joe had explained to her when she first started.

"Black, chrome, and red—makes guys think of muscle cars. And you girls represent those babes they think they can bag when driving cars like that."

"What about the big screen TVs? That doesn't continue the imagery," Bambi had said. She had taken note of the psychological tactics employed by the owner of The Booby Trap.

"This is a sports bar, Bambi. I couldn't have a sports bar without TVs."

"Then why not franchise a Hooters? Wouldn't that be easier?"

"I wanted to do my own thing. Plus, all that orange and white makes the girls look like college coeds, to my mind. I wanted to build a different vibe, you see. Sexy bar, sexy women—makes a guy feel like he could be dangerous."

"Doesn't that open things up for men taking advantage of the waitresses?"

"Maybe," Joe said, "but I don't take well to that. If a guy goes too far with you, you point it out. If he keeps it up, you tell me. We take care of each other around here."

In some cases, Bambi wouldn't have believed men like Joe. But she had known him almost her whole life. She had watched him protect his employees time and again from patrons who got a little too friendly.

She passed another waitress bearing a tray full of drinks. "Be careful, Lainie. Looky Lou's feeling a little touchy tonight."

"Thanks," said the statuesque black woman. "Gonna be a long night."

"Mine's almost over," Bambi said.

"Well then, you're lucky," Lainie said as she sauntered off. Watching her, Bambi wondered how she always managed to look so self-possessed, so in control of everything even when she worked at a place like The Booby Trap. She would definitely be a good subject. Despite being only a few years older than Bambi's 27, Lainie had a certain worldliness in her wise, brown eyes. And her model-like frame made all the other waitresses jealous, including Bambi, who always felt out of place in her skin-tight work outfit. Still, the guys who told their wives that they only went to a place like The Booby Trap to watch the game constantly admired Bambi's long legs, lush blonde hair, and wide blue eyes.

Bambi returned to Lou's table with the promised glass of ice water. For the rest of her shift, Lou managed to keep his hands to himself. Well, pretty much. But Lou was one of the regulars and Joe wouldn't take well to Bambi scaring him off. Especially given the favor he had done by hiring her and then promising to let her interview the other waitresses.

Bambi stopped in his office on her way out that evening. Joe sat at his desk with his gray head bowed over an accounts book.

"Hey, Joe, I'm heading out, but I just wanted to pick up my check."

"No problem, kid," he said, lifting his deep blue eyes to hers. "But remind me why, when I'm doing you some big favor for school, do I have to pay you, too?"

"Well, I have to make rent," Bambi replied. "And eat food."

"I guess that does come in handy. Here you are." He stood up, still strong despite the extra pounds he'd packed on since she'd met him, and handed her the check. Not much, but enough to supplement her grad school stipend and much more than she had made waitressing back in college. And her much more generous tips jangled in her purse.

"Thanks. And I also thought that maybe I could start in on the interviews next week," Bambi said. She had been at The Booby Trap for a year, enough time to gather information and put together a good list of questions, which she could consolidate over the weekend.

"Sounds good. Have a good night, Bambi."

"You too, Joe," Bambi said. She waited until she was out of his office to shrug on her thick brown stadium-length winter coat. Still in her heels, she raced from the warmth of The Booby Trap to her car, thankful that the weather recently had been dry. No black ice lurking somewhere to slip her up. She jumped in the beat up old boxy Volvo, turned the key, and pumped the air up to high. She was immediately hit with an icy blast, but by the time she had ditched her heels for the comfort of some furry Uggs, the heat was coming on strong. Bambi sighed in relief and wiggled her toes inside the boots, anticipating a hot cup of tea and snuggling under her big down comforter.

She drove through the streets of Everett and back toward her Cambridge home. She had no cute little apartment just down the street from Harvard Square surrounded by the college campus and comfortable bookstores. Rather, it was beyond that and toward the weird little shops that advertised "Fresh Chickens, Live Killed" and the South American bakeries and groceries with bars on the windows. Bambi crossed her fingers and prayed that there would be a parking space near her apartment, before finally giving up and parking three streets away. She thought about running the rest of the way home, but six hours on six-inch heels made the cold less motivating. She hobbled as best she could to her small studio apartment.

Bambi always left the light on, a habit she had acquired while growing up with her mom. She shucked off her Uggs, short skirt and black tights, and pulled on her old Columbia sweatshirt and some flannel pants left behind years ago by one of her mom's boyfriends. She flopped into bed and flipped open her laptop. She pulled up a document she had begun when she first started working at The Booby Trap. It was filled with observations about the climate and the women who worked there. Although she had only written a couple of sentences after every shift, it had become a 300-page document.

I really should organize everything one of these days if I ever want to get my dissertation done, Bambi thought. But tonight was too cold and the steam heater on the far side of the room just wasn't doing its job. Before stuffing her chilly hands under the comforter and relaxing to her forty-third viewing of *Love Actually*, Bambi decided to torture herself a little. She opened her browser and scanned her bookmarks until she found what she was looking for.

In front of an old painting of Lady Godiva riding naked on her horse, the website announced "Annual Women's Studies Conference welcomes the premier scholars to London, England. Special guests including Gloria Steinem, Eve Ensler, Patricia Hill Collins, and other lights of the feminist world." Bambi especially hoped to meet Gloria Steinem, whose essay about spending 17 days as a Playboy Bunny during the 1960s had partially inspired her own work at The Booby Trap. In fact, it was when she had mentioned Steinem's undercover work to Joe while contemplating ideas for her dissertation that he had offered her a job. He had always been a good sounding board, long after he and her mother had broken up.

Bambi sighed and paged over to the accommodations site to see the deluxe suites overlooking lush parks. She couldn't stop thinking about the conference in London. She had to figure out a way to get there. But currently, Harvard was only paying for fourth- and fifth-year graduate students to attend. If Bambi wanted to get around that rule, she would have to discuss it with her thesis advisor, Dr. Lois Williams. Only Lois could convince the head of the department, Dr. Martha Cheever, that Bambi should go. She decided to speak to her advisor on Monday.

Trip Whitley kicked back in the ultra modern offices of Belles and Beaux and surveyed the girl sitting across his desk. Definitely a 10. Red hair spilled in dark curls from her ponytail and curled around a face with wide green eyes. Freckles kind of took her from gorgeous to too girl-next-door for his taste, but Trip could overlook that.

"So you said you're interested in signing up for Belles and Beaux. Really," Trip widened his brown eyes, "I don't know what a girl who looks like you needs a dating service for." The redhead blushed and laughed self-consciously. *One point, Trip.*

"Oh, you're too nice. I guess I just haven't found The One. And I've kissed my share of frogs, you know? I was thinking maybe you could do the work for me." Her eyes glittered in invitation.

Trip ran his hand through his curling light brown hair. "Oh, I'm sure I could do some good work for you. Now, why don't you give me your information so we can get started?"

The redhead leaned toward him over the desk, displaying her

creamy white skin and just a hint of cleavage. "Here's my card." She slid it to him across the desk, their fingers grazing for just a moment. "It has all my information. And I can give you whatever else you need."

Trip pushed fantasies of red hair and white skin out of his mind long enough to create the profile and take her picture for the website portion. He slipped the business card in his pocket along with the three others he had garnered over the course of the day. Not so bad, he decided. He walked her out of the small office suite when the interview was over.

"Good luck with the service," he said, as he shook her hand and lingered to trace his index finger over her wrist.

"I'm optimistic." She pulled her hand slowly from his. "It's already exceeded my expectations."

As soon as the door shut, Trip heard a very snarky echo behind him. "It's already exceeded my expectations," Trip's friend and co-worker Pat mimicked in falsetto. "How many is that for you today, man?"

"Three," Trip said, eyes still on the door. He pulled the cards out of his pocket and displayed them nonchalantly without looking at Pat.

"If only I had your luck," Pat said.

"Oh, you're not doing so bad." Trip turned around. "I'm pretty sure you've gotten at least one good card today."

"Not a one." Pat hung his head, floppy dark brown hair hiding his hazel eyes.

"Maybe it's 'cause they can sense your happiness. I told you that you should never have proposed to Allison. Throws girls off the scent."

"Don't be absurd, Trip." Pat looked up, his hazel eyes sincere.

"I don't want any other girls on my scent. Well, except for the purposes of sticking it in your face."

"Your loss," Trip shrugged and said. "You ready to call it a day?"

"Give me Liberty or give me death, as Mr. Henry would say."

"Geez, Pat, just 'cause you live in Boston doesn't mean you have to sound like that. I should take you down to Faneuil Hall and leave you with Ben Franklin. But since I'm a good friend, I won't. Liberty Hotel bar it is."

Trip put on his cashmere camel coat and headed toward his father's office.

"Heading out, Dad," he said as he stopped at the door.

"Sounds good," said the distinguished gray-haired man sitting behind the desk. In his navy blue suit, he looked every inch the Boston Brahmin. Trip knew that his family had much more country roots. But Belles and Beaux had provided a good living for the family and depended on its high class image and clientele to stay in the black. "Oh, Trip," said his father, "I was just speaking to that marketing firm we hired. They have some excellent ideas to expand our plan. They'll be here in the morning to discuss the details. Make sure you turn up on time."

"Will do, Dad." Trip tried to conceal his exasperation until he had turned around and was safely on his way to the parking garage. He already thought his starring role in the Belles and Beaux advertisements was too cheesy. He could only imagine what else might be in store. His father was content to use him as a figurehead, even though Trip knew that he could do more for the business. *I'll deal with it tomorrow*, Trip resolved as he stepped out of the elevator into the chilly garage. He shivered, but by the time the valet brought the car forward, it was toasty warm.

After driving several blocks and leaving his car once more with a valet, he ducked into Clink, the cozy brick-and-wood bar at the Liberty. Amazing how something so posh could be made out of the city's old jail, but that was Boston. The city was filled with old buildings that various preservation societies refused to allow business owners to tear down. He walked up to the bar, ignoring the stares of admiration and recognition to order his usual.

"Double bourbon on the rocks?" the bartender asked. She was pretty, with an edgy, asymmetrical haircut and brown eyes lined with dark eyeliner that looked ready for fun. The black t-shirt stretched over her compact torso reminded Trip that her body was ready for fun, too.

"You know me too well, Marissa." He smiled at her and she smiled back. She set the drink in front of him. He enjoyed his grandfather's favorite drink as he waited for Pat. Trip's grandfather had come up to Harvard Business School from Kentucky and stayed to start the first iteration of Belles and Beaux.

"Excuse me," said a skinny blonde next to him at the bar, "but aren't you Trip Whitley? From the Belles and Beaux ads?"

He turned to her. "Why, yes, I am."

"Oh, I thought so!" she crowed. "You see, my friends over there thought I was crazy. But I would know those brown eyes anywhere." She blushed.

"Is that so? Well, shouldn't we go prove them wrong?" Trip picked up his drink in one hand and held out his arm for the blonde. She smiled up into his brown eyes and took his wrist as if it were a hand. Maybe younger than he had thought. He guided her smoothly through the bar toward her friends' table.

"Pleasure to meet you ladies." He smiled. "I hear there's been some confusion as to my identity. But I want to assure you that I am indeed Trip Whitley."

"See, I told you so," the blonde said.

"How do we know?" asked an outspoken petite brunette. "You look taller than the guy in those ads. And Meg could've just put you up to it."

"I did not!" said the newly christened Meg.

"Ladies, ladies," Trip released Meg's arm as she sat down to quibble with her friend. He reached into the back pocket of his trousers, pulled out his wallet, and held up his license for the girls to see. "That proof enough?" he asked.

"Let me see," the petite brunette said. "Wait a second! It doesn't say 'Trip' on here. It says 'Alexander Stuart Whitley, III.'"

"Let me assure you, we are one and the same," Trip retrieved his license. "Trip is my nickname. I'm the third."

"Oh," cooed some of the girls. The brunette did not share their agreement, but then grudgingly acknowledged he was right. "Oh, fine," she said.

"Thanks so much." Meg beamed up at him.

"No problem at all," Trip said. "And I just realized that I have my business card in here. Why don't I buy you ladies a round of Cosmos and maybe you can all give Belles and Beaux another look."

The girls yelped in glee. *That's at least another three customers*, thought Trip. He wasn't so sure about the brunette, though.

He said his goodbyes and made his way back to the bar, where Pat was waiting.

"Pick up any more numbers from the adoring fans?"

"Don't be silly, Pat. And why do you say 'adoring fans'?"

"Trust me, man, that high-pitched squeal travels. Even through a crowded bar. Ouch." Pat covered his ears.

"Way too young for me," Trip said. "Probably some Harvard undergrads from across the bridge."

"Whatever. So, you in for the bachelor party?"

"The Booby Trap? In Everett? I really don't know why you didn't make me your best man. Screw your brother," Trip said. "Trust me, there are classier places to be found."

"Classier? Did I mention this was a bachelor party? I'm pretty sure classy isn't on the agenda. Plus, Tim says the waitresses are hotties."

Trip laughed. "Hotties? Is that a Tim term? Doesn't matter. They're not my type." He winked at Marissa. "Tonight?" she mouthed behind Pat's head. Trip nodded.

On Mondays, Bambi TA'd class for Lois. Afterwards, she followed her advisor out of the lecture hall.

"Lois, do you have a moment to spend with me? I want to discuss my research with you."

"Bambi, honestly I'm rushing from one thing to another today. Could you walk and talk?" Lois wore her usual outfit of flowy peasant skirt, sweater, and combat boots. A long braid hung down her back, with generous amounts of silver shooting through the black. She was tall and in her mid-60s, although she had the energy and sharp eyes of someone much younger.

"Of course," Bambi said, gathering her bag and setting out across the Radcliffe campus after Lois. They speed walked and dodged the underclassmen heading to their next class. "I am very interested in going to the London conference in April.

Unfortunately, I don't have the money to pay to go myself, and I know that the University is only sending fourth- and fifth-year students."

"That's true." Lois nodded her head without turning toward Bambi.

"Well, I was wondering if there were any exceptions. I've been working at The Booby Trap for over a year now, and I feel that I'm ready to go forward based on the firsthand research that I've put together. In addition, I've developed some theories regarding erotic labor that I think will further inform the field on this form of women's work."

"I see." Lois turned to peer at her, slowing but not stopping. "Have you begun interviews with the staff yet?"

"I haven't. But I feel prepared to do so shortly."

"Could you expound on those theories at this point?"

"Well, as we've discussed before, the primary studies on erotic labor and sex work have thus far focused on more overtly sexual labor. Dominatrices, women who work in strip clubs, et cetera. I'm interested in exploring the gray area in sports bars like The Booby Trap. Do the waitresses understand their work as sexual? Or is it just waitressing? Do they employ techniques similar to waitresses in, say, a less sexualized environment? And what are the motivations for going into that kind of work?" Bambi wondered if she should go on or whether she had said enough.

"It sounds to me like you have more questions than theories at this point, Bambi." With that, Bambi felt her dreams of London fading.

"I suppose I do," she said, determined to rally her chances and make one last pitch. "But I really feel that a visit to the conference in London will help me refine my lens. For example, Gloria

Steinem will be there, speaking about her work in the Playboy Club nearly 50 years ago. I want to attend that talk and speak to her about those women."

There was a pause before Lois responded. "I can see how that and other opportunities might be beneficial to you."

"They will." Bambi could hardly contain her excitement.

"Well, then, I will speak to Martha about your attending." Lois continued in a business-like manner. "You will need to draw up a summary for her that details where you are in your work."

"Thank you so much, Lois! I will have the presentation to her by Friday."

"Very good. Now, I must get going." With that, she veered off the pathway and into another building. Bambi stood for a moment, just smiling. Then, she realized how much work she had to do in order to prepare the presentation for Martha Cheever. She turned and dashed in the direction of her apartment, thankful that she had no more classes to teach that day.

The next morning, Trip arrived early to the offices. Snow had been falling hard and fast for several hours. Trip had hoped that the marketing meeting would be cancelled, but he underestimated his father's commitment to appear to be a true Bostonian.

"Gonna let a couple inches of snow get in our way?" his dad had blustered over the phone that morning. "No way. You're in New England, son, not Kentucky. See you there at nine."

So Trip had hauled himself out of bed, into the shower, and was in the office by 8:45 a.m. He knew this day was going to be a doozy. He hated when the office was closed to walk-in clients.

He relied on those walk-ins to break up the monotony of his day, which was otherwise spent staring at a computer reviewing matches, invitations, and wondering whether he should head down to IT to tell them to tweak the compatibility criteria.

Around 10, still in a foul mood, Trip made his way to the conference room for the meeting. God bless Teena, their receptionist, who had placed hot coffee and an assortment of breakfast pastries on the table. Trip eyed a cinnamon scone as he went to shake the hands of their public relations team, Edward Weldon and a woman he had never seen before, Elizabeth Pinckney. Edward Weldon was middle-aged and had been working on the Belles and Beaux account since it had switched firms nearly 10 years ago. The woman was new. Plus size, 30ish, with short black hair and wearing a severe black suit. Perhaps she was an observer.

"Welcome," his father said. "We're eager to hear your ideas for the next campaign for Belles and Beaux."

"Excellent," Edward said. "I'm going to go ahead and turn things over to Elizabeth here. Frankly, we've been astounded by her ideas for your company, and I think she can tell you best in her own words."

"Thank you, Edward." Elizabeth was all business, speaking in clipped tones and using brusque gestures. "Well, I want to showcase the success and longevity of Belles and Beaux. A number of new dating sites have come onto the market over the past 10 years, but very few matchmaking businesses have transformed with the times as successfully as yours. The ideas that I'm about to suggest may be dramatic, but I do think they do the best at reminding customers of that longevity. And your family values."

Much more than an observer, Trip thought.

"Go on," his father said. Trip sipped his coffee, wondering if or when Miss Pinckney would get to the meat of the pitch.

"Thank you, Mr. Whitley," she responded. "Well, I think my firm has been wise to realize that one of your greatest assets lies within your own family tree: Trip. Women love him, men want to be him, and on camera, he's the best advertisement you have for Belles and Beaux."

Buttering me up isn't going to do you any good at all, Trip thought. *I'm this close to putting my foot down on those commercials.*

"I think we need to play up Trip even more. I think people need to see him in a serious relationship. This relationship would provide a real showcase for Belles and Beaux. In addition to spots we could do, your company would garner a significant amount of free publicity from local and national news outlets."

"WHAT?" Trip was surprised as all of the faces in the room turned toward him. Apparently he had not yelled only in his head. He paused, and then continued "Now wait just a second. You think I'm going to trade my freedom for a couple of shots in the *Boston Herald* or *Entertainment Tonight*? If so, you have got another thing coming."

"Excuse me?" Elizabeth Pinckney interjected. "Perhaps I should point out something else."

Like a completely new idea? Trip thought.

"Please," his father said.

"Well, I hesitate to say it, but your biggest asset could easily become your biggest liability. Trip's being out on the Boston scene has bought you a lot of free publicity over the years. But what does it say for a matchmaking service that fails to make a match for its own son, the most charming man on the planet?"

"Dad, are you going to let her continue like this?" Trip asked.

"Trip, I suggest you leave the room. Everyone else, too. I need to talk this matter over in private with Mr. Weldon and Miss Pinckney."

"I have a hard time understanding that, Dad. As something that significantly involves my participation, I feel I should be involved in this discussion," Trip said, trying to keep his anger at bay.

"Out," his father said.

Trip grabbed his coffee and scone and stalked out of the conference room. As he left, his father closed the door. Trip paced the hallway, hoping to hear some of the discussion inside.

"C'mon, bud," Pat tapped him on the shoulder. "I know you can't hear anything. Let's go back to my office."

Trip followed his friend but looked back toward the conference room, where people who wouldn't even let him in the room were determining his future. "What the hell, Pat?" he exploded once they had safely reached Pat's office. "I was looking for a bigger role in the company and they give me this?!"

"It's ridiculous, I know," Pat said. "And your Dad will see it, too."

"It's not just ridiculous, it's fucking insane!" Trip paced back and forth across Pat's small office.

"Calm down, bud."

"How can I? They won't even let me in the room."

"C'mon, Trip, you had to see this coming." Trip balked but Pat continued. "Think about your lifestyle."

"What about it?" Trip whirled and looked Pat directly in the eye.

"Look, you knew you were the face of Belles and Beaux. Some part of you had to know that that wouldn't just involve

THE BOOBY TRAP 17

dating women, it would involve getting serious with them, too."

"I'm doing that in my own time."

"Really? 'Cause Ms. Pinckney is right—"

"Don't you dare use her name and the word 'right' in the same sentence."

"Fine. It's appealing now, but what about in five years. Or 10? There comes a point when an old guy going on dates isn't fun anymore."

"Be careful there. I'm only 30. And Pat, you're the same age as me."

"And I'm getting married. To the girl I love. Have you ever thought about that? Be honest."

Trip scowled. "No."

"Well, maybe you should open yourself up to the possibility of it, at least. I know Connie Bradford broke your heart in high school, then Maddy Hart used you a couple years ago. I think they did a number on you, man. You need to get past it, give a girl more than a couple dates and a good lay."

"Whatever." Trip began to walk out the door.

"You still coming tonight?" Pat asked.

"Yeah," Trip said. "I'm gonna need to unwind after this day from hell. If they'll even let a decrepit old bachelor like me into the club."

"Trip . . ." Pat called, but Trip ignored him and made his way back to his own office to stew. Why didn't Pat have his back on this?

For the rest of the day, Trip was hardly able to get much work done. Although Belles and Beaux had opened to clients in the afternoon, only a depressing trickle wandered in from the snowy streets. Trip had the opportunity to get the number of a leggy brunette, but his bad mood killed any sparks between them. He was contemplating calling it a day and blaming it on the snow when his father appeared at his office door.

"Can I come in?" he asked.

"Sure, go ahead. Though why you asked, I don't know, because clearly my wishes don't mean anything to you."

"Now, Trip, that's absurd," his father said, taking a seat across from him. "I think Miss Pinckney was onto something there. I stayed back to hash it out because I knew you wouldn't be reasonable."

"Miss Pinckney, Miss Pinckney. Geez, you and Pat just can't stop talking about her."

"Trip, I need you to listen to me. Both for you and for this business, you need a little bit more stability in your life. You keep telling me you want a bigger role. But how can I depend on you when your social life is a mess? You can't keep dating a different girl every week, especially not these society butterflies who only seem to care about which designer dress they will wear to the next event."

"Oh, I'm shallow now, too, am I? I'll just start making a list. Shallow, decrepit, a liability . . . shall I go on?"

"That's enough." Trip heard something in that tone he hadn't heard since he was 15 and had "borrowed" his father's new Maserati for a joy ride that didn't turn out to be very joyful in the end. "I'm not asking you to marry anyone, and I think I'm being reasonable here. All I'm asking is that you date one woman for a decent length of nine months. If it works out, great for you, great for the company. If not, you can call it quits in August."

"Oh, only nine months of slavery," Trip mocked.

"Yes. Nine months."

THE BOOBY TRAP 19

"And just who am I supposed to be taking on these dates? I assume I don't get to choose there, either."

"I'm not unreasonable. Of course you can choose your own girlfriend."

"How generous—"

"Of course, she must be up to Belles and Beaux standards," his father interrupted. "If you'd like, I'll talk to Teena and have her pull up a list of eligible young women from our site."

"That won't be necessary."

"You could always take Connie out."

Trip grimaced. He and Connie Bradford had dated all through high school. His parents had the money and Connie's had the lineage. Both sets of parents had been thrilled, until they broke up at the end of their senior year. "Dad, it's not going to be Connie."

"Very well. You can use her as a guide. Your first date will be skating on the pond on the Common next Saturday. Be there."

"And if I'm not?"

"Well, Trip, your role in this company will diminish, not grow."

CHAPTER TWO

Bambi nervously smoothed the wrinkles out of her brown suit. Although it wasn't comfortable, she had bought it at Marshalls because it deemphasized her breasts and made her appear more academic. For the umpteenth time, she cursed her mother for naming her Bambi. That name on top of her pin-up body would prevent anyone from thinking of her as a professor. She double-checked her beat-up black messenger bag for the notes on her dissertation, knowing that her one shot at going to London would be this conversation with the department head.

She stood as Martha Cheever came around the corner. She was small and round, with short, curly, graying blonde hair. Her green eyes were piercing and her purple flowing clothes made her presence seem large and regal despite the fact that she was quite petite. Bambi had sometimes thought of her as the queen of the Amazons instead of the head of the Women's Studies

Department. "Bambi Benson, correct?" she asked. Bambi nodded. "Come on in."

Bambi stood and walked into Martha's office. It seemed classically academic. An oriental rug lay on the diagonal, bookcases were crammed with books, and a fern overflowing its pot brought a little of the outside in. Bambi knew from her limited experiences with Martha that the woman was much more organized than her office suggested.

"Welcome, Bambi. What can I do for you today?" Martha looked over her massive mahogany desk at Bambi.

"Thank you for seeing me, Martha," Bambi extended her hand and shook Martha's. She took a seat across the desk. "I came to see you about the London conference."

"Why, yes. We are all quite excited about this year's event. Harvard, of course, will be sending a large contingent."

Bambi let her hopes rise a little. A large contingent meant that she might join them. "That's just wonderful. As you know, I am hoping to attend myself. Of course, I would need some funding from the University."

"I see," Martha said. Bambi couldn't read her expression, so she plowed on.

"Yes. You see, I've just started my dissertation work, and I really believe that this conference will give me the opportunity to refine and focus my idea by speaking to a broad range of experts."

"I've seen your summary. I've also spoken with Dr. Williams. My question is: do you think you might have anything to present at the conference? Either from that or from your master's thesis?"

"I have some initial literature review information and firsthand observations that I have made into a presentation."

Bambi reached into her bag and pulled out the short presentation. She handed it to Martha.

Martha pulled the reading glasses from her head and quickly perused the presentation. Bambi fidgeted with her bag while waiting for the department head to finish.

"I see," Martha looked up. "I'm not entirely sure how much this can add to the discussion without the inclusion of additional interviews."

"I haven't yet started that process," Bambi said, but pressed on. "Even so, I've been working on my research for months now, and I'm confident that the conference's presentation regarding women in the workplace would be a big help as I continue down that road. So I really think—"

"Bambi," Martha put her hand up to silence Bambi. "I appreciate your enthusiasm, I do. But I think that there are more worthy candidates, further along in their research than you."

"Oh," Bambi said. She could feel a lump forming in her throat.

Martha continued, "Of course, I do agree that any gathering of experts would help someone in your position, but I'm afraid we don't have the funds to sponsor you. If you would be able to pay for travel, room, and board yourself, we might be able to help out with conference fees." Martha smiled at Bambi. Bambi struggled to smile back, knowing that Martha was trying to be helpful.

"I appreciate your offer. I'll have to"—she paused to swallow—"to see if I can get the money together to go. I'll let you know. Thank you for your time," she said, gathering up her bag and overcoat. Bambi walked swiftly out of the office, down the corridor, and took the stairs into the deserted tunnels below school. She felt grateful that there weren't many other students around to see her. Bambi took a few deep breaths to prevent the tears from coming. All of her dreams of spring in London died.

Bambi drove to The Booby Trap that night still stinging from Martha Cheever's rejection. The balls of her feet burned from her last night in heels, so from the beginning she knew that it would not be a good night. She grabbed the red shoes from under the passenger seat and decided to wait to change from her Uggs until the last possible moment.

"Hey Joe," she waved as she went past his office.

"Bambi, wait a sec."

"Yeah?" She stopped midstride.

"There's a big bachelor party coming in in about an hour. You think you and Lainie can handle them? About 20 guys."

Great. Perfect. Her night was just getting better. "Of course, Joe. We'll stay on top of them." She headed through to the small breakroom near the kitchen.

She sat down and groaned as she pulled off the Uggs.

"That bad, huh?" Lainie asked as she sauntered in.

"Worse," Bambi said. "I don't know how you do it. You were here even later than I was."

"Honey, my feet have almost become Barbie feet. It feels strange to wear flats."

"You hear about the bachelor party?"

"Yep. Joe tagged me on the way in. More tips, hopefully."

"More grabs probably." The girls laughed.

"Well, come on, honey," Lainie stuffed her purse into a locker and reached out to pull a reluctant Bambi to her feet.

"Okay. I'm coming."

Half an hour later, Bambi felt the burn in her toes all the way to her shoulders. She stepped her aching foot out of one shoe when she stood at the counter to give orders to one of the cooks in the kitchen.

When she returned to the seating area, she saw a tall guy who looked a little familiar make his way toward the table prepared for the bachelor party.

"Isn't that Trip Whitley?" Lainie sidled up to Bambi. "I don't know what he's doing in a place like this."

"Trip who?"

"Trip Whitley, honey. From those Belles and Beaux ads. I can't believe you don't know who he is."

"Oh, I guess I've seen him before. I don't watch a lot of TV."

Jeannie, the hostess, approached them. Younger than either Bambi or Lainie, she nonetheless managed the front of the house with organized efficiency. "He's here for the bachelor party," she said. "I figured since the table was already set up, I could seat him there. That okay?"

"Sure," Bambi said. "I got him." She stepped back into her left heel and plastered a smile on her face. She approached Trip Whitley. *Attractive as hell*, she thought. Long, lean body in clothes that looked like they'd been made for him. Brown hair with just a hint of curl. And brown eyes that could've turned liquid any moment. But not right now—they were hard as rock. Excellent—a guy who could finally tip her right and he was in the worst mood of his comfortable life. Well, maybe she could change that. "Hiya, angel, what can I do you for?"

"Bourbon on the rocks. Double." He didn't even glance up at her.

"Bad day?"

"My day," he said, looking up and raking his eyes over her body in a way that made Bambi wish more than ever that she were covered by more than the skimpy outfit, "is none of your goddamn business."

Bambi forced the smile to stay on her face. "Well then, I'll just grab you that bourbon and be back in two shakes." She intentionally swung her hips in an exaggerated motion as she walked off to show that she didn't give a damn about his bad mood. He wasn't the only one entitled to it. She would get him his drink and leave the poor little rich boy to his sulk.

"What's he like?" Lainie asked when Bambi had made it over to the bar.

"An asshole. Not surprising. Where do these guys get off?"

"Surprising to me. He always seems so laid back in the commercials."

"Lainie, please don't tell me that you believe everything you see on TV."

"Of course not, honey. I just hoped, is all. He is one good-looking asshole. It's a pity," she smiled.

"Well, I think this particular one might need some special attention tonight if we don't want him to ruin the mood of the whole party. We'll have to keep the bourbons coming and hope that he's not more moody drunk than he is sober."

Trip sipped his drink and thanked God that he was not one of the regular patrons of The Booby Trap. Other men might need a little liquid courage and a little fake companionship to make their days better, but not him. He knew plenty of girls who would listen to his problems and make all the appropriate noises.

But somehow, when he tore out of the office early, he hadn't felt like calling a single one of them. So he'd driven around in the snow, finally deciding that he needed a stiff drink even before Pat's bachelor party.

And boy, was he right. About forty-five minutes after he had first set foot in The Booby Trap, the party was in full swing. Pat's brother and high school buddies were drinking cheap beer by the gallon and eating an assortment of wings in chrome baskets that had been spread out on the table.

The one good thing he could say for the place was that the blonde waitress with the big boobs had managed to keep his glass full with some pretty decent bourbon. She seemed to read his mind, always appearing just as the thought of another glass was forming in his head. That said, those thoughts were taking longer to form with each passing glass. *Which wasn't a bad thing*, Trip thought, as he finished his third glass. Or was it his fourth?

"You look like you're feeling a little better." Pat had moved from one end of the table to the other to sit by Trip. He wore his goofy drunk grin along with a plastic ball and chain around his neck.

"Yep," Trip held up his empty glass, "This stuff seems to make everything a little better."

"I probably haven't gotten this drunk since college," Pat laughed.

Trip tried to focus on the glass still raised in his hand. "Me neither. But screw Ms. Pinckney and my father. I'm gonna have another."

"What'd you say, champ?" the blonde waitress had reappeared. She bent down between Trip and Pat, exposing a fair amount of cleavage. Pat stared openly.

"I said, I'm gonna have another," Trip said. "By the way, how do you always manage to be there?"

"It's my job." She smiled and turned to Pat. "Now what can I get you, groom-to-be?"

"Ummm," Pat seemed mesmerized by her boobs. Trip laughed at his normally straight-laced friend's regression into a 13-year-old boy. "Beer?"

She reached in one fluid motion for a pitcher across the table and emptied it into Pat's glass. "Let me get you boys another pitcher while I refill Mr. Whitley's bourbon." Before she could walk away, Trip reached out a hand to graze her hip bone. She stood for a moment before turning to face him. "Something else I can get for you, champ?"

Trip noticed she sounded a little annoyed, but he was confused. "How'd you know my name? And why don't I know yours?"

"Why, of course I know you," the waitress batted her eyes. If Trip didn't know better, he'd think she was playing him. "You're Trip Whitley, from all those ads. And even cuter in person."

"But what's your name?"

"Silly, you must know what it is. It's been right here all night." She tapped her name tag. "Bambi."

"Oh," Trip snorted. Now he knew he was being played. "Okay, *Bambi*," he said the name as if it were an inside joke between them. But as he watched her walk away again, he could swear he had seen her eyes roll. He didn't have much time to consider that before Pat punched him on the shoulder.

"Say, looks like you guys got something going on." Pat winked.

"I don't think so, bud."

"Well, she's real pretty," Pat said before he was distracted by the return of the tall, black waitress to the other end of the table.

It was all Bambi could do not to stomp all the way back to the bar. Guys like that really burned her. Not the alcohol-soaked groom, whose eyes lingered but whose hands stayed glued to his sides or the table, but that prick Trip Whitley. He wouldn't notice someone outside his own social circle if they kicked him in the shins. Which Bambi was ready to do after that nonsense about her name.

"Whoa, Bambi," Joe sauntered up to her. "You're gonna give yourself away if you take this job too seriously."

"Am I that obvious?" She turned toward him, taking her right foot out of the offending heel and rubbing it against her left calf.

"A little bit, sugar, a little bit. I thought you were used to this place by now."

"I did, too, until that asshole Trip Whitley walked in."

Joe rubbed her arm while taking in the Friday night rush. "Don't let guys like that push you around. Just remember, you're worth your weight in gold."

"Thanks, Joe."

"Order up." The bartender pushed the full pitcher and double bourbon toward Bambi.

"Well, that's my cue," she stuck her right foot back into its shoe, smiled at Joe, and took off again for the problem table. When she set the glass down in front of her bothersome customer, she noticed his brown eyes, cloudy with alcohol, had begun to clear, and he was looking at her strangely.

"Water next time, okay? Or coffee would be even better."

"You got it, angel." Bambi forced a smile onto her face. He kept looking at her. But although his gaze was aimed at her, it didn't seem that he was looking at her as a person. No big deal, usually, but with Trip Whitley, it made her uneasy. *What was going on in his head?*

Halfway through Trip's second mug of coffee, Bambi noticed that the party was winding down. The men fumbled for their wallets and tossed bills on the table. As she headed over to retrieve empty glasses and pitchers and press a glass of ice water on the groom-to-be, she heard Trip Whitley calling to her.

"Whatcha want, champ? I'll grab you a fresh mug of coffee as soon as I get some of this cleared." She had watched him as he sobered up. She had learned firsthand from her mother that most men were worse drunk than sober, but somehow, with those brown eyes boring into her, she had gotten more and more wary of Trip Whitley as he sobered up.

"Coffee's good, but I wanted to know when you get off."

"Too late for you," Bambi said with a smile. She had had to fend off numerous offers like this during her time at The Booby Trap. Trip Whitley was no different from any other guy.

Trip looked at her, eyes hard. "I doubt it," he said.

"Well then, too late for me. Taking care of all you boys tonight has left me one tired girl. But maybe you can come back Sunday? We have all those big screens showing football and I'll be here from four till closing." Always a good idea to get a paying customer back in, and especially good to get someone like Trip back into an environment Bambi knew she could control.

"Sunday, you say?" He still eyed her like a lab specimen.

"You bet." Bambi sighed and felt like she had dodged a bullet. For some reason, the prospect of being alone with this guy scared her a bit. She walked away with the tray full of empty glasses. Soon the table was free of the bachelor party, and, most important, of Trip Whitley.

"Thank God he's gone," she said to Lainie.

"Honey, I don't know what your problem was," Lainie said. "He seemed fine to me. Definitely not much of a toucher and less of a looker than most of the guys who come in here."

"I don't know," Bambi said. "He just got under my skin."

Trip shivered outside The Booby Trap and waited for "Bambi" or whatever her name was to come out. He thought about jumping in his car and taking advantage of the heat, but then worried that he might miss her if he did. Trip went over his plan again. Although formulated in something of a drunken haze, he congratulated himself on its reasonableness and potential effectiveness. Dating a cocktail waitress at a Hooters knockoff would send his father and that condescending PR rep into apoplexies. He found himself wishing that her name really was Bambi. Because that would make it even better.

When the lights went off, the waitresses began to leave the building in pairs. Most didn't pay attention to the lone man in the parking lot. Trip kept searching for the busty blonde, but as the trickle slowed, he began to worry that someone had tipped her off and that she was waiting him out. Finally, he spotted her, walking out with the other woman who had served their table. It was a miracle he recognized her at all, since she had covered herself with the ugliest brown coat he had ever seen and exchanged her heels for suede boots that were clearly designed more for warmth than fashion.

"Bambi!" he hailed her. She turned around, surprised to see him.

"I thought you'd gone home."

"I'm persistent. I told you I wanted to talk to you."

"And I told you Sunday was a better time. I'm tired. I'll see you then."

"I don't want to come back Sunday."

"Too bad for you." She stalked toward an ugly white Volvo that had clearly seen better days. "Bye, Lainie."

"See you, honey. You sure you got this?" Trip saw the other waitress nod her head toward him.

"She's safe with me," he said. "I'm a gentleman."

"Well, I don't know about that," Bambi said. "But yeah, I'm sure. I can handle this guy. Plus, Joe's still inside if I need reinforcements."

The friend looked as though she didn't believe Bambi, but left anyway. Trip saw her put her cell phone to her ear as she drove away, no doubt calling the guy, Joe, inside.

"Wanna talk in my car?" Trip asked. "Much warmer."

"Do you think I'm crazy?" Bambi asked. "Number one, I don't know if you are a gentleman, and an enclosed space is just an invitation. Number two, you drank so much bourbon tonight I don't want you anywhere near a wheel anytime soon. Talk."

"Okay, fine. I'm Trip, like you already know. And what's your real name? 'Cause I know it can't be Bambi."

She glared at him. "Well, it is. Believe me, because I'm not giving you any other name."

"Fine, Bambi." Trip could see her foot tapping and knew that he would have to choose his words carefully. Otherwise she would bolt into that car and he would have to find another girl, one not nearly so perfect. "I need you to help me out."

"You need a ride home? I can call you a cab."

"No. I need a date. Or multiple dates to be exact."

"Nice try, Trip," Bambi said. "But I get those offers all the time. Thanks but no thanks." She stuck her car key into the door.

"Wait," Trip said. "This is different." She turned back toward him with her hand on her hip. "I don't know if you know this, but I'm kind of the face for my family's dating company, Belles and Beaux."

"I've seen the commercials."

"Okay, well, they think that I need to start dating someone. Seriously."

"Excellent, bud. But I'm not interested in your personal life."

"It's not my personal life, at least not to them. It's business. Anyway, I want you to be the girl I date seriously."

"And why in the hell would I want to do that? You're one of the worst customers I've had all week. And in a place like this, that's saying something."

"I could pay you." At this, she closed her eyes and put her head in her hands. Trip knew instantly he had said something wrong. She looked up again.

"Listen, asshole, just because I work at this place doesn't mean I'm some kind of prostitute or escort or something like that."

"God!" Trip said. "I didn't mean it like that."

"Well, that's what it sounded like to me."

"I meant it like an acting gig. I mean, we would have to kiss and hold hands and stuff like that, but nothing beyond that. I swear."

"No way in hell."

"But . . ." Trip watched her unlock the car, slide in, and slam the door.

"No." She drove off, leaving Trip standing alone in the parking lot. He looked down at his shoes and wished that she had said yes. That would have been the payback he was looking for. *Oh well*, Trip thought, *I'll just have to think of another plan. But who else would fit the bill as well as a waitress named Bambi?*

CHAPTER THREE

The bone weariness Bambi had felt walking out of The Booby Trap had been replaced by energy from fury. Who did Trip Whitley think he was? His wealth didn't entitle him to treat people like objects, using them and paying for them. She was angry at herself for not driving away earlier, for spending some of her precious time talking to a man she knew she didn't like. Somehow, despite her best instincts, she had been drawn in by his bitter expression when he had mentioned that his personal life wasn't personal. Then he had turned out to be the snake she had known he was since she had first laid eyes on his lanky, athletic frame.

Boys like Trip, though, were pretty easy to deal with compared to the creeps her mother dated. Despite the heat in the car, Bambi shivered when she thought about the man in her mother's life just before she left for college. Like she always did, she wrenched her mind away from that night nearly 10 years ago and focused on the present. Besides, she knew that anger was much more empowering than fear.

Bambi maintained her anger during the treacherous drive home in the snow, probably going a little faster than was safe. It kept her warm on her walk up to her small apartment, and powered her through a cleaning frenzy despite the fact that her feet were screaming bloody murder. Mid-frenzy, she got the idea to chronicle Trip Whitley's proposition in the notes for her dissertation. If only she could humiliate him publicly. But when she flopped down on the bed and opened her laptop, sumptuous London hotel rooms from the conference page she had pulled up the night before stared back at her.

"Damn," she said out loud.

No funds for London. Bambi felt something that was steel inside her collapse into putty. She forgot her anger for a moment in the sting of Martha's rejection and her own broken promise to herself that she would be spending the spring in London. How would she get the money? Waitressing at The Booby Trap just covered her expenses. *If only . . .*

"Damn, damn, damn," she repeated.

Trip Whitley's proposition began to look pretty good. But could she really pretend to like that asshole for any period of time? *Once a pig, always a pig*, she thought. At least he would be predictable. But taking Trip Whitley's money wouldn't be enough. There had to be something else she could get out of this. She thought back to their scene in the parking lot, his smirk when he said her name.

Bambi sat up and heard herself say "Oh!" when the idea hit her. It could make everything worthwhile. When Trip Whitley had made his offer, he'd thought he was talking to some bimbo waitress. But for once, Bambi's name and appearance were working in her favor. The more she thought about it, the more Bambi realized that she just might be able to teach him how dangerous it was to make assumptions. That man was going to get more than he bargained for. Way more.

On Monday morning, Bambi pulled on the black-and-pink patterned wrap dress she almost never wore because it emphasized her chest. Then she grabbed her knee-high black boots with the kitten heels and headed off to TA her class. The few boys taking the course to fulfill a requirement ogled her, so Bambi knew the look was perfect.

After class, she hopped on the T at Harvard Square and took the Red Line into downtown Boston. On Cambridge Street, in the Back Bay, she found the offices of Belles and Beaux exactly where Google Maps had indicated. She pushed through the glass door into the ultramodern office suite, at odds with the quaint neighborhood outside, and marched to the reception desk.

"Hello," she said, widening her eyes. "I'm here to see Trip Whitley."

"Do you have an appointment?" the receptionist asked, clearly used to people coming in and asking for the guy in the ads.

"No, I don't."

"Well, I'm sorry, but Mr. Whitley is in a meeting right now and doesn't have any more free time today. I'm sure we could get you set up with Mr. McCready."

"I appreciate that," Bambi said as she turned on her brightest smile, "but I did run into Mr. Whitley over the weekend and he assured me he'd take care of me *personally*." Bambi forced a giggle and a blush. "I don't mind waiting. Do you mind just telling him that Bambi is here?"

"Bambi?" the receptionist seemed skeptical.

"Yes. Like the Disney movie." Bambi kept her smile bright.

"Okay. I will do that."

"Excellent!" Bambi clapped her hands a little, then decided she might be overacting. But not so bad so far. She walked over to one of several elegant, modern chairs, and sat down. She paged through the magazines and picked up a *Cosmopolitan* from the stack. It featured some scantily clad actress on the front and an electric blue headline that read "50 Ways to Drive Him Crazy in Bed." She thought of the article on the changing role of women in the household that she ought to have read by that afternoon. It would be much more useful to read than *Cosmo*, but she couldn't spoil the bimbo illusion for Trip. Not yet, anyway.

Soon, Trip Whitley and the groom-to-be walked through the lobby. The groom did a double-take when he saw Bambi, immediately recognizing her. Trip smiled at her without recognition and turned his flirtatious grin on the receptionist, but then the groom tugged on his shoulder just as the receptionist intentionally cleared her throat.

"Ah, Mr. Whitley, there's someone here to see you."

"Trip . . ." the groom interrupted the receptionist as Trip turned around. Bambi felt the full impact of his surprise.

"Trip Whitley," she stood and smiled. "I'm so glad you're in. And I see your friend works with you. How nice."

Bambi noticed that Trip recovered quickly, replacing his open mouth with a smile she imagined he used on girls all the time. To her taste, there was a little too much sense of the cat that got the canary. "I can't say I thought I'd see you again," he said.

"What are you doing here?" the groom asked. "Did we leave something?"

Bambi laughed. "No. After you boys left, Trip and I discussed some . . . business?" she looked askance at Trip to find out if that was the right word. "I came in today to give him my answer."

"Bambi's right, Pat," Trip said to his friend, who stared dumbstruck at both of them. Then he turned to Bambi. "Shall we complete this discussion in my office?"

"Sounds perfect," Bambi said with a smile. Trip narrowed his eyes at her, as if he expected her to stomp his toes with her kitten heel, but led the way back to his office. As they made the short trip, she noticed that he wore much the same outfit as he had the day before. He had exchanged the charcoal suit for a navy pinstripe and blue shirt and he wore a silver tie today, but he still had that expression that made him seem a little more dangerous than the average businessman.

Bambi noticed that the modern décor of the office extended into Trip's space. Glass desk, simple black chairs, sleek silver Apple laptop. Trip seemed to feel much more in control of things once he sat behind the desk. Better for her, she thought. Easier to catch him off guard.

"Based on our previous conversation, I hadn't expected to see you again, Bambi," he leaned back in the desk chair.

"Well," Bambi said as she reached a hand up to tangle a strand of blonde hair around her index finger, "perhaps I was hasty. I may not have thought things through. I thought maybe we could discuss details today a little bit more rationally?"

Trip smiled, playing magnanimous. "I'm glad that your brain got the better of your emotions," he said. Bambi wanted to spit at him, but kept her grin in place and twiddled her hair a little bit more for effect. "To be honest, you'd be doing me a real favor. Belles and Beaux is starting a new ad campaign, which would build on previous spots by portraying a lasting romance between me and some girl . . . which would be you."

"For how long?" Bambi asked.

"Nine months. Dates every weekend or so, affectionate PDA, but nothing tasteless. Of course, cameras will be around, that's part of the deal. In fact, we will be working with our own camera crew—still and video."

"So we act like we're falling in love?"

"That's the deal. For those cameras and whatever other cameras might be around."

"What about physical stuff?"

"Minor. Kissing, holding hands. I promise we won't have to release a sex tape."

Bambi fought the urge to wrinkle her nose. "Okay. What's the compensation?" There was no way she was going to do anything for Trip Whitley if she couldn't get the money for London.

"I'll pay you $500 a date."

That wouldn't work. Bambi wouldn't be able to get enough together before the conference. "I need $5,000 up front," she said. "Consider it a down payment for the first 10 dates."

"Fine," Trip said after a pause. Then he asked, "You got yourself in some kind of jam?"

"No," Bambi said. "Just planning a little something for myself."

"Okay," he pulled his checkbook from an inside pocket. "Who do I make it out to?"

"Bambi Benson."

"Got it." Trip finished writing and handed the check toward her. Bambi reached up to take it before realizing that she had forgotten one crucial detail.

"I still get to keep working at The Booby Trap, right?" No way was she going to shoot herself in the foot by giving up her dissertation research for the conference. "I mean, I need to make sure I still have a job after this is over."

Trip's smile spread a little wider, if possible. "I wouldn't dream of keeping you away. First date's Saturday at two p.m., Frog Pond, ice skating."

"I'll be there." Bambi took the check and walked out of the office. It had been easier than she had anticipated. Although, to convince the cameras, she was going to have to find ways to bear Trip Whitley for long periods of time without wanting to punch him.

From the exit of the Park Street Station, Bambi could see the hubbub already gathering around the Frog Pond. The closer she got, the more she realized the magnitude of this PR stunt. But there was no going back at this point. She had already spent a large portion of the $5,000 on plane tickets and hotel reservations for the trip to London. True to her word, Martha had found money from the University to cover the conference fees, but Bambi would still have to watch her pennies in the expensive city of London. Thinking of the lush hotel suite that promised a view of the Tower of London, Bambi marched toward the Frog Pond.

"Bambi!" Trip headed toward her and took her hand in his gloved one. "I'm so happy to see you." He looked every inch the spoiled rich boy she knew he was in a cashmere coat, expensive jeans, and designer sunglasses. She tugged self-consciously at her worn black coat.

"Who are all these people, Trip?" Bambi asked, trying to look adoring instead of irritated and frightened. They approached the waiting group of people.

"Well first, Bambi, this is Miss Pinckney," Trip pointed to a larger woman with a short black ponytail, about Bambi's age, dressed in a severe black coat over what looked like a black suit. "She's from the PR firm."

"Pleasure to meet you, Bambi," the woman extended her hand. "But to you I'm Elizabeth."

Trip steered Bambi away from Elizabeth Pinckney before she could respond. "And these two," he motioned to one man holding a large video camera and another holding a still camera, "are Jim and Jack Farrell. They're taking the shots of us. You ready to do some skating?"

"Sure, champ, let's do this." Trip reached for her hand and she tentatively let him take it. She followed Trip to a small structure where they rented ice skates. He kept his hand clenched around hers, only briefly removing it to pay the man at the counter.

"You ever done this before?" He grabbed the skates and headed toward a park bench not far from Elizabeth Pinckney and the two cameramen.

"Of course," Bambi said. "I grew up in Charlestown." He didn't need to know how few times she and her mother had been to the skating rink.

"Trip!" Elizabeth Pinckney called. "We need a shot of you helping her with her skates."

Trip bent down and cradled Bambi's calf in his hand. Which

felt entirely too good for any hand of Trip Whitley's. "Thanks," she said. Bambi wondered why her body was betraying her brain. She knew better than to be attracted to this guy.

"All part of the service," he said as he smiled up at her. "Now, let's hit the ice." He pulled on his own skates and took her hand as they tottered toward the ice. It was filled with shrieking children of all ages. Bambi watched girls and boys barely old enough to walk pushing upside-down plastic buckets for balance. Once her feet were on the ice, she felt herself go wobbly, but Trip steadied her by transferring his hand to her waist. She hadn't been ice skating in far too long. "Why did you change your mind after all?"

Bambi knew she couldn't tell him the truth. "Well, I realized that hanging out with a cute guy couldn't be the worst thing ever. Plus, I needed the money. For a girl's trip."

"Oh. Can I come along?" he winked.

"Give it up, Trip. Not going to happen."

Trip guided her around the small pond, deftly avoiding the careening children who seemed to skate either at a snail's pace or like hockey players across the blue line. He kept his hand snugly at her waist, and Bambi began to think she might get used to the easy rhythm that had developed.

"Wait a second!" She slapped Trip's hand from her body. Somehow, it had meandered from her waist to her bottom.

"Gotta keep it real for the cameras." He nodded in the direction of Jim and Jack.

"Not that real." Bambi skated away from him. Trip caught up easily since Bambi couldn't seem to skate more than eight feet without needing to cling to the railing.

"C'mon, Bambi. We have a deal."

"That deal does not extend to your hands on my ass."

"Fine. But the cameras are rolling. So will you at least take my hand?"

Conference money, London trip of your dreams, Bambi repeated to herself. She grabbed his hand and was amazed at how it seemed to steady her. Until they both looked ahead and realized that they were on a collision course with one of the small skaters pushing a bucket. Bambi grasped for the railing to stop herself while Trip tried to take them wide around the child, and they both landed hard on the ice.

"Ouch," Bambi said, rubbing her tailbone. But she was distracted from her own pain by the sight of Trip, limbs akimbo, sprawled across the ice. She began to laugh uncontrollably. Jim and Jack rushed over with their cameras to catch her glee. For a moment, Bambi saw irritation cross Trip's face before he realized the cameras were just over the railing. He began laughing as Bambi teetered over to him. "Can I help you up?" she asked. She sure liked this position, standing over him.

"I guess I have no choice but to let you be the chivalrous one." Trip accepted her hand, but Bambi noticed that he managed to pick himself up without exerting much pressure on her arm muscles.

"Women can be very chivalrous," Bambi said once they were both standing. "Think of Boudicca. She united the Britons in revolt against the Romans in 61 AD when they failed to respect her husband's will. Although . . ." Bambi paused, "I don't know if I would even want to be considered chivalrous at all. There was very little for women to do, you know, in the code of chivalry, aside from sit around and listen to all the adventures knights had. That couldn't have been any fun."

Bambi realized that she had been concentrating on putting

one foot in front of the other. But one look at Trip's baffled expression told her she had let her mouth get away with her. *Damn!*

"I don't think I've heard of this Boudy woman. You know a lot about her, though," he said.

Bambi turned crimson. "Oh, it's nothing. Just something I read somewhere . . . umm . . . how about we go sit down? I'm ready for a break. What about you?"

"Sure," Trip said. Bambi sighed, relieved that she had managed to distract him. Soon they were back on the bench, subject to the bright lights of Jim's video camera and the quick flashes of Jack's still camera. Or did she have them backwards?

Then she felt Trip's warm hand on her calf again. Something about that made her shiver. Bambi hoped it was the cold. Because there was no way it was Trip Whitley.

"I studied Boudicca in college," Elizabeth Pinckney piped up. Bambi had almost forgotten about the woman. "Is that where you learned about her?"

"College?" Trip asked.

Bambi slanted a look at Elizabeth. Then she turned a smile on him. "Just junior college." She saw Elizabeth glaring at her, but the woman did keep her mouth shut. "Come on, let's get back on the ice."

Trip followed her and soon they were skating. *Ooh, that was close.* Bambi was glad to have distracted Trip temporarily, but she didn't want any more uncomfortable questions. So she started babbling, trying to piece together some of the more inane conversations she had heard on Harvard's campus and inside The Booby Trap. "So my girlfriends and I went out last night and we thought we saw Tom Brady. Can you imagine? My friend Kelly swore it was him." She leaned in. "I think she even made out with him."

"That so?" Trip asked, but it was clear he wasn't invested in the conversation. His eyes had glazed over. Perfect.

"But when I looked at him, I was like no way, that is not Tom Brady. I would know Tom Brady. And besides, I told her, why would he be making out with a skank like you when he's got like the prettiest model in the world at home?" She babbled for the next half hour and gave herself a splitting headache.

When they got off the ice again, Bambi noticed that Elizabeth Pinckney was glowering as Trip smiled. He helped her off with her skates. "Well, this was nice, Bambi," he said.

"Thanks for asking me," she replied.

"Would you be up for the gala benefitting the Boston Pops next Saturday night?" Trip asked.

Could she really take that much more of this? *London, London, London,* she repeated. "That sounds wonderful." Bambi smiled for the cameras.

"Okay. See you then," he whispered, and moved in for a kiss she hadn't seen coming. It shook her all the way to her toes as his tongue darted and deftly washed her closed lips.

Damn, Bambi thought, *turns out that warmth comes from more than his hands.* When she ended the short kiss, she quickly turned away. "Bye Trip," she said over her shoulder so he couldn't see her flush.

Trip waved and smiled at Bambi as she made her way back to the T stop. Once she was out of sight, he turned to Elizabeth Pinckney. She stood with her black-gloved hands on her hips.

"Where the hell did you find her?"

"Oh, Bambi?" he asked. "She's wonderful, isn't she?"

"Not exactly the word I'd use. So?"

"The Booby Trap." He smiled. "It was Pat's bachelor party." Trip noticed Elizabeth's eyes widen at that. Bullseye.

"And what, may I ask, is that?" Her tone got even icier.

"It's a restaurant." Trip forced his voice to be light. "You know, like Hooters."

"So, let me get this straight. You found the girl you're going to date for this ad campaign, a girl named Bambi, I might add, in a titty bar?"

Trip took pleasure in Elizabeth's obvious anger. "Yes, and in fact," Trip improvised, "I think she might want to become an actress one day. I guess I have you to thank."

"Me?" Elizabeth widened her eyes.

"Yes. Without your plan, I never would have even thought about dating Bambi. Do you want to be the one to tell my father the good news, or should I?" She didn't respond, only glared at him as if she wanted to strangle him. Well, now they were even. "I should get going," he said. "Thanks for all your help, guys." He waved to Jim and Jack.

He smiled as he walked home. Bambi was perfect, his plan was perfect, and Elizabeth and his father couldn't do a thing about it.

CHAPTER FOUR

Back in her Cambridge apartment, Bambi had changed into sweats and was sitting on her bed eating dinner from containers of Thai delivery as she graded student papers on the feminist movements of the 1970s. So far, she hadn't dripped spicy basil sauce on anything. But when her doorbell rang, it startled her so much that she turned a container of chicken onto Amber Crossley's paper. She was considering the best way to get the stain out when she opened the door and saw Elizabeth Pinckney, about the last person she had expected.

"Hello," Elizabeth said. "I need to talk to you. I didn't mean to barge in, but someone opened the door for me downstairs. I figured I would just come up."

"You know where I live?" Bambi asked, flabbergasted at seeing the PR woman in her doorway. Elizabeth Pinckney was still dressed in her black suit, and Bambi wondered if she ever wore anything casual. "How do you know where I live?"

"You're in our commercials. It's my business to know where you live, among other things. Which is why I've come. May I come in?"

"I guess," Bambi opened the door wider and gestured to the café table and two chairs near the kitchen. Elizabeth walked toward the table, and her clipped strides in four-inch heels made Bambi realize just how poorly dressed she was. "Let me just go change. You see, I wasn't expecting company."

"Please, it's not necessary. I wouldn't be dressed like this myself if I hadn't come straight from the office. But we do need to talk about what happened today. You're pretty good, you know."

Bambi sat uneasily on the chair across from Elizabeth. "Pretty good?"

"Yes," Elizabeth said. "You almost had me going there, doubting myself, when you started talking all that nonsense about Tom Brady. You distracted him, but not me. I couldn't get Boudicca off my mind."

"What does she have to do with Trip?"

"Because she proved it. You lied about going to junior college. Why? Does Trip know that you're in graduate school? Getting a PhD?"

"Well . . ." Bambi debated how to play this. Clearly, Elizabeth knew more about her than Bambi had bargained for. Should she tell her the truth? Or play it off as something else? "You see, I met Trip at The Booby Trap, and guys have certain assumptions about girls they meet there."

Elizabeth snorted. "I bet they do, especially guys like Trip Whitley."

"You don't like Trip?" Bambi asked.

"Well . . ." It was Elizabeth's turn to be uneasy. "I should not have said that. But I suppose it's true. I did put him in an awkward position, so we didn't get along from the beginning."

"You came up with the dating idea?"

"Yes. He was not too thrilled, if you know what I mean. But I believe his playboy reputation has the potential to ruin Belles and Beaux."

"I see," Bambi said.

"But I've gotten off track. It's in the interest of my business to know why you're lying to Trip."

"Lying?" Bambi tried to pretend offense that she didn't feel.

"You said you went to junior college."

"You're right, I was lying. But I wasn't ready for Trip to find out what I did." Bambi prepared to give Elizabeth Pinckney the spiel about men not wanting to date women's studies PhD candidates because of all the uppity ideas they got about women's lib and working outside the home and the death of chivalry. But looking at Elizabeth, Bambi realized that she couldn't lie to her. First of all, someone as smart as Elizabeth would figure her out eventually. Secondly, Elizabeth didn't like Trip already, and it seemed that she could be a good ally. In fact, Bambi's plan would work that much better because it was clear that Trip was trying to upset Elizabeth's plans. But together, she and Elizabeth could both turn the tables on him. Bambi took a deep breath. "Trip was right when he said we'd met at The Booby Trap. But it wasn't exactly love at first sight."

"No?" Elizabeth leaned in.

"No. He acted like an ass. Like he didn't even realize that I was a person."

"Okay . . ." Elizabeth looked confused. "So why are you dating him?"

"Well, when I got off my shift that night, there he was in the parking lot. With an offer to play the part of his girlfriend for money. Which I refused. Quite adamantly. But . . ."

"But?"

"There's this conference. In London. I've never been out of the country before, and this conference brings in women from across the world. Gloria Steinem, who inspired my research at The Booby Trap, will be speaking about her experiences at the Playboy Club. I could meet people who could help send my career into outer space. But Harvard doesn't think my research is ready enough for me to attend. So I figured . . ."

"Maybe you would do what he asked?"

Bambi nodded. "And I figured maybe I could get some of my own back. I mean, why does a guy like Trip Whitley date a girl from The Booby Trap? I could think of two reasons. One is to get her into bed. But he said flat out that sleeping together wouldn't be part of the deal."

"And two?"

"Two is that he wants to freak out his family. Or someone. Which, I guess, in this case would be you. If that were his motive, then I could throw a wrench in his plans when I reveal myself and make him think twice about treating people like pawns. As an added bonus, I get the money I needed to go to the conference." Bambi searched Elizabeth's face for judgment, some indication that dating someone for money and revenge was tawdry, but she found nothing. Instead, Elizabeth's face broke into a smile.

"That's great!"

"You really think so?"

Elizabeth nodded. "Trip Whitley does need a lesson in humility. But this plan needs to be handled carefully so that it doesn't backfire. What's the next step?"

Bambi leaned toward Elizabeth. "Well, I do have some ideas." The two women began exchanging suggestions. Bambi brought her spilt Thai food to the table when the discussion went into its second hour. By the third, they had left Trip behind and begun talking about their own lives and dreams. In the fourth hour, Elizabeth traded her black suit for a pair of Bambi's pajamas, and the two of them lay on Bambi's bed to watch *Love Actually*. Yawning at 2 a.m., Elizabeth put her work clothes back on and left for her own apartment. Bambi fell asleep with the realization that she hadn't had a good girls' night in far too long.

The next Saturday, Trip waited in the lobby for Bambi to arrive at the Boston Pops gala. Jim and Jack stood by with their respective cameras, and Miss Pinckney fulfilled her role as guardian, prim in a black suit. But she seemed to be smiling a little more than normal, which creeped Trip out.

"You seem particularly happy today," he said.

"No. I am happy that you seem to be happy," she said.

Okay, that was even weirder. But Trip was distracted by Bambi's entrance in a gown that looked a little more appropriate for a high school prom than a gala, attended by all the blue bloods in the city. It was bright pink and sprinkled liberally with sparkly bits that Trip assumed were crystals. The slit that extended from Bambi's ankle to a spot on her thigh might be considered indecent. In short, he thought, perfect.

"Hey baby," he said, taking Bambi's hands. "You look fantastic."

"You think so, really?" her blue eyes widened. With all her hair piled on her head, her big eyes seemed even bigger.

"Of course. You're going to knock the socks off everyone in there."

Bambi giggled. Trip congratulated himself again on a wonderful choice. Those Brahmins were going to go crazy. Trip took Bambi's hand and slid his gaze over to Miss Pinckney, who was scrutinizing Bambi. At least that was better than happy.

"Okay, let's get this show on the road," he said, leading her toward the ballroom, the cameramen following behind. The room was glittering with subdued light and crystal. A string quartet culled from members of the Pops played sedate music in the background as members of Boston's elite toasted each other and their generosity. Almost all the matrons were dressed sedately in black, their younger protégées wearing gowns of taffeta or velvet in shades of deep crimson, midnight blue, or emerald green. Bambi stood out like a sore thumb. It was even better than Trip had anticipated. He steered her toward his parents.

"Dad," he tapped his father on the shoulder, pulling him away from some important businessman or another. "I want you to meet Bambi." His father excused himself from the conversation and he and his wife turned toward their son. Trip responded to the irritation in his father's eyes with a smile. "Bambi Benson, I want you to meet my parents. Mr. and Mrs. Alexander Stuart Whitley, Jr."

"Mr. and Mrs. Whitley, such a pleasure to meet you," she reached out her hand and pumped each of theirs. "Now, Mr. Whitley, Trip's told me about how he works with you at Belles and Beaux. So Mrs. Whitley, you must have to cook all day just to keep these two big, hard-working guys full!"

"Well, not exactly," Trip's mother said. Her brown hair was twisted up and she wore a classic black dress he wasn't sure he had seen before.

"So what do you do, then?"

"I manage a firm. We represent our clients' interests in government."

"Oh," Bambi looked confused. Trip was only too happy to clarify.

"Mom's a lobbyist," he supplied.

"Now, Trip," said his mother, "you know I don't like that term."

"Wow," Bambi ignored the exchange between mother and son. "That's so cool! Do you know the governor?"

Trip almost laughed out loud. He could enjoy this all night, but there were so many other people to see. "C'mon, Bambi. I think we should go get a drink."

"Oh, you're right," she said. Then she turned to his parents, "Well, so nice to meet you."

As they walked away, Trip could hear his mother ask his father, "Who is that girl?" in a tone that implied anything but a good first impression. He wished he could linger to hear his father's explanation, but he and Bambi had a full night ahead of themselves. He placed his fingers on the small of her back so he could feel her butt move back and forth. This reminded him, uncomfortably, that Bambi was an attractive woman. And tonight he genuinely felt it, with her color high and her eyes sparkling. He moved his hand up her back a little, away from the temptation to cup her bottom, and guided her toward the drinks table.

Once they found a free spot at the massive granite bar, a bartender hurried over to ask for their orders. Trip noticed that all that speed had not been for him, but for Bambi, whose appearance the bartender was clearly appreciating. Around her, the perfectly coiffed matrons and debutantes of Boston society had a different impression. Trip noted that Mrs. Bradford sniffed and quickly turned away.

"One for you, sir." The bartender handed Trip his drink without looking at him. "And one for the beautiful lady."

Bambi smiled back at him and took a sip. "Ooh my. The bubbles tickle my nose." Together, she and the bartender laughed. Trip looked on, not fond of the bartender's leering or Bambi's reaction.

"Come on, Bambi," he resisted the urge to tug her arm. "There's someone else I want you to meet." He headed for a knot of ladies surrounding the conductor of the Pops, all simpering at his stories. Their husbands and boyfriends stood by, with grins on their faces that didn't extend to their eyes. Trip wedged himself and Bambi into the cluster and the conductor turned around to see who was disrupting his tiny world. He apparently forgave Bambi the moment he glimpsed the expanse of leg peeking through the slit in the bright pink fabric.

"Signorina! Welcome," he gestured wildly with a handkerchief. Trip rolled his eyes. If the rumors about this guy were true, he grew up in the North End of Boston, not Northern Italy. But Bambi seemed taken with the man. "And what is your name, bella donna?"

"I'm Bambi," she said. "And who are you?" Trip almost burst out laughing at the expression on the conductor's face. Everyone in Boston knew Maestro Giovanni. At least everyone who was anyone.

"Bambi," he interjected, "this is Maestro Giovanni. He conducts the Pops."

"Oh really? How wonderful," she said. Trip watched the Maestro's indignation at not being recognized melt away.

After exchanging a few words with Maestro Giovanni, Trip led Bambi away and headed for another group of well-bred, well-heeled blue bloods. She somehow managed to create a sensation everywhere she went. She hung on Trip's arm and asked inane questions all night. As Bambi intricately explained some beauty secret to Connie Bradford, Trip's mind wandered. Something was bothering him, but he couldn't figure out what. The night was going just as he had planned. His father and Miss Pinckney would be upset, upper-crust Boston society in a roar, and he had had to restrain from laughing all evening at his joke on everyone.

The day after Bambi's command performance at the Boston Pops gala, Trip headed over to his parents' house for their bimonthly Sunday night dinner. He anticipated and almost relished the reaction his father would have to his new "girlfriend."

"Hello, dear. So nice to see you." His mother kissed him on the cheek. She looked much more approachable in a soft dress, with pink lips and with her hair down than she had the night before. "How are you doing?" But before Trip had a chance to answer, she said, "I thought we could make a change to our Sunday night dinners, so I've invited Virginia and Connie Bradford to join us! For this and for as many evenings as they wish."

"I see." Trip frowned. Spectators would mean that his father would subdue his reaction. "And what prompted that, Mom?" Trip asked but he thought he could pinpoint the reason.

"Oh, you know that Virginia lost her husband last year. We've been trying to help her stay active, of course. And you and Connie have barely spoken since, well, since college! I thought these dinners might give you a good chance to catch up."

Trip knew that "catch up" was just another way of saying "get back together." He didn't see any chance of that happening. He followed his mother to the living room where his father, Mrs. Bradford, and Connie were enjoying cocktails.

"Now, you all just wait here while I put the finishing touches on our dinner," his mother said, leaving him to make small talk.

"Trip, come sit by me," Connie said, indicating a spot on the couch. "When your mother mentioned dinner, it reminded me how long it had been since we've really talked. And with all of our families here, it will feel just like old times."

Trip couldn't see a way to politely avoid Connie's invitation, so he sat down next to her. She looked like a more sophisticated version of the high school girl he had known. She was still slim and he bet she still ran religiously. Her shoulder-length blonde hair was thinner than Bambi's, he noticed. "I hope it won't be entirely like old times," he said.

"No, of course not," Mrs. Bradford said. She looked much like she had years before. Substantial, with piercing brown eyes and dark hair dyed and pulled back into a bun at the nape of her neck. "Back then, you were just teenagers. Now both of you are grown and making such successes of yourselves. Isn't that right, Alex?" she looked to Trip's father.

"Of course," he answered, but it seemed to be perfunctory.

"Although Connie is setting the bar pretty high, isn't she?"

"Oh, stop, Mr. Whitley. Mom, you weren't supposed to tell anyone." Connie blushed. It was just as becoming as ever, but Trip felt more immune to it than he used to.

"I couldn't help myself. My own daughter, breaking records!"

Trip turned to Connie. "Breaking records? I think I'm behind the curve here."

"Oh, they're just being silly. I just got word that I might make partner in my law firm in the next two years. Which I deserve, given all the hours I work. It's no big deal."

"No big deal?" his father asked. "I would quibble with that. Trip, Connie has only told you half of the story. Should the offer come through, she will be the youngest associate offered a partnership in Hancock, Holmes & Lodge."

Just then, Trip's mother reentered. "Oh, Trip, did you just hear about Connie's exciting news? We are all so proud of her."

"I can see why," he said. "Connie, that is truly impressive." He meant it, but he couldn't help making the comparison with Bambi. And he knew this thought had crossed his parents' minds, too.

"Come along, everyone," his mother said. "Dinner's ready."

The adults exited for the dining room, but Connie held Trip back. "Thank you, Trip," she said, looking directly in his eyes. She moved her hand over one of his. "It means a lot coming from you."

"I don't know why," Trip said, withdrawing his hand.

"Oh, I guess because you knew me when I was just a gawky high school girl. I always thought back then that you could see the potential in me. It's nice to rise to those expectations." They stood for a moment, and Trip couldn't help but feel a little of the old electricity run through his veins. *But if she had really felt that way in high school, why did she dump me to move on to bigger and better things in college?* He didn't ask the question out loud, though, and the spell was broken when they followed the others into the dining room.

Over salmon and mixed greens, the conversation inevitably turned to the gala and to Bambi.

"Where did you meet this Bambi?" Mrs. Bradford wanted to know.

Trip saw the warning looks his father shot him from the end of the table, but ignored them. "I met her at my friend Pat's bachelor party. She was one of our waitresses."

"I see," Mrs. Bradford said with disdain. "Certainly, she's not anyone that I'm familiar with."

"Why were all those photographers following you around?" Connie asked. "I thought that the event was closed to press inside the ballroom."

"It's part of a promotion we're doing for Belles and Beaux," Trip's father answered. "Trip plans to carry on a long-term relationship with this woman to demonstrate the longevity of the brand."

"Oh, so it's not a real relationship," Mrs. Bradford said. "Thank goodness." Connie's face, which had fallen, perked up suddenly.

"It's real to me," Trip said, if only to watch his father's face. "In fact, I think Bambi's really very special. Who knows what could happen?"

"Don't be ridiculous, Trip," Connie said with a laugh, taking a sip of her Chardonnay. All the heads at the table turned toward her. "I mean, she seemed nice enough, but I spent five minutes with her and all we discussed was nail polish."

"There's more to Bambi than you realize." Trip smirked. "She has other . . . qualities that I find attractive."

"Don't be crude, Trip," his mother cut in.

"Charlotte, don't worry about it," Trip's father said. "Trip's decided to pursue this relationship for its physical virtues. I expect that, far before the arranged nine months are up, he will find himself less amused than he currently is by Bambi Benson. He's made his bed, now he must lie in it."

"Thanks, Dad. That's just what I'll do."

After dinner was over and the Bradfords had left, Trip helped his mother clean up.

"That was quite a scene at the dinner table. Both you and your father behaved badly, and in front of guests!"

"I'm sorry, Mom. He's trying to control my life. I'm 30, but he still treats me like a teenager."

"Be that as it may, I'd expect better from you—from both of you. And now, tell me honestly, what is the story with this Bambi woman? You can't be serious about her. If I didn't know better, I would assume that this is a cheap way to get back at your father."

Trip inhaled sharply. His mother had always been able to read him like a book. But he lied to cover her discovery. "I am serious, Mom. She's a great girl. It's not my fault if you're too stuck up to see it."

"I resent that. I could care less if she was an entrenched part of Boston society and you know that, Alexander Stuart Whitley the third."

"Wow. My whole name. Haven't used that in awhile," Trip said as he dried a plate.

"I haven't had to. But come on. I am not supportive of this relationship, but not because of what Bambi does, or where she comes from. It's because she has yet to demonstrate one pinky's worth of common sense or brainpower."

"And?" Trip didn't look at her.

"And? And?" His mother's temper was rising. "Trip, look at me. You deserve more than that. You deserve a partner, someone who can keep up with you. You don't want someone you can't debate with or make decisions with. That's NOT a life!"

"Someone like Connie? Don't think I didn't see your thinly veiled attempt to get us back together."

"Yes, all right, someone like Connie. Am I such a bad mother for that? You loved her in high school. Don't deny it, I know you did."

"Fine. I did. But that was over 10 years ago, mom."

"Well, that doesn't mean anything. Connie is bright and successful, and I can only imagine what you two could accomplish together. Whereas with Bambi," she shrugged, "I just don't know."

"Just because we're dating now doesn't mean I will marry her."

"I know, Trip. Please, just think about what I've said. Your father and I have a great partnership, and I wouldn't ever give it up. Don't pass up your own opportunity for something like that."

"I won't." Trip sighed. "I promise."

That evening, as Trip drove home, he thought about the day's events. It had been much easier to stand up to his father's criticism of Bambi than his mother's. He had always thought himself lucky to have such a strong and intelligent woman for a mother. Her distress that he hadn't picked a strong and intelligent woman for his girlfriend weighed more heavily on him than he had anticipated.

Bambi kicked off her heels and stumbled toward the bed after her tenth date with Trip in four weeks. This time, they had eaten dinner at L'Espalier, followed by a performance of the ballet. The dancing had been beautiful, even if Bambi had had to listen to Trip go on and on about the Boston Red Sox. The season hadn't even started! But she'd managed to simper like a fool throughout the whole evening. Her phone rang. Elizabeth was calling.

"Hey, Liz. Please tell me I don't have to do this much longer."

"You do not have to do this much longer," Elizabeth said.

"You're just leading me on." Bambi stripped out of her stockings, tossed them on the floor, and flopped onto the bed, not caring that her good black dress would wrinkle.

"I am not. Turn on your TV." Bambi searched in her bed for the remote. She couldn't find it.

"Do I have to?"

"Find the remote, turn the TV to channel 7 now."

Bambi hung her body half off the bed and looked underneath the bed skirt. She finally dug up the remote under the end of the bed. She glared at it before firing it on the television. She found channel 7, where a celebrity show was running. She recognized the jerky camera work of paparazzi and thought she might know the name of the blonde starlet they were following. "What the heck, Elizabeth? This is some trash entertainment show."

"Just wait. This is good."

Then, the show returned to the studio, where a svelte brunette wearing a too-short skirt began a report. "Turns out that everyone's favorite ad boy may be off the market. Trip Whitley, the face and some of the brains behind Belles and Beaux, has been spotted out at several Boston affairs with a new lady love."

"I told you it was good," Elizabeth said. Bambi didn't reply, watching open-mouthed as the reporter continued, pictures flashing above her right shoulder that Bambi recognized from Jack's camera.

"But take heart, girls. This Boston bachelor may not have settled down completely. The blonde bombshell he's been escorting around town? Well, she's not going over so well with the local blue bloods." An unhappy Mrs. Bradford flashed on, as Elizabeth snorted with laughter. "And his parents don't seem like they're big fans, either." The picture changed to the Whitleys on the day of the Pops gala, looking with distaste at Bambi's fluorescent pink gown. "Rumor is that she works as a waitress in a local watering hole known as The Booby Trap. Gentlemen, I'll leave more about that bar to your imaginations. It remains to be seen whether Trip will buck the establishment for this knockout beauty. Make sure to keep tuning in to *Access Hollywood*, because you know we'll have the latest on these two lovebirds."

"That was amazing, right?" Elizabeth squealed. Prior to that moment, Bambi had not imagined that Elizabeth could squeal. "I just love that picture of Mrs. Bradford."

"It was a good one." Bambi wasn't sure what else to say. "So this means we're on to phase two?"

"Don't get ahead of yourself," Elizabeth said. "I am working on getting you two on a local morning show to refute reports that you're breaking up. That will be the moment we get him."

"Super," Bambi replied. "I can't wait."

CHAPTER FIVE

The following weekend was Pat's wedding, and Trip was going to pick Bambi up Saturday morning for the short drive to Concord, where the wedding would take place. It was the first time in 20 years that Bambi had the chance to visit the legendary literary town, where Hawthorne, Thoreau, and Louisa May Alcott had lived. When she was 10, Bambi had just finished *Little Women* and was racing through Alcott's other books. Usually her mother could care less what Bambi was reading, but that summer they made a trip to Concord, visiting Orchard House, Louisa May Alcott's childhood home. After the house tour, she and her mother had lunched on the banks of the Concord River, near the Old North Bridge, the starting place of the Revolutionary War. Bambi yearned to return and maybe somehow capture the magic of that wonderful day she had spent with her mother.

But how could she tell Trip that she wanted to go through

museums and spend the day immersed in history, poetry, and literature? The Bambi he knew would not go for that.

At 10 a.m., Bambi locked her door and headed downstairs to wait in the annex. To her surprise, Trip stood outside his car, dressed casually in dark jeans and a soft sweater. The man did know how to fill out his clothes. Bambi navigated the steps to meet him with her overnight bag in one hand and dress bag in the other. Trip told her he had booked a suite with a pull-out couch, where he would sleep. Bambi smiled her fake smile, kissed him on the cheek, and handed him her bags.

"No need to play the part, Bambi," he said. "Jim and Jack aren't anywhere in sight."

What was that about? Bambi wondered. She swung herself into the passenger side of the black convertible. Not boxy like her trusty Volvo, this car was all curvy lines and plush leather seats.

"Everything okay?" she asked as soon as he got back into the car.

"Sure, it's fine," he said as he piloted the car out of the spot and onto the street. "So, what do you want to do today?"

"You sure you don't have any groomsman duties?"

"Nothing till six. I told Miss Pinckney I'd call her from the road to let her know where we were headed so Jim and Jack could meet us there."

Orchard House! Orchard House! Bambi's brain screamed so loud she thought for a moment that Trip might overhear. "Oh, I don't know," she said.

"We could visit Hawthorne's house. Or the replica of Thoreau's cabin on Walden Pond."

"Who are they?" Bambi heard herself ask.

"Famous authors. I guess you wouldn't know them. What about Louisa May Alcott? She wrote *Little Women*. I figured you might have read it since you're a girl. I think they also made a movie out if it."

Bambi thought on her feet—this was just the opportunity she was hoping for. "Oh yeah. They assigned that book in school. I just watched the movie." She cringed in spite of herself. "But Christian Bale was dreamy. Maybe we should go there?"

"You're on," Trip said. He got on the phone with Elizabeth, and within an hour, they were through with pictures outside Orchard House and had begun to wander through the rooms inside. Thankfully, flash photography was not allowed inside the old house, so Jim and Jack stayed behind, leaving Bambi and Trip alone with the tour guide.

Bambi found herself just as fascinated by the house as she had been as a child. She saw bits and pieces of her beloved *Little Women* everywhere, from May's delicate drawings in Louisa's rooms to the fold-down desk Louisa had sat at to write her manuscript. She stood with her eyes closed in front of that little desk, imagining some person between Louisa and Jo scribbling with a fountain pen, ink splotches on her fingers and forehead.

In the sunny parlor, Bambi thought of the gatherings that must have taken place in Concord back then. All of the Transcendentalists, discussing the most important issues of the day. Perhaps young Louisa had even taken part in the talks about women's suffrage! Bambi liked to think so, since she'd created a character as strong as Jo March.

"What are you thinking about?" Trip approached Bambi from behind and startled her.

"I was just thinking about what parties they must have thrown here. With all those famous neighbors, it must have been a great time."

Trip studied Bambi, and Bambi wondered if she had overstepped her persona. But then he smiled and said, "I can only imagine what they talked about. Did you know this home was a stop on the Underground Railroad?"

"Oh, how exciting and nerve-wracking!" Bambi said. "To think, any moment, the police might come in and send those poor slaves back South." She shivered at the thought of the people across history who had risked their lives to support their beliefs or gain their freedom.

Too soon, they were herded out of Orchard House for the next tour on its way through. Trip took Bambi's arm and together, they headed out into the garden, still dormant from the winter chill. "Where to next?" he asked.

Bambi thought of the picnic by the Old North Bridge, hoping she could luck her way into visiting another piece of her childhood journey. "Someplace pretty," she answered, crossing her fingers.

"Okay, I can handle that," Trip said. They found Elizabeth, Jim, and Jack waiting for them in the parking lot of Orchard House. Trip headed up to tell them the next destination, and Bambi trailed behind. But Trip turned to her and said, "Go wait in the car."

Bambi tried to avoid resenting being left out of the decision making as she made her way to their spot. When Trip got in next to her, he was grinning. But it wasn't just any grin. The smile transformed his face with boyish excitement. Bambi felt her scowl melting as they pulled out of the parking lot. "So, you going to tell me where we're going?" she asked.

"Nope, it's a surprise. But I promise it's pretty." Trip paused, as if considering something, then he picked up his thought, "Well, not as pretty as it is in the spring, but still something to see."

They whizzed through the town of Concord, seeming to begin a great loop past a sign indicating Ralph Waldo Emerson's house and cut through the tiny and quaint downtown until Bambi figured that they must be in the backyard of Orchard House, if it extended this far. They turned into a driveway marked "Sleepy Hollow Cemetery," which Bambi knew was their destination. Graveyard and final resting place of the Alcotts, as well as Emerson, Henry David Thoreau, and Nathaniel Hawthorne. She had always wanted to visit, but had never made the trip.

"Sleepy Hollow?" Bambi inserted some fear into her voice. "Is that like the place with the headless horseman?"

Trip turned to her and chuckled, "No, Bambi. 'The Legend of Sleepy Hollow,' with the headless horseman, was based in New York, not this cemetery. You don't need to worry."

"Still, it's a graveyard . . ." she trailed off.

"True. But it's daylight, and some of the major Transcendentalists and authors are buried here. Including Louisa May Alcott."

"Okay . . ." Bambi said, getting out of the car.

Trip took her hand and they strolled up a winding path. "You know, I used to come here when I was a teenager. During my dark phase—you know, wearing black, feeling like I was too soulful for this world."

Bambi was shocked. She had imagined teenage Trip as confident as adult Trip, clad in impeccably creased khakis and just-wrinkled-enough-to-be-cool button-ups.

"I used to come here and look around at all the old gravestones.

Especially the ones of the people who aren't famous. Trying to discover some deep meaning, commune with the spirits; I don't know what the hell I was thinking. I'm pretty sure some dead guy got pretty offended when I rested against his tombstone to write my bad poetry."

"You wrote poetry?" Bambi asked. She was truly surprised.

"Horrible, I know. Thankfully, I've since realized the error of my ways and leave the writing up to the experts."

They finished their hike at the top of a hill. Around her, Bambi could see the weathered tombstones marking the graves of Thoreau and the Alcott family.

"Did you know that this place was built during their time?" Trip gestured to the stones. "Concord was getting to be a big place, and they needed a cemetery. The guy who designed it met up with some of the Transcendentalists, and he understood what they were trying to say. He made this place kind of natural."

Bambi stared at Trip for a moment. She wouldn't have guessed that he knew so much, or cared at all about an old graveyard. He was right, too. She looked around herself at the richness, the beauty of nature enveloping its dead occupants. Leafless trees surrounded them, evoking the ghosts that lurked in the cemetery. She could see where daffodils had begun to come up, mistaking a recent warming in the weather for spring. And instead of feeling like man had imposed himself and his dead upon nature, manicuring lawns and inserting awkward water features, it felt like graves had been scattered throughout a natural landscape. She glanced over at Trip, who seemed as absorbed in the setting as she was.

"Okay, one last thing and I promise I'll stop boring you with history," Trip said.

"You're not boring me," Bambi said. She wasn't lying either.

Trip shrugged and said, "Emerson was here at the opening ceremony for the cemetery. He said something that kind of stuck with me because it became so true. He said, 'When these acorns, that are falling at our feet, are oaks overshadowing our children in a remote century, this mute green bank will be fully of history: the good, the wise, and the great will have left their names and virtues on the trees; heroes, poets, beauties, sanctities, benefactors, will have made the air tuneable and articulate.'[1] For a moment, there was silence. Then Jack's camera clicked. Bambi jumped a little, having forgotten they were being followed. Trip shook himself. "Stupid. But sometimes I feel like if I listen hard enough, I can hear their voices."

Bambi closed her eyes and stood, listening, "I think I get what you mean." Then, without explanation, Trip grabbed Bambi's hand and tugged her back toward the car.

"You don't have to be nice," he said. "Come on. I have to get to the wedding."

They didn't talk during the short drive from the cemetery to the Colonial Inn on Monument Square. No sooner had they checked in than Trip grabbed his tux and went off in search of Pat. After he left, Bambi still couldn't shake the feeling that she had somehow ruined his visit to Sleepy Hollow.

Trip cursed himself again for thinking about taking Bambi to Sleepy Hollow. Maybe it was a long time ago that he had sat among those tombstones and felt like the voice of Emerson spoke him, and maybe it had been a silly childhood fantasy. But the sight of that bimbo closing her eyes and pretending to listen to something so deep Trip could feel it in his bones somehow made his feelings cheap.

And once they were in the car, Trip couldn't erase the mental image she had created. It got worse when he thought of introducing Bambi to Allison. No matter how much grief he gave Pat, Trip liked Allison. She was smart and friendly and didn't mind the occasional late evening boys' nights Trip and Pat had shared ever since college. Parading his fake love around their real love seemed bad. Somehow the old Trip would have been better, the one who showed up stag and ended the night with a bridesmaid or a guest, whoever was prettier. For the first time, Trip regretted his decision to get involved in this scheme.

He barged into Pat's room in a foul mood and found Pat and his brother Tim already glugging from an open bottle of champagne. "Want some?" Pat asked, extending the bottle to him.

"No thanks, man. And you should probably hold off from drinking much more yourself."

"Buzzkiller," Tim said.

"Not a buzzkiller, just a guy who doesn't want to have to support Pat on his way down the aisle," Trip replied.

"Trip, you're the best," Pat slurred a little, smiling. "I was just getting loose before the big ceremony."

Trip could see that underneath the layer of expensive champagne was a happy man, and his bad mood disappeared, overwhelmed by Pat's good cheer. "I don't know what you need to get loose for. You should be thanking your lucky stars that a girl like Allison wants to marry you!"

"Well, maybe I'm worried that she's gonna jilt me!"

"No way, bud. I'd track her down. You're a catch yourself." Trip paused and hung his tux up in the antique dresser. "On second thought, Tim, pass me that champagne. I should finish it off so there's no danger for you boys." Trip took a swig from the bottle and laid it on the counter.

"So, you bring the lovely Bambi with you?" Pat asked.

"Yeah, I left her up in the room."

"Then, dude, what are you doing down here?" Tim asked. "If I had a hot girl up in my room right now you can bet I wouldn't be spending time with you jokers."

"It's not like that," Pat said, taking another swallow of champagne. "See, Trip's—" Trip cut Pat off with a swift slap on the back, causing the champagne to go down the wrong tube. Even if he had wanted to, Pat could not complete the sentence because he was coughing so hard. For a moment, Trip wondered if he would have to head over to Allison's room to tell her he had killed the groom.

"You okay, buddy?"

Pat finally stopped coughing and looked up with eyes watering from the exertion. "Yeah, fine." His voice was hoarse. Trip handed him the bottle of champagne, and Pat looked at him like he'd gone mad. "You trying to finish me off?"

"No, I promise." Trip offered the bottle to Pat again, and Pat took a swallow to clear his throat.

Tim broke in. "So anyway, what were you saying about Trip? Trip's . . . ?"

Sheepish, Pat replied, "Trip's . . . a gentleman. He told me they got two beds up there."

"Gosh, not what I would've guessed about Trip . . . especially with a girl like that," Tim said.

"Well, like they say, you can't always judge a book by its cover," Pat said.

"I don't know," Trip said. "She seems pretty much cover with no pages in between." He turned to Pat. "Not everyone can be as lucky as you, bud."

"True," Pat replied, and reached for the bottle of champagne. "Let's toast to my future happiness."

Trip grabbed the bottle from him, downed the rest of its contents in one quick swallow, and said, "I'm in. But this time, we toast with water."

Bambi lay in bed with her laptop. She was reading through a few articles for her dissertation that she had downloaded back in Cambridge, but she couldn't concentrate. Her thoughts kept drifting back to Sleepy Hollow and the boy Trip had once been—soulful and leaning up against those ancient tombstones. She laughed a little to herself about the earnest boy dressed all in black. But she couldn't laugh about the beautiful man, standing in the sunlight, reciting lines of Emerson. Was there more to Trip Whitley than it seemed? Bambi wondered if, in setting out to teach Trip a lesson about assumptions, she had made the same mistake herself.

She jumped when she heard a knock on the door. Looking down, she realized that she had spent the hour since Trip had left daydreaming instead of studying, having made it only five pages into the academic article on women's roles as personal caregivers in the workforce. She got up, closed her laptop, and slid it back in her overnight bag. Looking through the peep hole, she was surprised to find Elizabeth standing outside, and flung the door wide.

"Elizabeth! I thought I wouldn't see you until this evening."

Trip had agreed to allow Elizabeth and the cameramen to get shots of some of the dancing at the reception, although they wouldn't attend the ceremony.

"I know. I dropped Jim and Jack off at the hotel, but I thought you might want a break from being Bimbo Bambi. I thought I could psych you up for the rest of the night."

"That sounds wonderful," Bambi said. Even though she had never before felt guilty for concealing her true personality and interests from Trip, based on his misogynist assumptions, she did feel a niggling doubt deep in her gut at this moment. She thought she might be able to exorcise that doubt by being herself for a while, with someone who knew the real Bambi.

"And," Elizabeth said, "I have a great treat. The hotel serves afternoon tea! So we can prepare you for your trip to England at the same time!"

The idea of afternoon tea sounded like such fun to Bambi, but she worried. "Won't there be someone there who might see us? I mean, see me? Not acting in character?"

"Almost everyone is coming in from Boston and not staying the night, so they are probably not here yet. Besides, if we keep our voices down, no one will notice a couple of girls chatting."

Bambi wanted to believe Elizabeth. "Okay," she said, picking up her purse and the room key and heading downstairs with her friend. They arrived in the tea room and were seated at a white-linen draped table. Pink napkins fashioned into roses and a small vase of fresh flowers graced the table. Bambi thought how cute and quaint it all was.

"This is perfect," she told Elizabeth. "Just the escape I needed."

"Good, I was hoping so. Plus, I needed to get away from

Jim and Jack. Sometimes I just want to scream at them to stop wearing black just because they consider themselves auteurs!"

"You're one to talk," Bambi laughed, pointing at Elizabeth's trim black suit, another in the line of the thousands she seemed to own.

"Fashion experts say black is slimming!"

"Perhaps, but you would look beautiful in colors. With your dark hair and creamy complexion, you could pull off some really bright colors. Not like me, permanently stuck in the pastels."

"I'm not sure," Elizabeth blushed. "Besides, I thought women's studies majors wanted people to focus less on outward appearance and more on inner beauty."

"True. But any smart woman realizes that what she puts on the outside changes what people think about her. To your point, a smart man would ask the simple questions to see beyond that."

"And Trip has not asked the smart questions."

"He's barely asked any," Bambi replied. "And I guess I thought he totally lacked curiosity. Didn't care about discovering anyone's story but his own."

"But?" Elizabeth said.

"You think there's a but?"

"I know there's a butt," Elizabeth winked. "But I meant your 'but.' You said you were 'beginning to think.' What changed your mind?"

They were interrupted by a waiter bearing a crate of teas, followed by a man in a business suit. The man was the tea sommelier, who had extensive knowledge of the Inn's tea collection and baffled them with his intricate information about the individual flavors. Elizabeth selected an exotic jasmine green tea, while Bambi chose the Lady Grey, a variation on the classic Earl Grey.

"Women's lib in all things, I say," she said.

"Appropriate for your field, I guess. But don't think you can distract me." Elizabeth picked up her periwinkle china tea pot decorated with delicate yellow flowers, then poured some tea into her cup.

"Distract you? From what?" Bambi said.

"I see how it is." Elizabeth laughed with the cup midway to her lips. "You play dumb with everyone else, so you think that you can pull that act on me. Well, nice try. But I know better. So what's the but?"

"Okay." Bambi sighed and poured her own tea, loving its flowery scent. She took a sip before answering. "Well, sitting there in that cemetery, I began to wonder. You know, if there might be more to Trip than I had previously thought. Maybe I haven't been asking the right questions, either."

"Wait a second, do you have feelings for Trip Whitley?"

"Of course not!" Bambi slammed her tea cup down. Then she remembered that china may not be the best material for slamming in emphasis. She peeked at the cup and sighed with relief when she found it in one piece.

"Good. But you are starting to empathize with him? Trip Whitley?"

"I guess. A little."

"Just because he was a soulful poet as a kid?"

"Well, he did quote Emerson in what amounts to Transcen-dentalist headquarters."

"You're being irrational. One quotation doesn't change who

Trip Whitley is today." Elizabeth peered over her cup of tea at Bambi. "Oh God. You're probably having second thoughts about your great plan."

"Well . . ."

"Come on, Bambi. I would say 'man up,' but I know that would offend your sensibilities and it sounds misogynistic now that I'm thinking about it. But for God sakes, woman up! Poor baby got everything he wanted and yet he still felt the need to garb himself in black and hang out in a cemetery," Elizabeth said.

"When you say it like that . . . it sounds kind of stupid." Bambi flushed.

Elizabeth's expression softened. "Look, it is not stupid. It is just that he is not a wounded kid. He is a grown man who thought he could use you, deceive me, and misuse his own company because he did not like a PR stunt."

"You're completely right," Bambi said. What was with her if she'd managed to take one nice afternoon with Trip and spin it into complete forgiveness?

"But I did not bring you down here for us to spend time thinking about Trip," Elizabeth said, reaching under the table to pat Bambi's knee. "It is for us to have a grown-up conversation between two unbelievably smart and goal-oriented women."

"And for food," Bambi said, eyeing the three tiers of tea that their waiter was carrying toward them. Dainty finger sandwiches filled with egg salad and cucumber and cream cheese, scones with clotted cream, and bite-sized portions of tarts and cakes made her mouth water.

"Amen," Elizabeth said. "Let's eat."

The two women oohed and ahhed as they spread liberal

amounts of clotted cream over scones that threatened to disintegrate with the slightest touch and luxuriated in bites of heavenly chocolate dessert. They didn't spend one more word on Trip Whitley, but by the time Bambi headed back to her room to change for the wedding, she felt as though she were changing into her anti-Trip armor. No way would he get under her skin tonight.

CHAPTER SIX

But boy, did he look good in a tuxedo. Trip even pulled off the tuxedo with tails, which she had imagined would make the men look more like waiters than groomsmen. But that seemed to be the order of the evening. Everything was even more splendid than Bambi had imagined it would be, partially because it wasn't the massive and overdone affair she had anticipated. Instead, soft candlelight bathed the wood of the old room in soft light. Bambi estimated attendance at about 150, fewer than what she had expected. The only place where the bride had spared no expense was the flowers. All whites and creams, they spilled out of vases along the aisle, adorned every chair, and cascaded over the arbor which decorated the front of the room and framed the bride and groom as they took their vows. And yet with all of those blooms, the fragrance managed to be soft instead of overpowering.

Pat and Allison, a lithe woman with hair that seemed close to fire-lit gold, exchanged Irish claddagh rings instead of traditional wedding rings. Instead of traditional vows, they said to each other: "By the power that Christ brought from heaven, mayst thou love me. As the sun follows its courts, mayst though follow me. As light to the eye, as bread to the hungry, as joy to the heart, may thy presence be with me, oh, one that I love, 'til death comes to part us asunder." Allison wore a tulle A-line gown with lace appliqué, lace sleeves, and an exquisite long lace veil. Bambi thought it was, by far, the most beautiful wedding she had ever attended.

She lingered to watch the picture taking after the ceremony since she would be seated with Trip at the table for the bridal party. She smoothed down her deep red dress and sat quietly, comparing the flickering candles to the harsh flash of the photographer's bulb. When the happy couple broke off to do some shots alone, Trip walked over.

"Feels weird to let someone else have the camera for a bit, doesn't it?"

"What?" Bambi had never thought about it that way. "No, of course not."

"So . . ." Trip leaned back on his heels during the awkward silence. "Nice wedding, huh?"

"It was beautiful," Bambi said, standing up to meet his gaze. "I mean everything. The candles, the claddagh rings, and the flowers. Oh, the flowers!" She spread her arms wide as if to encompass the whole room and spun a little.

"You thought so?" Trip asked.

"Of course!" Bambi said. "Why, did you think I wouldn't like it?"

"I guess it just seemed a little . . . soft for your tastes."

"How would you know?" Bambi said. By the look of shock

on Trip's face, she realized that she may have let too much anger out with that question. So she widened her narrow eyes and forced the scowl from her lips. "I mean, I do love color, but this was so pretty even without it. Don't you agree?"

"Yeah. I do. Allison's got an eye," he said. "Well, I gotta go. Be introduced and whatnot. See you later." He pecked her on the cheek.

Bambi made her way into the reception, already deafening with people chatting, an amazing 10-piece orchestra playing, and a vocalist singing the greats of the Big Band era. Bambi picked up her place card and took a seat at her table. Soon, the bandleader called everyone to their seats for the entrance of the bride, groom, and wedding party. Bambi laughed when the band launched into "Makin' Whoopie," while the bandleader acted as MC and introduced everyone.

Uniformed waiters appeared with bottles of wine to pour and trays loaded with food that tasted as delicious as it looked. After dinner, Pat and Allison had their first dance, a restrained foxtrot to "Fly Me to the Moon." But unquestionably, the highlight of the traditional dances was that of the bride and her father. They took position as if to do a sedate waltz, until the music began. To everyone's surprise, "I'm Shipping Up to Boston," by local Boston favorites the Dropkick Murphys, filled the room. Allison and her father slipped into a frantic Irish jig to the upbeat music. Everyone laughed and clapped along to the music, and midway through, the bride's sister and mother joined in to make it a foursome. By the end, they had beckoned Pat's family onto the floor, and the newly joined families danced together. Bambi had tears in her eyes from laughing so hard. She caught Trip's gaze a couple of times and noticed that he was enjoying Pat's attempts at the high-paced dance, calling out half-encouragement, half-taunts every so often.

Afterwards, Pat grabbed the microphone from the bandleader. He used his wheezing to comic effect. "Well, I don't know about you people, but I'm out of breath!" He wiped sweat from his brow as the guests cheered. "I'm going to need a drink. Which means it's a great time to start the toasts!"

As if on cue, the waiters stood at their tables with trays of champagne flutes balanced on their shoulders. Tim rose and gave his best man's speech, making everyone laugh about the times when he was younger and Pat would trap him under a laundry basket, sitting on the basket so Tim couldn't get away. After Tim, Allison's sister Katie toasted the bride and groom, talking about how excited Allison was when she met Pat, and how Katie could tell that they would spend the rest of their lives together.

Bambi thought the toasts were over, but to her surprise, Trip got up after Katie and took the microphone into the center of the room.

"I know I'm not the best man, but Pat told me I could say a few words since I was actually there when Pat first met Allison. Back in those days, we were degenerate and unrepentant flirts. And sometimes, a pretty girl would walk into the offices of Belles and Beaux, looking for a setup. Well, we figured, why weren't we as good a setup as some of the guys on the site?" Here he paused and looked to Pat, who acknowledged his statement with a nod. "I remember distinctly the day that Allison walked into Belles and Beaux. It was nasty outside. Rainy or snowy or something like that. I saw her standing in reception and, with that red hair, she looked like a beam of sunlight. I was about to head in, do my thing, when I noticed Pat was already on the way. Like a compass seeking true north. I thought to myself how lucky he was to get the girl that time. Just think how things would have turned out differently had I been the first one to reach her!" The audience chuckled, and Trip let the laughter die down before he continued. "But seriously, if I had reached her first, she would have dumped me in no time and found her way to Pat. Because he's her true north. And vice versa. Congrats, buddy." Trip raised his glass. "To Pat and Allison."

Bambi felt herself softening toward Trip as she raised her glass and watched everyone else do the same and repeat, "To Pat and Allison." Trip ran over to hug the groom and kiss the bride on the cheek. When he joined the table once more, he was congratulated on his toast.

After the toasts, the dancing began for real. Trip eyed Bambi with a suggestive gleam in his eyes. "You up for it?" he asked.

"Sure!" Bambi extended her hand. She wasn't the most coordinated person, but how could you not dance at a wedding? Trip took her hand and led her to the floor, where the band had moved from the 1940s to the 1960s, playing Motown and early rock 'n' roll hits. She and Trip twisted and did the monkey, and Bambi couldn't help laughing when he played the ham and got into the dancing. Any awkwardness between them that lingered from the scene in the cemetery was gone. She was laughing when she noticed the flashbulb going off near her face and recognized the familiar faces of Jim, Jack, and Elizabeth, there to do their shots for the evening. One look at Elizabeth reminded her of their conversation earlier. No matter how much fun Trip was as a dance partner or how good he was at giving wedding toasts, he still wasn't a great guy. But hey, she could have fun dancing with him without falling in love.

That was easy to remember for awhile, even after he grabbed her hands and led her in some sort of intricate twirl that ended with her backed up to his chest. Or over his knee in a daring dip. But then, the song changed to the Righteous Brothers' "Unchained Melody." Trip pulled her close and the whole length of him against her set her body twitching and wishing for more. At a distance, her head had always won out over her hormones. But now, he stood too close and his body felt too good. Her hormones were quickly gaining the upper hand.

And then, Trip leaned down and kissed her. Although she knew that it was just for show, all for the cameras and the people watching, her head lost the battle for that moment. His tongue tickled her lips and she opened her mouth to him, melting even deeper against his hard body. Almost against her will, her hands threaded up into his hair, willing him closer, wanting the kiss to go on and on and on. As their tongues danced, the rest of Bambi's body felt as if there were a live wire of electricity running through it, jumping with uncontained energy, dangerous and exciting.

But Trip broke off the kiss. He stared at her for a moment, their lips just millimeters away from each other, then pressed her head down to his chest. The live wire died.

Just for show. She repeated it to herself over and over, to remind the hormones that had taken over. It had all been just for show. So why had it felt so real?

Damn. Trip hadn't meant for the kiss to be quite like that. They had acted like teenagers on the dance floor at his best friend's wedding. Maybe the champagne had gone to his head.

He thanked his lucky stars, the bandleader, and whoever

else might be worth thanking that the next song was a fast one. Martha and the Vandellas sang about a heat wave, which seemed appropriate because Trip felt like he was on fire. It seemed like sweat was pouring out of previously unknown pores. He needed a drink, and fast.

"I'm getting a little thirsty," he yelled to Bambi over the music. "Want something?" He could've gotten in a little closer, whispered in her ear, but there was no way that was going to happen. Not after the kiss.

"Sure," she yelled. And then, apparently doing just fine, she leaned in to his ear. "How about a rum and diet Coke?"

The sensation of her breath on his neck caused Trip to recoil as if he'd been bitten. She looked at him strangely, but there was nothing he could do about it now. He led her back to the table. "I'll be right back," he said.

With every step between them, he began to feel cooler, so that by the time he reached the bar, he was feeling much better.

"One Sam Adams, one rum and diet Coke." Trip leaned on the bar and dared a glance back at Bambi. To his surprise, she was staring at him. Probably wondering what the hell he was thinking, kissing her like that. He narrowly missed meeting her eye before turning back toward the bartender.

"Trip."

The voice startled Trip. He composed his face before turning to face the man and the voice. "Hi, Dad. Good to see you. Enjoying the wedding?"

"It's wonderful. Allison is a lovely girl," his father said. "Very tasteful."

Trip understood the implied dig at Bambi, but didn't rise to his father's bait. "Yes she is."

"You know, your mother and I are seated just a few tables away from you."

"That so?" Trip asked, taking the drinks from the bartender.

"It is. I would think that you would have had time to say hello before you started playing tonsil hockey with that woman on the dance floor."

Trip fumed. His anger at his father grew for pointing out what Trip already knew had been a mistake. He struggled to keep the mocking tone from his voice. "I'm sorry you felt left out. We'll definitely make a point of saying hello to Mom later."

He walked with the drinks back toward the table, where he saw that Pat and Allison had begun their rounds of the room. Pat stood chatting with Tim and the bridesmaids, while Allison sat in Trip's seat, deep in conversation with Bambi. Although maybe "deep" wasn't the right word to use in reference to Bambi. He found himself quickening his pace, whether to save Bambi from Allison or the other way around, he wasn't sure. He just knew that the two of them wouldn't get along.

In the back of his mind, he wondered whether Allison knew about the plan. Probably yes, since Pat knew and Pat told Allison everything. But con or not, Allison would not approve of Trip's choice of a blonde bimbo cocktail waitress. As he approached them, he heard Bambi say, "Well, so that's the plan. You don't think it's too much, do you?"

"Hello ladies," Trip placed Bambi's drink in front of her with a flourish. He noticed that she jumped a little in her seat. "What's the plan? And what's too much?"

Allison smiled up at him. "Bambi was just asking me whether she should get her highlights done a shade lighter. And if it would be too much—I mean, I don't want to make her look like a bottle blonde."

"Oh." Trip was disappointed. He had wondered what had the two women seeming to be on such good terms, but it was just more girl talk.

"What do you think?" Allison asked, and then switched her concentration to Bambi's face. Or hair, he guessed.

"Oh, I don't know," Trip said, baffled why his opinion mattered. Allison wasn't the type of girl to ask these questions. Maybe she was just being polite. "She probably knows better than I do."

"How true," Allison said. "Bambi, I think it's a wonderful plan. And not too much."

"Thank you." Bambi's face shone with a smile that transformed her face and lit up her eyes. It made her beauty, which Trip was trying to forget, impossible to ignore. "Your opinion means a lot to me since you know a lot about . . . hair color."

"Well, you can't be married to Pat and not know a lot about the topic," Allison said. By that time, Pat had made it over to his bride and shot a questioning look at Trip. Trip shrugged his shoulders. He had no idea what the two women were talking about now, because he couldn't imagine Pat took any more interest in hair color than he did.

"Ally, ready to head on to the next?" Pat laid his hands on his bride's shoulders.

"That I am, Pat." Allison smiled. She stood up, and Bambi stood with her. "It was nice to meet you, Bambi."

"Nice to meet you, too," Bambi replied.

"Bye, Trip," said Allison. "And good luck." She had turned around and been caught by another well-wishing guest by the time that Trip thought to ask what he needed the good luck for. He turned to Bambi, her eyes still on Allison.

"Sorry it took so long getting the drinks," he said.

Bambi looked at her rum and diet Coke. "Oh, that's fine. I enjoyed meeting Allison. She's really something."

"Apparently full of information I never knew she had," Trip said. "You girls have so much to worry about."

"Hmmm?" Bambi seemed distracted. "Oh yes. Hair color." She giggled. "Yes, we do." She reached down and took a long swallow of the drink.

Soon the dancing broke up for the cake cutting and the bouquet and garter tosses. Trip cheered when the girls headed for the bouquet toss and saw Bambi take a spot in the middle toward the front of the group. She was much too close and Allison's toss soared right over her head. She didn't even reach up to catch the flowers, which was not what Trip expected. She seemed like the kind of girl who would buy into all the traditions. Instead, Connie Bradford caught the bouquet. At first, she seemed a little surprised, but then seemed pleased as the other girls congratulated her.

When it was his turn to join the other single men on the floor for the garter toss, he figured that he should adopt Bambi's strategy. He did not want to end up dancing with Connie Bradford. With the tension over Bambi and the PR campaign, he didn't need a dance with Connie that his parents would insist represented fate intervening.

Trip stood at the front of the group of men, and was looking over the crowd when something hit him smack dab in the chest. He looked down and there was the blue ribbon-and-lace garter lying innocently at his feet. He glanced up, saw Pat looking at him, and glanced down again.

"Trip," Pat said, "I think it's all yours."

Trip bent down and picked up the garter and the men cheered. Pat came over and held out his hand for the garter. Trip handed it over, and his friend stretched the elastic so he could string the thing around his head.

"There ya go, bud," Pat said, pleased with his handiwork.

"Sure I look okay?" Trip asked, figuring there was nothing left to do but play along.

"Never better," Pat laughed. Then he raised his voice, "How about that dance?"

Everyone cheered and Trip saw Allison pushing Connie toward him as the band launched into "Strangers in the Night." He bowed exaggeratedly toward her and took her in his arms. She blushed. Probably just as embarrassed as he was, he figured. Together, they began to dance a foxtrot, the simple steps from cotillion coming back to them as they circled the floor.

Bambi watched Trip and Connie Bradford move around the floor smoothly. For some reason, it surprised her that dancing was one of his talents. His oversized moves when they were boogeying earlier had her convinced that he was more proficient at the white man's overbite than the waltz. But she had been wrong.

They looked like they belonged together, she thought. Although Constance, like Bambi, was blonde, the resemblance ended there. Connie's blonde hair fell in a waterfall past her shoulders, expertly highlighted. Bambi knew she could never get her hair that straight. Connie was waiflike, thin like a model so that her undoubtedly expensive dress hung on her frame and highlighted the tone in her arms and the flatness of her belly. Bambi had always curved, from the chest that made her a believable hire for Joe at The Booby Trap to the hips and ass she had in vain tried to diet away. She would never achieve the slimness that seemed to come naturally to Connie.

"Don't they look lovely together," she heard Mrs. Bradford saying a little too loudly to the person behind her. "You do know they used to date?"

"I didn't," the woman replied.

"They broke up before college. He went off to Stanford while she was in New Hampshire at Dartmouth."

Bambi moved away to avoid hearing the rest of that conversation. She watched the dance to its bitter end, where Trip dipped Connie low—she was clearly thrilled to have him near. But although their lips came perilously close to touching, Trip hauled Connie up to the sound of applause.

He returned to the table and propelled Bambi through the crowd. Lost in her thoughts, Bambi hadn't bothered watching where they were going; now, she saw that Trip was steering her toward his parents. She plastered a smile onto her face. Not very much protection, but it was the only armor she had going into this battle.

"Mom, Dad," Trip said. "Sorry we didn't make it over earlier. You remember my date, Bambi Benson?"

"So nice to see you again, Mr. and Mrs. Whitley," Bambi said.

"And you, Bambi," Mrs. Whitley wore a smile Bambi could tell was fake about as easily as Mrs. Whitley could spot the fake diamonds sparkling in Bambi's ears.

"Now, Trip," said Mr. Whitley, ignoring Bambi, "I know you've come to this wedding to have fun, to enjoy a date with your . . . er . . . Miss Benson, but you have to keep in mind that you're representing the company, too. Excessive public displays of affection are so tawdry."

Trip stiffened.

"Mr. Whitley," Bambi piped up, "It was actually my fault. Can you really blame me? We were having so much fun and I was listening to the Righteous Brothers and, well . . ." she glanced shyly into Trip's eyes. Then she turned to Mrs. Whitley. "Did you ever see *Ghost?*"

"No, dear."

"Well, you should. Then you would understand how that song just sucks you up into it and you really have no control over your actions."

Bambi could tell that her little speech had made the Whitleys uncomfortable, but she had achieved her goal in taking the focus off Trip. And, she hoped, in diverting some tricky questions that she and he might have to tackle later. Like whether that kiss was everything it seemed to be.

"Well, just remember where you are," Mr. Whitley said.

"Oh of course, Mr. Whitley."

Any other opinions that the Whitleys wanted to share on public displays of affection were silenced by an announcement that guests should join in saying farewell to Pat and Allison at the front of the hotel. As they headed in that direction, Bambi caught Trip studying her curiously. But he didn't say anything, and soon they were in the midst of the excited crowd. Guests gathered along the porch and the walk toward the sleek black limo that would carry the couple to Boston for the night, before they left for their honeymoon in Bali. Bambi tore her gaze from Trip as Pat and Allison hurried toward the car.

CHAPTER SEVEN

As the car circled past the city square and on to Boston, Bambi felt Trip rest his coat on her shoulders. "Thanks," she said.

"I should be the one thanking you for helping me out with my parents. You know, I could've handled it."

"I'm sure you could have. But they already dislike me, so what's one more thing?"

"I guess." Trip didn't sound convinced. "You ready to head up to the room?"

"Yes." Bambi sighed. They went back into the hotel, up the stairs, and to their room. Once inside the door, she shrugged the coat off her shoulders and held it out to Trip. He took it wordlessly and both set about preparing for the night. Bambi unpacked her tank top and flannel pants as Trip stripped out of his tuxedo, leaving him in blue and white striped boxer shorts and his undershirt.

She watched him go into the bathroom and could hear him run the water and begin to brush his teeth. She returned her attention to the tank top and flannel pants, debating whether to wait for him to vacate the bathroom or just change in the room. Although she had ditched her shoes the minute she had stepped in the room, Bambi itched to get rid of her confining pantyhose. He probably had a good couple minutes in there of brushing his teeth, so she decided to strip quickly. The dress came over her head in one smooth motion and she worked the offensive hose down her hips. *Gosh, that felt so much better.* Glad to be free, she threw her arms up in the air and did a big stretch before undoing her bra, dropping it on the bed with the dress, then putting on her pj bottoms. Finally, she pulled the tank top over her head, picked up the dress, and headed toward the closet to put it away. But there, in the way, stood Trip. His eyes wide and toothbrush motionless in his mouth made it clear that he had been there for at least a little while. Long enough to have seen too much. Bambi felt her face flood with embarrassment, more so when she glanced at the mirror that would have given Trip an even better view.

"What the hell, Trip?" she pushed past him to hang the dress in the closet, slamming the hanger on the rod with a clang. "You could've said something."

"I . . . uh . . . sorry." Trip blinked as if he had just woken up and took the toothbrush out of his mouth. "I just came out here to see . . . wait, hold on a second." He ducked back into the bathroom and Bambi heard him spit out the toothpaste and rinse his mouth. "Just thought we should maybe talk about when to leave. I didn't mean to, you know, see anything."

"Sure." Bambi tossed her hair and stalked past him, grabbing her toiletries from her bag. She had the joy of shoving past him once more as she headed for the bathroom. She began to shut the door when he put his hand on the other side.

"Bambi." He ducked his head so that he could see into her eyes. "You know, you're beautiful."

She blushed again, but covered it with what she hoped was a brusque "Whatever." She slammed the door closed and began to wash her face. *Dumb, dumb, dumb,* she thought. Why couldn't she just have waited? Somehow, she couldn't escape the thought that that was something the dumb Bambi character she was playing would have done. Maybe intentionally, maybe not. She was going to have to see Trip less often because she felt like she was losing a little of herself in this persona.

When she left the bathroom, she found Trip safely tucked in his bed, propped up and reading a hardback book with no dust jacket.

"What's that?"

He looked up. "*Mayflower.* It's by Nathaniel Philbrick. Pretty good, too."

"Reading up on your ancestors?"

He laughed. "Not by a long shot, at least as far as I know. I descend from hill people in Eastern Kentucky, much as my parents like to pretend otherwise."

"Oh."

"Yep. My grandfather Whitley somehow figured out how to make it out of Boltsfork, Kentucky, and up to Harvard Business School. Where he promptly decided that these people needed a little more romance. Hence Belles and Beaux."

"Did you ever ask him what he did to change his life?" Bambi was intrigued to learn about the Whitleys' humble ancestry.

"No, unfortunately. I don't think I cared until it was too late."

Bambi could sense the hurt in his voice. "When was that?"

"Three years ago this April."

"I'm sorry."

"Aww, it's okay. But Gramps is the reason I'm reading this book. He had a lot of respect for the Pilgrims, if not some of their descendents. How they took a chance, based on faith, for a better life. I figure he fancied himself a modern-day Pilgrim. Maybe that's why he stuck in Boston."

"Sounds like an interesting man."

"He was." Trip smiled and turned back to his book. But he looked up again. "Listen, Bambi, about earlier . . ."

"Don't worry about it."

"I want to. I should've moved or said something. I don't know why I didn't. I guess my brain wasn't talking to my feet."

"Apology accepted," she said. She grabbed the romance novel beside the bed and settled in to read. This was at least one hobby that worked with both of the Bambi personas she had going. Although she had always felt weird carrying romance novels around the Women's Studies Department, she loved them. She understood the archetypes and the inherent fallacies, and she knew there were plenty of books out there that romanticized misogyny. Of course she hated those. But for the others, she couldn't resist the happy endings. If that made her a traitor to her discipline, so be it. She thought back to Trip's story about his grandfather, about seeing the need for romance. Well, maybe they had some similarities.

But despite the sharp dialogue between hero and heroine, Bambi couldn't keep her eyes open for long. She fell asleep with the book across her chest, bedside lamp still burning.

Trip took much longer to go to sleep. He tried to concentrate on his book, which really was good and had managed to distract him for several hours, but his eyes kept sliding over to the bed next to him and the beautiful girl lying there. And when his eyes weren't betraying him, his brain was, flashing images of Bambi, dressed only in the pink thong, stretching. Her breasts lifting, just begging to be cupped on their way down. He hadn't meant to stay, had meant to say something. But then she rose on her tiptoes, stretched her arms above her head, and arched her back. Frankly, she had been lucky he couldn't move. Because his feet certainly wouldn't have taken him back into the bathroom after that.

He wasn't sure what he was supposed to do with these inconvenient images. His and Bambi's relationship had been based on the initial transaction. One of its advantages was that there were no feelings involved. And it had been easy to keep feelings out of the whole thing when she played her part. But this weekend, she had seemed to transform into someone different.

If he didn't know better, he would swear that she had read *Little Women*. She had walked through that house, pointing out May's paintings, or drawing parallels between young Louisa May Alcott and her character Jo. Trip had never seen the movie, but how could they squeeze so much into two hours?

And then she defended him to his parents. She slipped back into the ditz as if she were wearing some kind of costume. He watched her do it as a calculated move, knew that she was playing a part.

But what about that kiss on the dance floor? The one that had gotten them into trouble in the first place. There was nothing pretend about that. He would swear on his grandfather's grave. Come to think of it, that had been his worst decision of the whole weekend. Trip blamed that kiss for his later immobility after stepping out of the bathroom. And his inability to get Bambi, her soft lips, or her beautiful body out of his mind.

When Trip finally fell asleep, she followed him into his dreams, too. Taunting, teasing, he reached out to touch her but his fingers fell through the illusion of her body.

He woke up the next morning with a monster headache and enough morning wood to build a fire. Trip turned onto his side toward the wall, thanking God that Bambi still slept peacefully on the other side of the room. He prayed that things would subside by the time she woke up. They would have to check out sometime, after all.

An hour later, with Bambi still asleep, Trip decided he needed to get out of the room. He had stuffed tennis shoes and workout clothes into his bag at the last minute and he hoped that a punishing run would work off his frustration. Out in the cold morning air of early February, his head began to clear. He ran past the Old Manse and the bridge where that fateful clash between redcoats and minutemen had signaled the beginning of the Revolutionary War. He circled over the river at a different bridge, then past some place marked the "Calf Pasture" before running back toward the hotel.

Trip walked into the room and heard Bambi singing Aretha Franklin's "Respect" in the shower. That wasn't so good for his newfound concentration. Nor was her entrance into the room just a few minutes later dressed only in a towel, wet from the shower and smiling at him.

"Good morning. I thought I heard you come in. I had wondered where you went, but I guess it's pretty clear now."

Trip could feel her eyes taking in his sweaty body. He felt self-conscious. "Sorry, I must stink to high heaven."

"That must be an expression of your grandfather's," Bambi said.

"Yeah, I guess. I'll just jump in the shower. If you're done, I mean."

"Let me just grab a couple things in there." She walked past him and back into the bathroom, and Trip thought how easy it would be to just grab some of the towel as she went by, unwrapping her like a Christmas present. But that would be incredibly ungentlemanly. Still, his fingers itched. To keep them occupied, he grabbed the dopp kit from his bag and rushed into the bathroom, locking the door behind him, more to keep himself in than to keep Bambi out.

Standing in the scalding hot shower, Trip struggled for control for the second time that morning. This was not how things were supposed to go. He groaned and ducked under the stream, wishing that it could make his problems go away.

When he got out of the shower, he saw that Bambi had crawled onto his bed and appeared to be searching for something.

"Lose something in my bed?" he asked.

"Oh!" she yelped. "You scared me. No. I just heard your phone ring. Sounded like it was over here, but I haven't found it."

Trip headed over to the bed to assist in the search, but as soon as he got close, Bambi jumped off and made toward the other end of the room as if she were a frightened rabbit. *Odd.* Trip turned back the covers and pulled up the pillows, but no luck. Finally, he spotted the phone between the nightstand and the bed. Realizing the towel around his waist was coming undone, he lay flat on the bed and stuck his arm into the gap.

"Got it." He looked down at his phone to see whose call he'd missed. Ah, Elizabeth Pinckney. Trip contemplated ignoring the blinking message, then thought better of it. First of all, she would track him down. Secondly, he could think of no better coolant to his libido than the snarky PR agent.

Sure enough, he started thinking less and less about Bambi naked the moment he heard Elizabeth's cheerful voice.

"Hi Trip," she said. "Just got word of a great opportunity for you and Bambi and Belles and Beaux. Have Bambi swing by the office tomorrow morning around 10 and I'll fill you both in on all the details."

"Fill you in on all the details," Trip mimicked. "Gah!"

"What's that?" Bambi asked, sticking her head out the bathroom door.

"Oh." Trip was embarrassed that she'd caught him acting so childishly. "Just picked up the message. It's from Miss Pinckney. She said she's got something for us. Wants you to meet us at the office tomorrow at 10."

"Hmm . . . I wonder what it could be?"

"God only knows." Trip rolled his eyes. "But I wouldn't get too excited if I were you."

Trip grabbed his clothes and headed into the bathroom to change, wondering what "great opportunity" Elizabeth Pinckney had managed to lay her hands on. No doubt it involved his sacrifice of dignity at the altar of Belles and Beaux. And no doubt his father would be on board, especially after their tense conversation at the reception.

Trip grumbled all the way down to breakfast, where the

upcoming meeting seemed to be all that Bambi wanted to talk about. She speculated about everything from dinner at some new restaurant opening that week to a cameo on a TV dating show he had never heard of. There was only one positive thing about her babbling: Trip could slide by with just the occasional "oh" or "uh-huh."

He thought that they had reached a new place in their relationship, even though it was a sham. There had seemed to be more to Bambi. But he must have been wrong. Elizabeth Pinckney had not only shattered what was turning out to be an unusually fun weekend with Bambi, she had also turned Bambi back into a dithering idiot. The more he thought about how she had ruined his Sunday, the angrier he got. His mood darkened further when he carried Bambi's bags up the stairs of her building and saw something behind a bush across the street. The black-clad figure with his face concealed behind a video camera approached.

"Trip, you just get back from a long weekend with Bambi?" the photographer ducked out from behind his camera.

"Mind your own business." Trip hustled Bambi toward the door. Just his luck to run into one of them. There weren't many paparazzi around Boston, and those that hung out in the city tended to follow the star quarterback of the New England Patriots and his supermodel wife. Apparently he and Bambi now rated as a story.

"You are my business, at least today." The small, skinny man continued taking shots as he said it.

"Who is that, Trip?" Bambi asked. She looked startled to discover a man taking pictures of her on her front stoop.

"Just some paparazzo. Wants to get some shots of us. Just

smile and wave." She did as he asked and gave the guy the shot he was looking for.

"Okay, you got your shot, now beat it."

"Aww, I can't leave before you do. I'd miss all the good stuff."

"Look," Trip turned from Bambi and headed down the stairs toward the guy. "You need to go. We gave you something, now I need you to leave."

"Like I said . . ." the paparazzo answered.

Trip began to bear down on the man. He was in the mood for a good fight, but he doubted that the guy would bother raising his fists. Probably would just end up suing Trip for the well-deserved punch he was going to get in the face. Trip gauged the man, wondering how he could hit his face and not the camera. He was enjoying the photog's expression, which had morphed from jerky confidence to fear as Trip got closer.

"Trip!"

He heard Bambi calling him from the door. Clearly, she didn't want a fight. And it was her street, after all. But he wasn't going to let her spoil all his fun. He stopped right in front of the man, using the inches he had on the shorter guy.

"Go." He almost whispered, knowing it would be more intimidating that way.

"Uh, you got it, Mr. Whitley." The man turned and headed back toward a beat-up black sedan. Trip waited in the street until he had driven out of sight.

Some of his anger had burned off in that exchange, and he turned back to finish helping Bambi to her apartment. But she no longer stood on the step. He had been so wrapped up in the scene with the paparazzo that he had failed to hear her door close.

CHAPTER EIGHT

"Of all the stupid, brainless, idiotic, testosterone-filled things to do!" Bambi yelled at Lainie that night. She was stomping around The Booby Trap in her red heels, not even noticing the pain although she had been in them for the better part of six hours.

"I don't know." Lainie eyed her from the bench in the locker room. "Sounds like he was being pretty chivalrous to me."

"I don't need a knight in shining armor, Lainie. I can damn well take care of myself! And sure, I was a little surprised to see the photographer there, but Trip didn't need to practically threaten him with a duel to get him to leave."

"I know you can take care of yourself, hon. But sounds like you all had a pretty nice weekend. Why are you fixated on this one thing?"

"He just makes me so angry sometimes." Bambi paced the

small area of the room. "Why do men constantly need to prove they're more macho than other men?"

"Bambi, if you figure that out, you'll have uncovered one of the secrets of the universe. I imagine that belching and farting go along with it."

Bambi laughed, which took the edge off her righteous indignation. She realized her feet were killing her and sat down next to Lainie, slipping off her shoes. "Men," she said.

"You gonna break up with him?"

"No." Bambi groaned.

"Why not? Seems like you might want to."

"It's complicated."

"Always is. Well, I think you make a pretty couple, especially from all those pictures I've been seeing in the paper and on those shows."

"God," Bambi groaned again. "It's ridiculous, isn't it?"

"Yeah." Lainie laughed. "But I got a good story since I know how you two met. Spitting at him then, just like you're spitting at him now. Say, how did you ever get over that?"

Bambi was startled. What should she say? "Well . . . I guess you could say we came to a sort of agreement."

"What sort of—" Bambi glared at her and Lainie cut herself off. "Oh, I see how it is. All right. No more questions."

"Thanks, Lainie."

"No problem, sugar, anything for you."

"Anything?" Bambi perked up. This might be the perfect time to talk to Lainie about her dissertation. She had been putting off interviews since the whole Trip thing started. But if she wanted to have at least a little something ready for the conference, which is why she'd gotten herself into this mess in the first place, she needed to dive in soon. And although Joe would be a great help in getting the girls to talk, Bambi knew that Lainie would be an even more invaluable resource.

"Something on your mind other than Trip Whitley?"

"Actually, yes. You know I'm working my way through school. Well, things are a little bit more connected than that. You see, I'm working on my PhD."

"Wow, girl! That's amazing."

"Thanks." Bambi blushed and continued. "Anyway. I'm writing about The Booby Trap."

"Is that so?" Lainie scrutinized her.

"Yep. About women's roles in professions that have traditionally taken advantage of their sexuality, transformed them into sexual objects for men. I want to look at how women cope with the environment, how they maintain or lose their power, and what effect professions such as these have on wider gender dynamics. I'm also interested in how this fits into the wider discussion of erotic labor."

"Okay . . ."

Bambi could sense Lainie's wariness. "Look, it's a lot of big words for saying that I need to interview the women who work in The Booby Trap. If I can, I'd also like to do some interviews with our repeat clientele."

"What do you want to find out?" She looked Bambi in the eye.

"To be honest," Bambi said, "I don't know. I hope it's something about this world that people have never thought about. People come in here or think about the people that work here in all kinds of ways even though they don't know any of us. Maybe the women derive a certain sort of power from working here. Maybe they don't. I want to know."

"What do you need me to do?" Lainie asked.

"First, I just need you to answer my questions. As openly and honestly as you can. I'll change everyone's names for my writing, so you don't have to worry about anything coming back to bite you."

"And second?"

Bambi took a breath. "I need you to help me with the other girls. Convince them that they should talk to me."

There was a beat of silence. "Joe know about this?"

"Definitely. And he knows that I want to start my interviews soon." Bambi refocused her eyes on Lainie's deep brown ones. "Will you help?"

Lainie was silent and Bambi feared the worst. She wasn't sure how to tell her friend that she wasn't looking to slander the women who worked at The Booby Trap. Or even its clientele. She just wanted to give the world a broader understanding of all of it.

"Okay, I'm in."

"Thank you so much!" Bambi pulled Lainie into a hug.

Lainie laughed. "When do we get started?"

"Soon. Very soon."

Getting up the next morning hadn't been quite as easy as usual since Bambi had closed The Booby Trap Sunday and spent the hour afterwards talking with Lainie. After putting their heads together, she and Lainie decided she should call all the girls together and explain to them what she was doing. Since next week was the big pre-Valentine's Day meeting with the whole staff, Joe had said she could do it then. After that, she had gone home and started planning.

On her way to the Harvard Square T stop, Bambi had indulged in a Dunkin Donuts iced coffee and coconut doughnut to combat her grogginess. She arrived at the Belles and Beaux offices as she slurped the last of the coffee, and dropped it in the waste bin before approaching the receptionist.

"Hi, I'm Bambi. I think I'm supposed to be in a meeting this morning?"

"Oh, Miss Benson," the receptionist was all smiles, "of course. You're a little bit early, but I'm pretty sure the conference room is ready. Just follow me."

Bambi followed the woman through the small office suite into the conference room, where exposed brick and leather office chairs lent the room a very official air. Unsure of where to sit, she chose a spot near the end of the table and picked up an orange from the fruit basket. Probably wise to supplement all that sugar and caffeine with something healthy.

Soon, Elizabeth and an older man, whom Bambi knew was Elizabeth's boss from her description of him, walked in. Bambi smiled and waved at them, but it was clear they were in the middle of some discussion; although Elizabeth lifted her hand in greeting, they stationed themselves at the opposite end of the table. About five minutes later, almost precisely as the clock on the wall struck 10, Mr. Whitley entered. He chose a seat at the center of the table and gave a curt "good morning" to her and to Elizabeth and her boss. To Bambi's relief, he wasn't interested in morning chit-chat.

She sat at her end of the table and ate the orange slices slowly as the minutes ticked by. Five minutes. 10. She could see Mr. Whitley growing redder in the face with each tick of the clock. Fifteen minutes after the supposed start to the meeting, when

Mr. Whitley looked like he might explode out of the chair, Trip sauntered in.

"You're late," Mr. Whitley said.

"Oh am I?" Trip grabbed a danish. He bit into it and talked around the bite. "I'm sorry. I got roped in by a client and things took longer than I expected."

Bambi suspected that nothing of the sort had happened, but she wasn't interested in playing Trip's game. He slung a careless arm around the back of her chair and she said, "Well, since Trip is here now, maybe we can get started? I worked all night last night and I'm really tired."

Mr. Whitley raised his eyebrows, but Elizabeth took the cue. "Excellent. Glad we all could make it." She glared at Trip. "As you all may have noticed, people have fallen in love with Trip and Bambi. The promos have increased business for Belles and Beaux not only here in Boston, but nationally. Am I right, Mr. Whitley?"

"They have." Bambi noticed that a reminder of increasing profits seemed to soothe at least some of Mr. Whitley's ruffled feathers.

"In addition to the ads, the affair has begun to garner interest in the national media, which was exactly the point, as a way to multiply your advertising dollars. We are approaching a very sensitive time in the next week, as you may know."

"Valentine's Day," Elizabeth's supervisor, Mr. Weldon, said.

Oh. Bambi hadn't even given a thought to the most romantic day of the year except as it pertained to her dissertation research.

"Yes," Elizabeth said. "And we've been thinking of ways for Trip and Bambi to celebrate the holiday that will highlight the romance and 'different worlds' story they have, which will play nicely into Belles and Beaux. But just last night, I received a call from Madison Hart's people. They're doing a show on local celebrity couples. How they met, how they make it work, how they are celebrating Valentine's Day. And they want Trip and Bambi."

"Madison Hart," Mr. Whitley said. "I've heard that name before."

"Yes, sir," Elizabeth answered. "She has worked as the *Boston Daily*'s gossip columnist, and has parlayed considerable success there into her own show about local culture. *Hart of Boston* features restaurant reviews, suggestions for things to do around the area, and interviews with locals and local celebrities. I think it would be a great way to plug Belles and Beaux."

"'Scuse me? But do we have any plans for Valentine's Day?" Trip asked, leaning back in his chair as far as it could go and licking the icing off of his fingers.

"I am still working out the details," Elizabeth said. "But we will have them to you by the time you need to do the interview. It is on Thursday."

"Oh, I'm so excited!" Bambi said. She couldn't imagine any bimbo that wouldn't be interested in being on TV.

"You think that Madison Hart will make them look good?" Mr. Whitley asked Elizabeth. Bambi felt his disapproving gaze directed at both her and Trip.

"Of course. It's a total puff piece, Alex," Mr. Weldon said. "Nothing to worry about. After all, it's Valentine's Day. Who wants any hard-hitting reporting on the day of romance?"

"Don't I get any say?" Trip asked.

"You don't show me the courtesy of coming to the meeting on time, so no, you don't get to say anything," Mr. Whitley barked. Then he turned with more good favor to Elizabeth and Mr. Weldon. "Thanks for your good work. This sounds like a wonderful opportunity."

Mr. Whitley stood up to leave and Bambi figured that there was no need for her to stay. "You'll let me know when you need me?" she looked first at Trip, who was studying his fingernails, then at Elizabeth.

"Wait, Bambi," Elizabeth said, "let me walk you out. We do have to iron out a few details, you know." Once Bambi had said her goodbyes to Trip and Mr. Weldon and they were out of the room, Elizabeth lowered her voice. "This is it. Can we talk tonight?"

Bambi nodded.

"Excellent. See you at eight." Then she made her voice louder again, "Don't worry, Bambi, you will be great on camera."

That evening, Bambi heard a knock on her door. "Come on in! It's open!"

Elizabeth walked into the small apartment and immediately began talking. "Bambi, this is going to be it."

"I thought Mr. Weldon said it was just a puff piece." Bambi eyed the spaghetti noodles in the pot critically, wondering if they were done yet.

"Edward Weldon, for all his wonderful qualities, does not know a thing about Madison Hart. She is a climber. And she is always looking for the best stories."

"That so?"

Elizabeth wandered over to the stove and grabbed the fork Bambi had been holding over the pasta. She dunked it in, fished out a noodle, and dropped it in her mouth. "Mmmm. Yes. And I have to give her credit; she does have a nose for secrets. That is what made her such a good gossip columnist."

"You think it's done?" Bambi asked. At Elizabeth's nod, she drained it in the sink, added the store-bought pasta sauce to some onions and ground beef she had been cooking, and mixed them together.

"She will find out about your education, I guarantee you. If only to make it a better interview."

"Well, I'm not exactly trying to hide anything. I mean, I haven't asked anyone to lie for me."

"Except me." Elizabeth looked Bambi in the eye.

"I guess you have a point there. But what I'm saying is that it'll be something easy for her to find."

"True. I found it myself." Elizabeth grabbed some plates from the cabinet and ladled the pasta onto them as Bambi finished mixing the sauce. "That makes it even better. Even Madison Hart will be playing into our hands."

"How so?"

"As I mentioned, Madison Hart is great because she digs. No one at Belles and Beaux will suspect any ulterior motives from either of us. Plus, she won't think she's revealing a big secret, since the information is so easy to find."

"How can you be sure she'll find it?"

"You know me. I do not leave anything up to chance. I just sent an anonymous tip from a newly created email address to the producers of the show."

"They might not read that—those guys must get millions of emails a week."

"Oh, I am sure they will, especially with your name on it.

They are always looking for the newest stuff. They cannot afford to pass this up."

"What did you send?"

"The transcript of your Class Day speech from the *Columbia Spectator*. And a mention of your graduate work at Harvard."

"Oh, geez."

"I thought it was great. Particularly the part about women making their own fairy tales. Finding their own happy ending, where love isn't the sole determinant."

"I might just be in over my head." Bambi dropped her head into her hands.

"You will be perfect! I know you are intelligent and can think of plenty of things to say, but I thought that you might need a little preparation on the questions they would ask. For that reason, I made you a binder. It's just some of Maddy's history, transcripts of some of her past interviews, potential questions." Elizabeth left the table and headed over to her briefcase, from which she retrieved a red binder. "Festive, right? I figured if it were red, you would remember what it was for."

Bambi looked at the binder filled with about 100 pages of what she assumed were questions and answers. She almost choked on her food. This was bad timing. How could she prepare for that and her presentation to the girls at The Booby Trap at the same time?

"Is that all?" she asked.

"Oh, this is what I thought to throw together at the office today after we—" Elizabeth stopped mid-sentence. "Oh. You were kidding. Well, I am sure you won't need half of this, since it *is* your subject."

"Don't worry," Bambi said, taking the binder from her friend. "I'll look through it."

Elizabeth seemed to sigh in relief. "Oh, good. You know, this media thing is a whole new world for you. I just want you to do as well there as you've been doing in academia."

"I appreciate it, Liz, I really do."

"And maybe we should go over it a bit tonight? Then I thought we should have another study session, when you've had an opportunity to familiarize yourself with more of the materials. You know, in case you have any questions."

"Sounds great," Bambi said. But as she finished eating her pasta, she wondered how she was going to prepare for both her meeting with the girls at The Booby Trap and the interview with Madison Hart. Probably with a lot of sleepless nights.

She forced her concentration back on her friend, who was looking at her expectantly. "Should we get started?" Elizabeth asked. "I mean, only if you're ready."

"I'm as ready as I'll ever be," Bambi replied. She could tell by the look of determination on Elizabeth's face that this was going to be the first of many long nights.

Bambi stopped by Joe's office on her way out Wednesday night since she wouldn't be back until the following Monday, the day of the big pre-Valentine's Day meeting.

"Hey Joe."

"Bambi. Come on, sit down for a sec. You look a little tired tonight. Have I been working you too hard?"

"No of course not." Bambi took a seat, figuring she could take a moment before dashing off to her last prep with Elizabeth. It definitely felt good to take a load off.

"Well, what about that fellow of yours? You could've gotten

those circles thanks to some extracurricular nighttime activity, if you know what I mean." Joe winked.

"Joe! I'm certainly not going to be discussing my extracurricular nighttime activity with you, that's for sure. You're practically a father figure to me."

"Well, how is your relationship going?"

"Trip's . . . fine." Bambi wondered what Trip would be like after the interview tomorrow. Probably not fine. But that was not her problem.

"Fine. What an endorsement."

"Don't worry, Joe." Bambi tried to keep the exasperation out of her voice. She knew Joe was just looking out for her.

"Okay, okay. But at least tell me what's on your mind. School keeping you awake?"

"Not really. I guess I'm nervous because Trip and I are appearing on this show later." And after all the preparation with Elizabeth, Bambi still wasn't sure she wanted to take on Madison Hart.

"Bambi, can I ask you something?"

"Sure, Joe, anything."

"Seems to me like the media aren't painting a very accurate picture of you. Sometimes I just want to punch the TV. Mostly, I just change the channel. Why's that?"

Bambi was taken aback. She hadn't expected that Joe would be watching any of the gossip shows. "Oh, I guess it's just the media. They want to see what they want to see."

"That's what I don't get. Even if I hadn't known you since you were an anklebiter, I would know in one second that you are one smart cookie. How can they not see it?"

"I don't know, Joe."

"Listen, if this is something about your mother or what that jerk did to you . . ."

Bambi put her hand up. "It's not. I promise."

"Okay, well, I just want to say one more thing, then I won't bug you anymore. No matter how great this Trip Whitley is, no matter how rich, you shouldn't have to change yourself for him. You're smart and beautiful and damn near perfect. If he doesn't love you, that's his fault. If he hurts you, I'll punch him in the nose."

Bambi's emotions were running high thanks to the lack of sleep, but she wasn't sure whether to laugh or cry at Joe's statement. "Thanks, Joe."

"Anyways." Joe cleared his throat. "You ready for Monday? If that's what's bugging you, we can put it off."

"No, no. I'm not ready yet, but I will be. Thanks for that, too."

"Aww, that's nothing. And you'll be great. Most of the girls love you. And those that don't are still pretty impressed by you being on TV and all, dating some big shot celebrity. Stupid, I know, but maybe you can use that in your favor."

"That's a good idea. I just might." Bambi stood up. "Well, I gotta run. Got to finish preparing for the interview tomorrow with Madison Hart."

"Well, I hope Miss Hart will see through all the bullshit."

Now Bambi laughed. "Me too." She circled around his desk to give him a hug around the neck. "Bye, Joe. See you Monday."

"See you Monday, kid. Get some sleep."

CHAPTER NINE

Trip walked into the studio for *Hart of Boston* at five till three, a whole five minutes before his call time. He may have been more than comfortable leaving Elizabeth Pinckney waiting, but he knew better than to get on the bad side of Maddy Hart. She had dug into a few of his friends back when she was writing for *Boston Daily*, and once she decided she didn't like someone, she had no qualms about using her proverbial poison pen.

A girl he assumed was an intern led him through to the green room. On the way through the studio, they passed the make-up room, a glass box situated toward the back of the studio. Trip saw Maddy inside, appearing to be spray-painted with some odd contraption. She was looking straight ahead, murmuring lines, oblivious to the chaos around her. Her thick brown hair was partly pulled off her face, the rest of it falling in romantic ringlets. He couldn't see her clothes, but he imagined that they fit the picture: romantic, girly. He knew better than to be deceived.

"Hold on a sec," he called to the intern. Then he headed to the make-up room.

"Wait, you can't go in there," the girl said to his back. Trip ignored her and pushed through the door.

"Hello, Maddy."

"Trip Whitley." She didn't move but rather eyed his reflection in the mirror in front of her, her green eyes both sharp and cruel. "Good to see you. I would do the whole kiss kiss thing, but as you can see, I'm otherwise occupied."

"I'll forgive you this once."

"Glad you were able to do the show."

"Well, thanks for having us. And my people said that I could do a plug for Belles and Beaux."

"Of course. Least I can do. I must say, I never thought I'd see you doing the Valentine's Day episode. When we ran in the same circles, you seemed to be more content to be a bachelor. That is, after Constance Bradford broke your heart."

Trip winced but tried not to show it. "You don't forget a thing, do you, Maddy?"

"My mind is a steel trap. I even remember wonderful moments we shared together at JER-NE. Oh, and a couple lovely evenings just upstairs in the suite at the Ritz. No better way to get in with the in-crowd, I say, than to get in with Trip Whitley. But I understand that the Liberty Hotel is the new spot."

Trip thought back to those encounters with something approaching disgust. Maddy had used her athletic body and full lips to wrangle invites and information from Trip. He had thought they shared something. Then, he found out she was just exploiting him.

"Was the old jail, you know. You should come out sometime," Trip said. "I know you'd feel completely comfortable there."

"What fun would it be without you there with me?" Maddy finally turned around and looked him in the eye.

"I'm sure there are plenty of other saps to take my place."

"Perhaps." Maddy turned back to the mirror. "I doubt the new girl of the week would have much fun there, anyway. I must congratulate you on her, Trip. She sounds like a real catch."

Trip bristled. Maddy's tone had been sincere, but he knew there was always sarcasm underneath it. No matter his feelings for Bambi, she didn't deserve to be looked down on by this bitch. "We're very happy. And excited about Valentine's Day."

"That so? Not what I would've guessed, given everything I know about her."

"Well, maybe you don't know the whole story," Trip said.

"I'll just have to look forward to finding it out, then. See you in an hour, Trip."

Trip knew when he was being dismissed, and he didn't like it. But he had nothing to add to the discussion, so he walked out without saying goodbye and met the impatient intern at the door. She frowned at him before she started on her way again.

Oh well, Trip thought. *One customer down.*

Bambi stood in the green room discussing camera outfits with Elizabeth. It felt like she had brought her entire wardrobe to the shoot, with pieces spread on every available surface of the room. Add one more stressor to a day that was promising to be a doozy. Then, Trip walked into the chaos.

"Oh, good, you are on time," Elizabeth said.

"Wouldn't miss it for the world," he said, looking calm and unruffled. But then, he probably didn't know what a shark Madison Hart was reputed to be. And he definitely didn't know what Bambi was going to hit him with during the interview.

Elizabeth turned to Bambi, "So, he's wearing khaki pants and the pink button-down shirt, meaning you should not wear the red." She turned back to Trip, "By the way, when were those pants last ironed?"

"Ironed? Hell, how should I know?"

"Well, you cannot go out like that. Give me the pants."

"What?" Trip looked offended that he might have to take his pants off in front of Elizabeth Pinckney.

"The pants, Trip. Now. I have to run them over to wardrobe to see if they'll iron them for you. You cannot go on TV looking like that. Your family owns a successful business and yet you fail to iron your pants?"

He looked at Bambi for some support. But she didn't have any to give. She was busy making sure her hands didn't shake so much that she dropped the dress she was holding. Eventually, he gave up, took off his pants, and handed them to Elizabeth.

In his boxers, he walked over and put his hand on Bambi's shoulder as she stood in front of the mirror. She jumped. "A little nervous?" he asked.

"I guess you could say that." She tried to look braver. It would not do if even the dense Trip Whitley could figure out how she was feeling.

"You'll do just fine. Don't let Maddy get to you."

"Maddy . . . do you know her?" Bambi traded the gray wool skirt and v-neck sweater she was holding for a navy sweater dress with a cowl neck.

"Just a little bit. I guess you could say we ran with the same crowd starting about the time that she began working for *The Boston Daily*."

That was more than Elizabeth had told Bambi. And it was interesting enough to temporarily reduce her apprehension. "That must've been awkward. I mean, her writing about you guys and hanging out at the same places. It sounds incestuous."

Trip smiled. "It was fun for a while. Back then, most people, me included, got pretty excited to see their names in the paper. Good or bad."

"Seems like things aren't very different now."

"That's where you're wrong. None of this was my idea. I would get out of these ridiculous ads if I could." Bambi turned to look at him. That was definitely unexpected. She would have thought that a guy like Trip Whitley would love the publicity—and all of the perks that came with it. He continued. "I want to take a much bigger role in the company, be something more than a figurehead. So personal publicity isn't a big thing anymore. At least not for me."

"But still for Maddy."

Trip laughed. "Yep. You hit that nail right on the head. Still for Maddy."

Bambi was uncomfortable with their shared assessment of the waiting interviewer. She changed the subject. "Which one do you think I should wear?" She held out the gray skirt outfit and the navy sweater dress. "I just can't decide."

"Definitely the sweater dress. We're supposed to be pretty informal here."

"Do you mind turning around while I put it on?" She

thought back to the night last weekend at the Colonial Inn, when he caught her naked.

Trip turned and closed his eyes. "This good? You just give me the word when you're done."

"Okay," Bambi said as she pulled her shirt over her head. She wasn't sure she trusted him, so she jerked the dress over her body. "Almost there . . . okay, you can turn around."

Bambi stepped in front of the mirror, still worrying about choosing the correct outfit. She pulled on a pair of low-heeled brown boots that hit just below the knee, and cinched her waist with a dark red belt. She bent down to retrieve jewelry. Her hands trembled, and she struggled to pin the silver hoops into her ears. She failed completely with the clasp of the silver necklace.

"Here, let me help." Trip strode over. Bambi couldn't see that she had a choice and gave him the necklace. She lifted her blonde hair from her neck to help him do his job. He clasped the two ends together, but he didn't immediately take his hands away. Instead, he settled his thumbs into her shoulders and massaged them.

"Thanks," she said. "That feels good." And it did. Probably more than she wanted to admit. She let her neck drop and Trip continued his work. He moved his hands up and down her neck and out to her shoulders. But she knew she shouldn't let it last too long. "Trip?" Bambi pulled her head up and turned to look at him. Then, she noticed their lips were scant inches apart and forgot what she had to say. It wouldn't take any effort whatsoever to close the remaining distance and have his lips on hers.

"Thank God those people were able to do something with these pants." Elizabeth bustled back into the room. Trip jerked back from Bambi, the spell broken. Not aware of the tension in the room, Elizabeth thrust the pressed pants at Trip. "Here you go. And then you both need to head into make-up."

Bambi silently thanked Elizabeth for saving her from doing a very unwise thing. She retreated to the other side of the room as Trip accepted the pants and tugged them on.

"Bambi, that dress is perfect." Elizabeth continued to babble as Trip left and headed to the make-up room. Once he left, Bambi felt like she could breathe again.

Trip returned to the green room after make-up. Bambi was gone—he had seen her sit down in a make-up chair just before he'd left. Elizabeth was straightening the area when he walked in.

"Need any help?" he asked, although he didn't have a clue where anything went.

"Almost done. You should have a seat, Trip. I wanted to talk to you about the interview."

"I've done stuff like this before."

"As the face of Belles and Beaux, I am sure you have. But this time, it is a little different. You are going to be talking about the personal, not the business. I want to go over a couple of things."

"Do we really have to do this?"

"Yes, we really do. Look, I've reviewed some questions with Bambi, and now it's your turn. That is what your family pays me for."

"Fine." Trip sat down and Elizabeth sat next to him.

"First, can you tell me what your plans are for Valentine's Day?"

"Dinner at Upstairs in the Square, which is in Cambridge,

near Bambi's apartment. Then we're headed into Boston to watch a production of Shakespeare's *Twelfth Night*."

"Good. You are going to need to elaborate more when you are talking to Miss Hart, but I am pleased you've got it down."

"I can memorize things, you know."

Elizabeth's eyes flattened and she looked down her nose at him even though he was a good foot taller than she. "I know. But you haven't always put much effort into doing what I've told you."

"I've got this down pat, don't worry." Why couldn't she trust him an inch?

"Fine." She persisted, "You know Madison will ask you about how you met."

"Yeah, I'm ready for that one, too."

"And about what Bambi does. No doubt, she will have some serious questions to ask. She is . . ."

"Not going to take it easy on me, I know." Trip looked her in the eyes, trying to let her know that he understood Maddy Hart and women like her.

"No. Or Bambi." Elizabeth paused, as if to think something through. "You need to make sure you say that you support Bambi in what she does no matter what. Do you think you can handle that?"

"Got it." Trip stood.

"They are going to tape for an hour or so and use the best bits for a five or 10 minute segment during the show. That means they have a lot to play with. Don't give them too much." Elizabeth pointed at him to emphasize her point.

"I said I got it. Listen, I'm not my dad. I know Maddy."

"Good, I just wanted to make sure we are clear."

"Crystal." He caught Elizabeth's gaze and then turned and left the room.

Bambi made her way onto the soundstage. It was set up to look like a cozy living room, with a plush chair for Maddy and coordinating couch for guests. She sat down for a moment to get her bearings, but it felt as if the couch were stuffed with rocks, so she rose. The usual set, which she had seen in the previous interviews she had watched for research, had been dressed up with red and white roses, and she saw glass arrangements with candy hearts inside them on various side tables.

Lights glared on the stage and obscured Bambi's view into the rest of the studio. From that blackness a tech emerged to fit her with a microphone. Bambi was just beginning to feel the blood pumping through her veins as the adrenalin kicked in. She would have to be on her toes throughout the interview.

Soon, Trip joined them and was fitted with his own mic. Maddy arrived and really sent Bambi's nerves into overdrive. Maddy had swapped her usual power suit for a floral dress that wrapped around her toned figure with sleeves that belled out by the wrists before ending in a small cuff. She had clearly been styled to look like a romantic heroine, her thick brown hair pulled off her face and cascading in ringlets down her back.

"Bambi, so nice to meet you." She stretched out her hand. "I'm Madison Hart."

"Nice to meet you, too, Miss Hart." She gave Maddy a firm handshake and let the woman take her measure.

"Oh, please call me Madison. I'm not Miss Hart to anyone,

especially Trip's girlfriend. You do know that Trip and I go way back." She reached out to rub Trip's shoulder.

Bambi realized she hated Madison Hart. Her soft pink dress and the soft make-up couldn't hide what this woman really was: a villainess. Bambi supposed it would be better if she could think of Madison as her ally, since the woman was unwittingly helping her to reveal something to Trip and the world that Bambi herself wanted to share. But something about Madison's smile turned her off. And that condescending comment about how she and Trip went "way back." Please. As far as Madison Hart knew, Trip was off the market now, no matter how far back he and she or Constance Bradford or anyone else went. She looked down her nose at Madison. Two could play that game. "He told me already."

"Well, great." She looked around, signaling to a cameraman. "Why don't we all take a seat? I imagine my team or yours has briefed you on the plan, but I'll repeat it. We're going to spend about an hour or so talking about you, your relationship, and your plans for Valentine's Day. It should be a fun conversation, so relax and throw your worries to the wind."

Trip snorted, but Maddy ignored him and continued. "What I'm saying is, pretend it's just friends out to dinner or something, and we're having a chat. Unfortunately, we won't be able to use everything we talk about, but a significant portion of the interview will be aired on Valentine's Day. Does that sound good to you, Bambi?"

"Yes. Perfect. I think there are a lot of misconceptions out there about me and about our relationship. Hopefully, you can help me correct some of them?"

"I'm sure I can," Maddy said.

Bambi composed her face into a bright smile and arched her back. She was ready, and Madison Hart should have learned a lesson from her research: not to underestimate Bambi Benson.

Trip looked back and forth between the two women. Maddy's green eyes twinkled and he wondered what she knew. He also wasn't sure what Bambi had meant about misconceptions. Before that moment, he didn't even know she knew the word. She couldn't mean the transactional, rather than romantic, nature of their relationship. Thinking of that, Trip broke into a cold sweat. He looked to Bambi, who smiled sweetly back at him.

"Let's get started," Madison chirped. "First, I have to do a quick intro, but then it will be all about you two lovebirds." Trip wouldn't have a chance to ask Bambi what she had meant.

He looked at her adoringly for the camera. But instead of an adoring look back, he saw some determination or spark in Bambi's eyes that he had never seen before. He knew, though, that it was futile to hope that Madison Hart had met her match. He just prayed that she would take it easy on Bambi. He watched as the camera panned and ended with what he assumed was a close-up on Madison.

"Hello, Boston! And welcome to *Hart of Boston*." Madison spoke into the camera as if it were an old friend. "Happy Valentine's Day. I'm Madison Hart and today we're interviewing some of Boston's favorite couples. We'll hear about how they met, how they keep the romance alive, and what their plans are for the big night tonight. My first guests have been cropping up all over the city on their dates and all across the country as entertainment shows try to get all the gossip on their blooming romance. But we here at *Hart of Boston* decided to get our information straight from the sources, Trip Whitley and Bambi Benson."

Trip grabbed Bambi's hand as he watched the camera pan toward them.

"Now, Trip," Madison continued, "We all know you from your appearances in ads for Belles and Beaux. Did you and Bambi meet on the site?"

"No, sadly, although that would be a great story to tell and a great endorsement for Belles and Beaux," Trip responded. For once, he was glad of his starring role in the commercials. They had gotten him ready to respond and react to the cameras.

"So tell me, how did you meet?" Madison leaned in.

"It's an unlikely story, just like so many of the matches we make on Belles and Beaux," he said. "We actually met at The Booby Trap."

Bambi chose that moment to chime in. "He was there for a friend's bachelor party. I noticed that he was feeling a little down."

"Rough day at work," Trip shrugged. Elizabeth had told them to stick close to the story of what had really happened.

"Happens to us all." Madison also mugged for the camera.

"I didn't even know who he was, not until my friend told me," Bambi said.

Trip picked up the story. "Well, you can imagine that when I could see enough beyond my funk, I noticed this beautiful girl serving me drinks."

"So, did you ask her out right then and there?" asked Madison.

"No, it wasn't long after the party broke up that the bar closed. So I just waited outside for her."

"It must've been pretty cold. Boston winters can be frigid," Madison said.

"What can I tell you? I guess, as they say, I had my love to keep me warm." Trip smiled indulgently.

"So what happened next?"

"When she came out, I begged her to go out with me. And she said yes. How could she resist this charm?" Trip turned to her and stole a kiss.

"It wasn't quite like that." She poked him in the chest to push him back. "Normally, I have a policy of not dating customers. But he wore me down till I just couldn't say no." Bambi leaned past Trip and beckoned Madison closer. "Plus, he is pretty cute and charming, although don't tell him I said so."

"Your secret's safe with me," Madison said as she leaned back. "What a cute little story. Well, you two have certainly set gossips around the country buzzing, thanks to Trip's status as one of the most attractive bachelors under 35. And, I don't mean to be rude, but about your workplace, Bambi."

"No offense taken," Bambi said.

"But it seems they haven't gotten the whole story, am I right? You've been labeled an airheaded cocktail waitress when you're anything but."

What? Trip wanted to chime in. But he kept silent.

"It's true; I've found that people have stereotyped me just because of where I met Trip. Just like any other stereotype, this one is unfair to women who work in places like The Booby Trap."

"And you're particularly qualified to make that statement, aren't you? As a PhD candidate in women's studies at Harvard?"

Trip was blindsided. He withdrew his hand from Bambi's and turned to stare, mouth agape. How had he not known? Why had she not told him this? And why in hell had she chosen this moment to expose herself?

"I am only a third-year student, so I don't know how qualified I am, but yes, that environment is one of the things I'm focusing on in my studies. As for the gossips you were speaking about, I find that some people make snap decisions about who you are without asking the right questions."

Trip caught Bambi looking at him significantly. *Oh, I see how it is. You wanted to teach me a lesson?* He hated her at that moment. True, black hate. But there was nothing he could do on camera, in front of Madison Hart.

"Well," Madison said, "let me see if I can ask you the right questions. But first, I want to talk to Trip." *And it was about to get worse.* "Trip, tell me how you felt when you found out that Bambi was not just another pretty face."

"Uh," Trip blinked several times and took a deep breath. How was he supposed to respond? Maybe honesty would do. "Surprised. As you can imagine . . . but . . ."

"But what, Trip?" Madison asked.

"Proud of her." He exhaled, took Bambi's hand, and looked her in the eye. He wasn't going to let Madison Hart win this one. She had pegged him as a playboy five years ago. Things had changed. "Of course a PhD is a big deal, a difficult thing to get."

"That's true. But a lot of men are uncomfortable with dating and marrying women who are so ambitious. What about you? Certainly most of the other women you have dated in the past haven't been quite as . . . accomplished."

Trip narrowed his eyes at Maddy. He thought of what his mother would tell him to say. "True. But I want a partner to share my life with, not just a one night stand."

"I see. Glad to see that Boston's playboy has grown up. How do you feel about a woman making more money than you?"

"Frankly, I find it unlikely with Bambi," he smiled, "since she's in academia. But I don't understand why the husband ought to be the primary breadwinner. My mom probably makes more than my dad, although I've never asked."

"Your mother is quite the power broker in local politics, isn't she? I suppose she's had a strong influence on your thoughts about women."

"I'd like to think so," Trip said, glad to move off the topic of Bambi and toward one he knew more about.

"But those are big, life questions. What about the more practical impact of Bambi's views and lifestyle on how your relationship works every day? Does she allow you to open doors for her?"

The respite had been too good to last. Trip breathed. "She's never mentioned any objection."

"And I imagine that Bambi's work has had an impact on how you pursue your relationship? And how you're going to celebrate Valentine's Day?"

"Insofar as . . ."

"Well, of course her views on romance are definitely atypical." Madison smiled. She thought she had gotten him. "My producers pulled up her editorial from the *Columbia Spectator*, titled 'Smashing the Glass Slipper.' Maybe you haven't read it, Trip, but I'm sure Bambi's talked about it with you. She does say that women need to start forgetting the fairy tale ideal that a man will come along and transform their lives from drudgery to hearts and flowers. She said that women are responsible for their own lives and their own transformations. But isn't the transformative power of love and romance at the heart of Valentine's Day?"

"Well . . ." Trip was thrown for a second, albeit smaller loop.

He was not only dating a PhD student, but one who had written an article called "Smashing the Glass Slipper"? This could not get any worse. He tried to think quickly, feeling unusually tongue-tied.

Bambi watched Trip flounder. Part of her enjoyed it, but she couldn't bear to watch him be completely humiliated in front of Madison Hart. Even Trip didn't deserve that. She jumped in. "Madison, you're right. It does make our relationship a little different from the others you might have on your show today. I don't buy into the Valentine's Day production, but that doesn't mean that Trip and I can't have a nice night together. In fact, we're going to see *Twelfth Night*."

"Is that so? One of Shakespeare's, right?"

"Yes. Like many of Shakespeare's comedies, it features a woman who dresses like a man to achieve her goals. Some scholars have suggested that Shakespeare used his work to play with gender stereotypes using confused feelings of love." Bambi watched Madison's eyes glaze over and stopped herself.

"I see," Madison said. "Well, what do you say to young girls who are watching you cavort around town, becoming a princess?"

"I wouldn't say that I am." Bambi tucked a strand of hair behind her ear.

"Hasn't Trip taken you on dates to the theatre, the opera, and to exclusive benefits?"

"He has. And I of course couldn't pay him back. But girls need to figure out what they want out of their relationships and if they feel comfortable with boys paying all the time. I certainly don't. And maybe I can't do the big productions because I am a graduate student, after all. But I can contribute to this relationship."

"And for Valentine's Day?"

"Listen, I think there's too much emphasis put on Valentine's Day. I want to tell the girls out there that you don't need a guy to be happy. You can make yourself happy."

"Okay. Would you consider yourself a feminist?"

"I would," Bambi said.

"Well then, what is the role of modern feminism? Aren't men and women treated equally nowadays?"

Bambi responded to that and a barrage of other questions. Trip sat next to her the whole time, holding her hand, but he may as well have been a block of wood for all of the emotion that he was sharing with her. When Madison signaled that the interview was over, Trip yanked off his microphone and stormed off the stage.

"I wonder what his problem is," Madison said.

"No problem," Bambi said. "Maybe I ought to go check on him." Without another word, she followed Trip into the green room where Elizabeth was waiting.

"What the hell was that?!" Trip slammed the door behind her. "You didn't think you needed to tell me about all of that?"

Bambi's sympathy vanished. "You made an assumption. You didn't care. I just became what you wanted. "

"So you thought it would be a good idea to drop the charade in front of Madison Hart?"

"It's not my fault that she cared more about researching me than you did. When have you ever asked me about my interests?"

"You bring this up now?" He paced across the room.

"Trip, Bambi," Elizabeth interjected. "Maybe we should calm down, talk rationally."

"You knew!" He pointed a finger at Elizabeth. "You knew. Don't deny it because I can see it all over your face. What was this, some kind of conspiracy?"

"Not a conspiracy, Trip," Elizabeth responded. "Just an opportunity for you to learn more about your girlfriend. Whom you supposedly care enough about to ask about her life."

"Whatever." Trip headed toward the door. "I'm out of here. This is over."

"Trip, it cannot be over," Elizabeth said. "You should have seen the two of you out there. It was gold. And the face of Belles and Beaux cannot be seen breaking up with a girl who just stood up for womanhood."

"Screw that! She hates romance."

"Come on, Trip. She is the ultimate symbol that you can have both romance and a career! That there can be two powerful people in a relationship! The two of you just earned a spot as Boston's favorite power couple."

"Fine. Whatever. It's clear that my life isn't my own anymore. But I don't want to see her," he pointed to Bambi, "until Tuesday night."

He slammed the door so hard on the way out that Bambi cringed. What had seemed like such a good idea before didn't look so great right now.

CHAPTER TEN

Trip raced out of the studio, the humiliation and anger burning like physical pain in his chest. He picked up his phone to call Pat, then realized his friend was still on his honeymoon and threw the phone across the car.

He raced down the streets of Boston at speeds that were not safe. He knew he was lucky that he didn't run into any cops, because he wasn't sure that he could control the rage that surged through his veins.

When he got home, he headed straight for a cabinet that held his liquor and grabbed a bottle of bourbon and a glass. He tumbled a few ice cubes into the glass and poured in a liberal amount. He knocked it back with a vengeance. The hot trail it paved down his throat was just the sensation he needed at that moment. He poured himself another drink, grabbed the bottle, and made his way to the couch.

Why did she have to humiliate him in front of Maddy Hart, of all people? And how was it that Madison Hart knew more about his girlfriend than he did? Granted, the relationship was fake, but Trip never wanted to see Maddy get the upper hand.

Trip took another gulp as he considered the events back in the studio. Both women had taken him by surprise. Maddy was a shark and she would smell the blood in the water. It had taken everything he had not to show his surprise, his ignorance, his shock. But the moment the pressure was off, Trip's shock at the information had quickly transformed to anger. How dare she not tell him? What right did she have to blindside him like that?

Trip decided that the glass was slowing him down and discarded it in favor of drinking straight from the bottle.

When he awoke the next morning with the worst headache he'd had since his twenty-first birthday, Trip surveyed the damage. He had finished the bottle of bourbon, but the glass had overturned onto his rug, leaving a big, wet stain.

Holding his head, he wandered into the kitchen in search of paper towels. A ringing phone made his head feel like it was about to explode. Without looking at the caller ID, he picked it up and immediately regretted his decision when he heard the voice on the other end.

"Trip, where the hell have you been?" his dad shouted.

Trip winced. His father's shouting voice was almost as bad as the ringing phone had been. "Dad, can you quiet down a little?"

His father lowered his voice about one decibel before continuing, "I've been calling you all morning on your cell phone."

Trip realized that he had left the cell phone in the car, and it had remained wherever it had landed when he'd thrown it. "Sorry, Dad. I didn't charge my phone last night."

"Well, it's a good thing I made you get the land line, then."

"Sure, Dad." Trip wasn't about to get into an argument about modern technology with his father when he was pretty sure his brain was functioning at far less than normal capacity. "What were you calling for?"

"Dinner tomorrow night. You coming? Virginia and Constance Bradford will be there again."

Trip winced. Sunday dinner every two weeks. Was the last one already two weeks ago? It seemed like it had been much more recent. But he never missed one of his mother's dinners without a truly good excuse.

"Trip?" his father asked. "You there?"

"I'm here, Dad. I'll be there."

"Good. See you at six."

His dad hung up the phone without saying goodbye. Trip headed back into the living room to lie down on the couch when he saw the stain on the rug again. He returned to the kitchen to grab more paper towels.

As he scrubbed, his thoughts turned back to Bambi and Maddy Hart. Much as it pained him, literally, to think about them, he couldn't get the interview out of his mind. He had been dating Bambi for nearly four weeks, and although he hadn't fallen in love with the woman, he would never have put her in the same category as Maddy Hart. Aside from seeming to be way below Maddy's intellectual level, he wouldn't have guessed that Bambi had a similar mean streak running through her.

He thought back to their trip to Concord, the way she had oohed and aahed over the connections with *Little Women* at Orchard House, the surprise in her eyes after he had quoted Emerson in the cemetery. Maybe he should have noticed then that there might be something more to Bambi Benson than he had originally thought.

And then there was Allison. In the short time that he had left them alone, she and Allison had seemed to get along. And Ally was no dummy, nor would she stand for airheads. Trip tried to think back to the wedding. In his mind, he saw Allison saying it was a pleasure to meet Bambi. He searched his memory of her face for any trace of the insincerity or simple politeness that he had seen on his mother's face or Mrs. Bradford's face that night of the gala. There was nothing but genuine appreciation for having met a lovely girl.

That brought Trip up short. If Allison had been able to find Bambi's intellect, why hadn't he? He recalled their previous dates and couldn't remember a single topic of conversation. That had him feeling pretty bad.

The more he thought about his and Bambi's relationship, the more he realized that he might have shared some of the blame. He didn't agree with her decision to throw all that on him in front of Maddy Hart or the thousands of people watching the program, but he could get over it.

Trip's anger had cooled considerably by the time he knocked on his parents' door Sunday evening.

"Hello, Trip. Glad to see you're on time." His father looked casually elegant in dark jeans, a white button-down, and maroon cashmere sweater.

"Good to see you, Dad." Trip shook his father's hand and made his way into the kitchen, where his mother was taking a roast out of the oven.

"Trip," she turned around and saw him. Once she had set down the pan, she kissed him on both cheeks. "Alex, will you carve that?"

"Mom. Smells delicious."

"Oh, it was nothing. But where's Bambi?"

"Bambi?" Trip was taken by surprise. His mother had made her feelings toward Bambi pretty clear.

"Your father told me. I don't know why you kept that from us, you silly boy!" She swatted Trip with a potholder.

"Dad?" Trip was getting more suspicious by the second. His father looked up from the roast with a twinkle in his eye.

"Elizabeth called me about the interview. Sounds like it went even better than we had hoped. Maybe you did pick a winner, son."

Damn Elizabeth Pinckney. His scheme was shot, he felt humiliated and embarrassed, and his father was happy.

His mother walked into the dining room to make sure the table was set properly. "We're so eager to hear about her research. I mean, I have a million people she ought to meet and some wonderful ideas for her dissertation."

"She is going to take Boston by surprise," Trip's father said.

"So, darling, exactly how far along is she in her research process?" his mother asked.

Trip's goodwill toward Bambi was vanishing in the face of questions he couldn't answer. Then the doorbell rang. Trip thought it was probably the first time Mrs. Bradford had managed to have such good timing.

"Oh, that's Virginia and Constance. Hold that thought."

She headed for the front door and Trip took a deep breath. When he looked up, his father was studying him.

"It's a good surprise, Trip. But I can't help but wonder why you conspired to keep us all in the dark. I mean, perhaps you were trying to make some sort of point, although I can't imagine what it was. But you could have let your family know."

"I wanted to let Bambi tell people in her own time." Trip searched his mind for a better explanation. "She seemed to think it would be helpful to her research."

"Well, next time, I would appreciate being informed. I am, after all, head of Belles and Beaux."

"I know, Dad."

Just then, the women came into the kitchen. They stayed there only briefly before Trip's mother shepherded everyone into the dining room. Mrs. Bradford took no time making her way to Trip.

"Trip, I'm glad that Miss Benson isn't here. Frankly, I'm not sure about her. She doesn't seem to be of your caliber."

"Virginia, I thought the exact same thing. Until I heard about the show. Oh, wait, I just realized you haven't heard the good news!" Trip's mother said.

"Mother, how would she have heard? The show hasn't even aired yet." Trip smiled at his mother through his teeth.

"Haven't heard what?" Mrs. Bradford's eyes darted between Trip and his mother.

"Maybe we should save the surprise for later," Trip said, trying desperately to avoid spending the entire night discussing the subject.

"Nonsense, darling," his mother replied. "They're practically family."

Trip rolled his eyes as his mother shared the new information about Bambi.

"Are you sure?" Mrs. Bradford wasn't convinced.

"Of course, Virginia. I called Jane's husband—he works in the administrative office at the University—and he confirmed it all!"

"Well, isn't that interesting."

"I think it's quite funny!" Trip noticed that Connie had started giggling, her first contribution to the conversation. "Just think, she toppled all of us from our high horses."

"Constance!" her mother admonished.

"Oh, come on, mother. Trip must have been laughing inside the whole time. Weren't you, Trip?" She walked over and placed a hand on Trip's arm.

"I guess." Trip thought back to the Pops gala, how he had been laughing at everyone for falling victim to his con. He hadn't realized at the time that he was the butt of the joke.

"Well, you must tell us all you know, now." Connie kept her hand on his arm.

"Why don't we head into dinner where we can discuss this?" Trip's mother suggested as she motioned everyone to the table.

There Trip had to field questions about Bambi that he didn't know how to answer. He silently cursed her once more for leaving him in the dark. But as his anger against Bambi grew, so did his sympathy toward Connie. Connie saw some humor in the whole thing. And with her, he could begin to see it, too. No thanks to Bambi Benson.

He had forgotten how pretty Connie was. Her sleek, blonde hair was pulled up in a smooth ponytail. She had serious brown eyes and a mouth that had haunted his teenage dreams. And she was easy. Always easy. Easy to talk to, easy to get along with. Being with her, his anger with Bambi stayed at a dull roar rather than a sharp screech. Trip never had to worry about where he stood with Connie. If he wasn't mistaken, that hand on his arm meant she might be ready to pick things up where they had left off 10 years ago. Trip considered the possibility that he might be ready, too.

After dinner, Connie sidled up to him. "Why don't we ditch these guys and go for a drink?"

It was the best idea Trip had heard in a long time. He winced a little at the thought of the way he had spent the last night. "I'm in. As long as I can have something other than bourbon."

"You're on." She smiled. "Let me get my wrap. Clink?"

"You're a woman after my own heart."

"Don't give a girl any ideas."

Trip made his goodbyes and went to bring his car around. His mother followed him to the door.

"Are you sure that you want to spend an evening alone with Connie?" she asked.

"I just can't please you, can I?" Trip snapped. "First, you want me with Connie. Now you don't."

"I thought you and Bambi had something. I was wrong about her, and I feel horrible. But I don't understand why you feel the need to take Connie out. All of Boston knows your history."

"Good. Then all of Boston will know that we are two old friends, grabbing a drink." Trip turned away from his mother and went to start the car. Soon, Connie appeared, with fresh lipstick and a flush high in her cheeks.

"You ready?"

"C'mon, Trip. Let's go."

When they got out of the car at the Liberty Hotel, Trip glanced across the river at Cambridge. Bambi's apartment was over there. But right now Trip didn't care what Bambi was doing.

"Trip? Are you coming?"

He turned away and put his hand on Connie's back to guide her into the building. At Clink, Trip found a secluded booth and joined Connie in a martini. Midway through the evening,

Connie slid her hand over his and left it there. He didn't mind. His brain was going fuzzy and her hand felt good.

As they made their way out of the bar, Trip thought he recognized a familiar figure clad all in black. But when he turned around to figure out why he'd seemed familiar, the man had disappeared.

The martinis were wearing off, but his head still felt a little fuzzy. After so much talking, Connie seemed content to spend the ride back to her apartment in the Back Bay in silence. Trip stole glances at her when they stopped at traffic lights. When he pulled up in front of her building, he asked, "What's on your mind, Connie? You have the most mysterious smile."

"Oh, nothing. Just thinking about Bambi. You know she's a lucky girl, Trip." Then she leaned over the console and brushed kisses over both cheeks. Trip felt her warm breath on his face, and it took all his willpower not to turn his head so that their lips would meet. She pulled back and sat there for a moment before dashing out of the car and out of sight.

On his drive home, Trip wondered why he hadn't kissed Connie. Something had kept him from it. Next time, he resolved, he wouldn't miss the opportunity.

On Monday, Pat was back in the office after his honeymoon. Trip wasted no time after he came in to flop onto his friend's office couch with his morning coffee.

"Man, you look sickeningly tan and happy. You make the rest of us look bad," he said.

"What can I say? The weather was great. The beaches were great. The hotel room was even better." Pat winked.

"We'll be lucky if we can get you to do any work at all today without calling Allison every five seconds, I know."

"Getting married was the best decision of my life. I would do it over again and again if I could get eight more days like I just had. Man, let me tell you—"

"Don't mean to cut you off, bud, but I did not come in here to talk about you."

"What do you mean? I'm the one with stuff to tell!" Pat acted offended. "I went away for a whole week to an exotic and tropical isle, while you stayed at home. And you're the one with stuff to tell me?"

Trip shrugged. "A lot happened!"

"Fine. Lay it on me."

"Well, things seemed like they were changing with Bambi at your wedding. Then, the second we're back, Elizabeth Pinckney says that we have some big interview scheduled with Madison Hart."

"*The* Madison Hart? From 10 years ago Madison Hart? The one who practically screwed up your entire life? That Madison Hart?"

"The one and the same. Whatever, it wasn't a big deal. We can make nice now. At least in front of a couple of cameras."

"Okay . . . so what's the big deal?" Pat scrutinized Trip.

Trip detailed to his friend what he had begun calling in his head Bambi's coming out party. How she had left him completely flat-footed and what she had failed to tell him before he sat in an interview with Maddy Hart.

"Oh, man, that's bad," Pat said, glancing down at his computer.

"And then—wait a second, Pat." Pat didn't look away from his computer when Trip called him by name. "Working on something important?"

"Uh . . . just realized I had some emails to get to," Pat said, not looking up. "Haven't been here for a whole week, you know. I should probably get going on them before your father hears about it."

"You've got to be kidding me. I tell you that story, and you tell me you have to check emails? Pat?" Trip waved his arms. "Look at me!"

Pat finally turned away from the screen. He looked incredibly guilty. "Sorry. We'll talk about it later, I promise. But I think there's a crisis brewing that I need to take care of."

"Fine." Trip got up and made his way out of Pat's office. He had been waiting for his friend to return to give him some good advice, and it hurt to be brushed off like that. Pat had never done that before. He'd always been solid. And yeah, they didn't spend a lot of time discussing their feelings, but when Madison Hart had wreaked her havoc, Pat had been the one to help him get his life and relationships back in order. It just didn't make sense. Maybe marriage had changed him.

Then, Trip stopped in the hall. Marriage hadn't changed Pat. And that guilt he had seen in his friend's face hadn't been over dropping him for a looming crisis. He stormed back into Pat's office, where he found his friend on the phone.

"You knew?" he yelled.

"What?" Pat didn't even cover the phone.

"You knew what she was going to do to me!" Trip slammed his fist on Pat's desk. "And you didn't even give me a friendly heads up!"

Trip noticed that Pat directed his attention back to the phone. "Yeah, it is, honey. I'll call you back later."

Trip threw his arms in the air. "Allison knew too?"

Pat nodded.

"Bitch. She turned all my friends against me."

"Honestly, Trip, I didn't know," Pat pleaded. "Not until we were in the air and on the way to Bali. She must've told Allison at the wedding."

"Are you telling me they didn't have phones in Bali?"

"Ally wouldn't let me. I swear."

Trip shook his head. "That is cold, man."

"I'm sorry." Pat looked miserable.

"You know what? I was beginning to feel sorry for Bambi." He spit out her name. "Feel like I had some blame in all of this for whatever, judging her by her outside. But she turned my own best friend against me."

"Trip—"

"Don't even talk to me. I don't want to talk to you. Ugh. I'll let you get to your so-called crisis."

With that, Trip walked out and slammed the door. He couldn't believe that his best friend had treated him that way. Or that Bambi had managed to turn Pat against him. He wasn't sure how he could stand seeing her the next day. If anyone thought this relationship was going to last, they had another thing coming.

CHAPTER ELEVEN

When Bambi got home the evening after the interview, she decided not to think about Madison Hart, Trip's reaction, or the upcoming Valentine's date that she was sure would be just this side of unbearable. Instead, she threw herself into preparations for her presentation to the girls at The Booby Trap. She knew that she would have to strike just the right note to encourage them to participate in her study by answering questions. She would have to convince them that she wasn't going in with any preconceptions or any judgments. In that, she knew she had honesty on her side. During the time she had spent working at The Booby Trap, she had become friends with most of the girls. Of course, some of them appeared to fit the stereotype of stupid women who had relied on their bodies to get what they wanted out of life, but most of them were thoughtful, smart, enjoyable women. Their approaches to the job, which depended on the objectification of women, were endlessly interesting to Bambi.

When she arrived at The Booby Trap on Monday night, girls crowded around her, interested in her relationship with Trip. Bambi had heard from Elizabeth that the promos for the Valentine's Day *Hart of Boston* show were already running multiple times a day, and most of the women had caught a glimpse.

"Gosh, Bambi, you're so lucky," said one.

"He seems like such a dream. If only I could get that much support from my boyfriend," another said.

"Lucky girl. I wonder what would have happened if I had been working that table that night."

"Knowing my luck," one said, "he wouldn't have given a damn about me."

Bambi wanted to tell them that wasn't the case. Probably any pretty girl who had brought Trip drinks that night would have done the job for him. But she kept her mouth shut. As Elizabeth had said, their relationship was more important than ever to Belles and Beaux right now, and Bambi had made a deal. But she felt like a fraud. These girls were using her as a model for the perfect relationship. If only they knew the true circumstances.

"Tell us more about him, Bambi," Lainie said. "What doesn't everyone know about Trip Whitley?" Bambi knew she was trying to be helpful. The better rapport Bambi could develop with the girls now, the better off she would be in getting their help on her project.

"Well, I guess part of Trip is just what you'd expect," Bambi said. "He's smart and attractive. He likes to read, especially about Massachusetts history." She figured the last part was right, remembering his quoting Emerson in Sleepy Hollow Cemetery and *Mayflower* as his nighttime reading material. She began to realize how little she knew about Trip, despite the fact that they had been on several dates together.

"Is he a good kisser?" someone shouted out.

Bambi blushed in remembrance of the kiss she and Trip had shared on the dance floor at Pat and Allison's wedding. The crowd oohed. "He must be something," said another girl.

"Yes," Bambi answered, blushing even more as she said the word. "And he's a good dancer."

The girls then pelted her with a million questions at once. Where had they been on their dates? When had they had their first kiss? Did she like his friends? What about his family? Bambi was not sure how to answer all the questions, much less which to answer first. Luckily, she was saved. "Break it up girls," Joe said. "We need to get this meeting underway."

The girls expressed their disappointment but made their way to their seats. Joe stood at the front of the room and went over the schedule for Valentine's Day. It was always one of their biggest days of the year, and every girl would be working. Bambi had learned from Joe that they rotated every year which girls worked in the evening. Sometimes there were arguments, but she had noticed that a certain camaraderie had developed between the girls so that they would do some shift switching if they knew a friend had a big night planned.

When everyone seemed to be clear on the military precision with which Joe planned to run the night, he turned the floor over to Bambi.

"Hi, ladies. I hope not to keep you very long, but I'm going to ask for your help." Carefully, Bambi laid out her plan and watched the expressions of the women in front of her. By the time she opened up the floor to questions, only a few women looked interested.

"What kinds of questions are you going to ask?" one asked.

Bambi pulled out a sheet of paper with questions printed on it that she had made for the occasion. "Here are some of the questions. Feel free to think about them beforehand. There are no right answers, and I'm not going to be grading you. But you should also be aware that I want this to be a little bit of a conversation, so some questions will come up that aren't included on the sheet."

"Who's going to read what you say about us?" one asked.

"Well, I'm making it into my dissertation, which is kind of like a big final paper. That means that my committee will read it. That's three professors. I'll probably try to turn at least some of it into an article that could be published in an academic journal that mostly students and professors of women's studies read."

"Would anyone we know read it?"

"Well, of course I'd make a copy available to anyone here who wants to read it. But odds are, no. Unless something crazy happens and it gets picked up by a bigger magazine. That almost never happens."

"You said you were going to change our names. Are you going to change the name of The Booby Trap, too?"

Bambi responded to this and other questions. She watched more women become reassured, but wondered if there would be enough participants to make her research relevant since there were only 20 women there. Then Lainie stood up. "Is it okay if I say something?"

"Sure." Bambi ceded the floor to her best friend.

"Listen girls, we've all gotten to know Bambi in the time that she's worked here. She's slogged through the trenches with us, and I think you get a pretty good measure of a girl when you see her deal with the stuff that we have to deal with here. And we all knew she was smart, even before we knew that she was at Harvard. And she's right. People think a lot of things about most of us that are wrong just because of where we work. Now, we have an opportunity to set them straight. And we know we can trust Bambi not to twist our words. She'll report what we have to say accurately. Isn't that right?"

Bambi noticed Lainie looking to her for an answer. "That's absolutely right. And I'll do it not only because I know you, but also because it's an ethical standard required by my research. I would be cheating if I manipulated what you have to say."

"So I think we should help her out. I know I'll be doing it."

Lainie had just done her a huge favor by making that speech and publicly offering to participate. Bambi smiled at her friend in gratitude. "Thanks, Lainie. Well, I hope you girls will do it. I'll make some sign-up sheets and we'll begin over the next week."

The meeting broke up and Bambi hung back from the crowd. Even so, one woman after another approached her to say that she would be happy to help her out. She was on her way.

The next day was Valentine's Day. Bambi ran from one thing to the next. First, class in the morning, then the lunch shift at The Booby Trap. When she raced home around 4 p.m., she knew that she would really have to scramble to get ready for her date that night. Absorbed in her thoughts about seeing Trip again and wondering if he had cooled down, she hadn't noticed the black-clad figure hanging from a tree branch across the street.

"Excited about your date tonight, Bambi?" he called. She jumped and screamed, thinking for a moment that perhaps she was about to be mugged. When her rational mind took over, she recognized him as the paparazzo that Trip had fought with after they returned from Concord.

"Should be great!" she yelled across her shoulder in answer but didn't slow her progress toward her building. She heard the camera snapping as she turned the key in the lock and made her way inside.

An hour and a half later, Bambi slowed her frenetic pace and took a moment for a deep breath. She was showered, dressed in a figure-hugging, fire-engine red jersey dress, and her make-up was done. In a couple of minutes, Trip should be pulling up in the pre-arranged limousine. She plugged Elizabeth's number into her cell.

"It's going to be fine, right?" she asked once her friend picked up. "He's cooled down some, right?"

"Some," Elizabeth didn't seem entirely convinced, which wreaked havoc on Bambi's nerves.

"Oh God."

"Don't worry." Bambi heard Elizabeth's tone change from one of worry to her typical confidence. "It will be great."

Bambi heard the door buzz. "That's him. I gotta go. Wish me luck."

"Good luck," Elizabeth said. Bambi hung up, grabbed her coat and headed down to the front door of the building where Trip stood waiting.

Bambi felt like her heart stopped in her chest when she saw him in the exquisite charcoal pinstripe suit and forest green tie. The tie brought out glints of green in his brown eyes that she had never noticed before. She looked into them for some clue about how he was feeling.

"You look beautiful." He handed her a bouquet of red roses. Then he leaned down to kiss her. She couldn't resist coming up on her toes to meet him, her body tingling in anticipation. But this kiss lacked any fire whatsoever. So he was still mad. He pulled away after what seemed a calculated amount of time and shifted his mouth to her ear. "We have company."

Attempting to ignore the way his breath felt on her neck, she whispered back. "I know. He's been there since I got home this afternoon."

Trip stepped back from their intimate position and offered his arm. "Shall we? I mean, if it's okay I take your arm." He quirked a brow and continued sarcastically, "I wouldn't want to upset your sensibilities."

She accepted his arm and struck a calming tone. "Trip, you look . . . amazing."

He ignored her comment. "Smile and wave at the paparazzo. And Jim."

Bambi did as she was told, seeing that their cameraman had joined the party and was riding up front with the chauffeur.

Trip handed her into the limo, then followed. Once they were seated close together, he asked the driver to put up the privacy screen. Bambi's brain filled with visions of things that a man and woman could do in the back of a limo with the privacy screen up. She involuntarily shivered in anticipation.

"Trip, we don't have to do this," Bambi said. "Won't the driver get suspicious?"

"That's why this plan works so well. He'll get suspicious that we're lovers who want some privacy on Valentine's Day. When we in fact we won't be doing anything." Trip moved away and took a seat as far away from her as he could manage in the small space.

"I wasn't asking for—" she began.

Trip cut her off. "I'd prefer it if we didn't talk." He shifted his gaze out the window. The short drive to Upstairs in the Square was filled with tension. Bambi knew it was going to be a long night.

As the limo driver slowed to a stop in front of the restaurant, Trip slid back into the seat next to her. Then, after he'd helped her out of the car, he kept a firm hold on her hand. Bambi wondered how it was that someone could be so close yet feel so far away. She had never liked Valentine's Day anyway.

The restaurant, however, was decked out for the occasion. Normally, she thought of Upstairs in the Square as a wonderland where Lewis Carroll's Alice would have felt at home. The bright pink walls and zebra carpet looked slightly less whimsical in the soft candlelight. A series of windows ran the length of one room, outside of which the lights of Harvard Square winked through falling snow that had already made a carpet on the grass. Pink roses sat on every table, where couples discussed their days or gazed into each other's eyes.

Once they were seated, Trip immediately said, "I can't believe how beautiful you look." Bambi knew that he was playing to the crowd, because the sincerity in his voice wasn't echoed in his eyes.

"Thank you," she said, her voice small.

A waitress came over to take their drink orders. Her eyes grew wide when she saw who her diners were, but she managed to play it off.

"What would you like? Some wine?" Trip played the solicitous boyfriend.

"You choose. I don't know much about wine. I like reds, though."

Trip turned to the waitress, assaulting her with the brilliance of his smile. "Is there anything you can recommend tonight? Something in a red?"

"Oh, of course." The waitress smiled back. "We have a wonderful Pinot Noir from the Loire Valley. Or a full-bodied California Cabernet."

"We'll take the Pinot. Oh, and one more thing." He beckoned her closer to whisper something into her ear. When he was finished, the waitress straightened, blushing.

"Of course, Mr. Whitley."

"I'm not Mr. Whitley. That's my dad. Call me Trip."

"Of course then, Trip." The waitress wore a goofy smile as she turned away and headed back to the kitchen.

Bambi watched her go with rising anger. How could Trip create such closeness with a girl he had known under five minutes, yet freeze her out so completely? When he turned back to her and took her hands across the table, she looked into eyes that regarded her as if she were gum stuck to the bottom of his shoe.

"Trip, you can't do this to me."

Trip's eyes flashed a warning as his hands tightened on hers in a grip that hurt instead of soothed. He nodded his head in the direction of the other couples enjoying their dinners. "How was your day, honey?"

"Trip, we need to talk about this. We can't go on this way. We won't convince anybody."

Trip caressed her hand. Bambi noticed a few diners surreptitiously taking glances in their direction. A couple of the women even sighed.

"I think we're doing just fine," Trip said through his teeth. "And last time I checked, you didn't care to bring up a certain subject when it would have been convenient for me. So I ask you again, how was your day, pumpkin?"

Bambi knew that Trip was throwing in the endearments to bother her. Fine. If Trip didn't want to talk to her, she could use some time to figure out her next step in the interview process. She hadn't been able to run her ideas past Elizabeth since she was busy working with Madison Hart's people on the Valentine's Day segment. She couldn't go to Lainie, since Bambi knew Lainie's interview would be integral to her presentation. If Trip didn't feel like responding, at least Bambi would have the benefits of hearing her thoughts out loud.

"I had a really busy day. You see, I asked all the waitresses at The Booby Trap yesterday to be interviewed for my dissertation work. Today, in addition to class in the morning and probably the busiest day of the year at work, I fielded questions from a couple of girls about the interviewing process."

Bambi found herself pouring out her concerns and questions about the interview process to the man in front of her. She talked as the waitress brought the Pinot Noir and continued her speculation on the best questions and interview techniques as she sipped the wine. Trip responded with the occasional "huh" or "really," but never joined in what was turning out to be a running monologue.

Trip sat back and did the best he could to block out what Bambi was saying without appearing as though he'd done so. Apparently, when he'd shown up at her doorstep, she'd thought they could have a quick discussion and everything would be fine. Well, nothing was fine. Pat had dropped by his office that morning, tail between his legs, attempting to apologize again. Trip had shut him out. Shut everyone out, really.

His father had also dropped by to warn him not to make a mess of the big Valentine's Day date, and Elizabeth Pinckney had called to remind him of the plans for the night. Trip thought she might have been trying to tell him something, but he growled so hard when she called that he could have sworn even she was a little bit scared of him.

Halfheartedly, he listened to Bambi discussing her study of the girls at The Booby Trap. Maybe he had something in common with them. She probably deceived them, too. But at least they didn't have to find out from national television.

As Trip brooded, he realized that he had never heard Bambi so animated. She gestured with her hands and furrowed her brow when she worked out problems. For a moment, he wished that they didn't have such a contentious history. He was beginning to think that he might have gotten to like this version of Bambi. Against his better judgment, he turned his full attention over to her, resolving that he would treat it as if he were watching a movie. Something in which there was no need for participation.

"I feel like I have all this to prove to Martha," she continued. "That I'm worthy of being there. I mean, sometimes I feel like she doesn't really believe that I'm a serious student. I mean, I don't exactly look like the prototypical PhD student, much less one in women's studies. Just ask all of Boston."

That much Trip knew was true. If you had asked him to paint a picture of a graduate student in women's studies before he'd met Bambi, he would have given the woman breasts that sagged without the aid of a bra, hairy legs and underarms, unplucked eyebrows, and ugly glasses. And perhaps one of those t-shirts that read: "A woman needs a man like a fish needs a bicycle."

And thinking that, Trip thought back to the interview with Madison Hart. Leave it to a back-stabbing journalist to dig a little deeper. Sometimes, you came up with shit. But in Bambi's case, you came up with gold. Trip himself hadn't bothered to look below the surface, much like this Doctor whatever her name was. He spoke up. "Bambi, I'm pretty sure that it's your knowledge and your research that determine whether you're a good PhD student, not your looks. But more to the point, you can't let people like that Martha—or me—determine how you view yourself or your competence."

"I know." Bambi touched his hand across the table and it felt like he'd been shocked. He looked up to answer her.

"We doing all right here?" The cheerful waitress interrupted his thoughts and gave him time to stall. "Let me just take those plates away and I'll get you started on dessert."

The waitress cleared the plates and the busboy deposited a chilled bucket of champagne by their table. All of this activity gave Trip more time to think, and the more he thought, the angrier he became at himself.

"Excuse me." Trip stood up. "I'm going to the bathroom."

He headed out of the dining room and instead of walking upstairs to the men's room, went downstairs and outside. The blast of cold air he met coming through the door helped a lot to clear his senses. Why had he been prepared to forgive her so quickly? Something about Bambi Benson always got him twisted up. She knew just what to do to drive him crazy. Unbidden, Trip's brain turned to the bedroom, and he wondered whether she would know just what to do there, too.

He shook his head to clear the unwanted images. Trip now realized he had made a huge mistake in choosing her for his scheme. The thing he had to do now was figure a way out of it, without letting her tangle him up in her life.

Feeling significantly better, he walked back into the restaurant. He saw that Bambi must have enticed the busboy back to open the champagne since she sat drinking a glass. She looked up hopefully.

Trip didn't intend to give her an inch. "Listen, Bambi, you and I both know what this relationship is. We'll smile, you'll kiss me once I'm done talking. But we don't belong together. We're both looking for a way out. At least we'll be honest about that."

He touched her cheek and kissed her tenderly, steeling himself as much as he could to the sensations she aroused in his body.

CHAPTER TWELVE

Bambi sat down at a small table in the breakroom of The Booby Trap. She checked that her small recorder was working and tapped her fingernails nervously against the table. This would be her first interview with any of the women, and even though it was with Lainie, Bambi couldn't help but feel a little antsy. She shuffled through her notes, reviewed her questions one more time, and waited for Lainie's shift to be over. She was cursing herself for coming in so early when her friend walked through the door.

"Hey, Bambi." Lainie waved with her fingers. "Want me to close this?" she indicated the door.

"Sure, that would be great. Are you ready to begin? I'm going to turn my recorder on if so."

"I guess. I've never done this before, so I'm not exactly sure what I should do. Let me know if I mess anything up, honey."

She pulled out the chair across from Bambi and took a seat.

"You can't mess it up. And it's my first time, too, so we're both new to this." Bambi smiled to put her friend at ease. "Well, let's get started. Can you please state your name and age?"

"Lainie Harrison, age 32."

"Great. And Lainie, when did you start working here at The Booby Trap?"

"Hmm. I started here when I was 20, I guess. Hard to believe I've been here that long."

"Has anyone else been here for as long or longer?"

"Nope. Well, unless you count Joe."

"You've been working here quite a while. I imagine you were at a very different point in your life when you started than you are now. Can you tell me why you began working here?"

"Man, you are right. I was a different person back then. I grew up in North Carolina and I stuck around there for a few years after high school."

"Did you attend college?"

"No. No money and, to be honest, not much interest. Anyway, I was working as a waitress down there and met a fry cook named Shaun. I fell hard for that boy." She shook her head.

"I've never heard of Shaun."

"I guess I don't talk about him much anymore. But back then, I couldn't get him off my mind. He was something else. Not a bad cook, either. In fact, he could make the best fried fish you ever tasted. And his hush puppies . . . well . . . I can't even describe them."

"So if things were going so great with Shaun, why would you leave North Carolina?"

"It was Shaun's idea. He was going to bring his cooking

expertise north. We figured on Boston because there's easy access to fish, plus it's not quite as big as New York."

"So you moved?"

"We did. Drove his car the 12 hours and started our lives up in Boston. He worked as a short order cook in Salem and I was back to waitressing. We were saving up money for our restaurant."

"So, if regular waitressing was working out for you, why come to The Booby Trap?"

"It wasn't working out so much. We were just making ends meet. I looked around to take on a second job to make more money. One of my friends at the other job told me about this place. Said they were looking to hire. So I applied."

"Did you have any thoughts—positive or negative—about this type of waitressing?"

"I just needed the job. Joe runs this place tight, so I knew I wouldn't be in any more danger than I was at the other job. He knows what this place is, but he doesn't let anyone get too frisky. Then, when I started working, I made more money. And, honey, I have no problem taking money from guys who get a charge from seeing a little more leg and a little more boob."

"Did you consider stripping? Surely it must be more lucrative."

Lainie recoiled. "Hell no! I'm a waitress here, and there's a big difference between what I do and stripping."

Interesting, Bambi thought. She wondered if Lainie's bright line was so bright with all of the other girls. Exposure of a woman's body played into both professions, so where did other women draw the line between decent and indecent exposure for money?

"What are you thinking about over there?" Lainie asked. "Stripping? I don't know why people always equate that with what I do."

"People? Who other than me?"

"Shaun." Lainie sighed. "I was so excited about this job, the opportunity to make more money, get our restaurant up and running even sooner. But Shaun didn't see it that way."

"I see."

"I can still remember him going on and on about how my ass was out, how my boobs were out. How guys were taking advantage of me. I told him, no—I was taking advantage of them."

Bambi took note of the reverse exploitation theme that Lainie seemed to gravitate toward. She was empowered by her body's ability to exploit some kind of weakness in men. Bambi redirected her attention toward her friend when she realized Lainie wasn't finished with her story.

"He didn't hear what I had to say. Wouldn't hear it, I guess is more accurate. Finally, he got real quiet and said something like, 'Nobody can look at my woman like that. I'll kill anyone that tries, and I forbid you from working at that place.' Well, I thought to myself: I see how it is. The man thinks he can forbid me. No. No one owns me. And anyone who thinks he does is a problem."

"So what did you do? Weren't you in love with him?"

"I walked out that night. I was in love, and I cried for about two months straight, but I never looked back. Love doesn't convey ownership."

"Did The Booby Trap mean that much to you?"

"Of course not. It was about me being my own person. And it's taken me a while to get to where and who I want to be, but in a weird way, I feel like this place has helped me get there. It's definitely made me more confident."

Bambi continued to ask questions. She learned more about how Lainie understood the distinction between selling the sex of the job versus the business of waitressing. She delved more into the question of exploitation and its relationship to empowerment. She found Lainie's perceptions to be infinitely more nuanced than even she had thought they could be, but Lainie's personal story kept nagging at the back of her mind.

"One more question," Bambi said.

"Sure. Shoot."

"Do you know whatever happened to Shaun? Did he get his restaurant?"

Lainie smiled. "Ever hear of Beacon?"

"Are you kidding? All of Boston is going nuts about that place. That's Shaun's?"

"Yeah." Lainie chuckled.

"Geez . . ." Bambi took a breath. "Do you ever regret it? Your decision to walk away?"

Lainie smiled. "Only in my darkest moments. Wouldn't it be so easy to be sitting on top of the world right now?" She shrugged. "But my life is all right. I'm getting my MBA and pretty soon Shaun Parker will be looking up the ladder at me."

"Really? That's amazing." Bambi got up and circled the table to give her friend a hug.

"You're not the only one who can keep a secret. Besides, I can't work here forever."

"Well, let me know if you need any help at all. You've been so wonderful to me with the interview and speaking with the girls that I hope I can return the favor sometime."

"I will. We smart girls need to stick together. By the way—are we off the record now?"

Oh." Bambi had almost forgotten she still had her recorder running. She reached out to stop it. "Yeah. What's up?"

"I wanted to see how you and Trip are doing. Seeing as I've been blabbing about myself for the last hour."

"You haven't been blabbing. You've been helping me out—and doing a really good job."

"Thanks." Lainie smiled. "But that doesn't mean I don't want to check in with you. So, how are things going? The last paper I picked up had you and Trip canoodling over coffee."

Bambi looked down. "Everything isn't as it seems."

"Trust me, honey; I know that better than the back of my hand. And I know you do, too. So, it's the man?"

"I just don't feel like he sees me anymore."

"Then why don't you break up with him?"

"It's complicated."

"You keep saying that. Listen, Bambi. I know that it's nice to date a guy with a little cash to throw around. You get kind of comfortable. But that's no way to live."

"It's not that at all." Bambi looked at her friend, wishing she could divulge everything.

"Okay." Bambi felt Lainie surveying her critically. "Well then, how can we fix the problem?"

"I don't know. I think I kind of threw him for a loop when I told him about the whole PhD student thing."

"That must've been ages ago, though. You can't tell me he hasn't gotten over that by now."

"It wasn't exactly ages ago. In fact, it was just during the interview."

"Bambi! You can't start a relationship by leaving out such a big part of your life."

"I told you around the same time I told him!" Bambi knew Lainie was right, but she still felt the need to defend herself.

"Honey," Lainie held up a hand, "there are several key differences between me and Trip. One, we're not dating. Two, I know what it's like to have people look at you sideways 'cause of what you do. Clearly. I just spent 20 minutes telling you my sad story."

"Your story has a happy ending! But I guess you're right."

"Three, you let all his people believe you were this bimbo. He's probably been doing damage control ever since."

"I'm not so sure about that. His mom went from wishing she could force Trip to break up with me to wanting to adopt me into the family."

"Maybe she's different." Lainie put her hand on Bambi's knee. "But most people don't appreciate being made fools of. They don't know you; maybe they feel embarrassed about their assumptions about you so they haven't confronted you. But don't think that doesn't mean they haven't torn into Trip. They would've expected him to know."

"I never thought of that."

"Yeah."

"So how do I fix it now?"

"Sounds to me like you two need to have a serious talk. Neither of you knows what to expect out of the relationship. Put everything out there. No more lies or 'I'll tell you when it's convenient to me.'"

"You're so right." Bambi nodded.

"Of course I am. Come on, let's get out of here and do something fun."

"Sounds great," Bambi said and began packing up her things to go.

Trip pulled up in front of Bambi's apartment on Saturday afternoon for their next date: candlepin bowling. Apparently, Elizabeth just wanted him to look ridiculous. As he walked up to Bambi's doorway, Trip waved to the paparazzo hanging in the tree and the man responded by trying to conceal himself even further. He saw Bambi at her doorway when he looked back to her building. She wore jeans and a short black coat, blonde hair in a swingy ponytail. *Beautiful, as always*, but thoughts like that didn't get him anywhere in his current plan.

"Hello." He dipped her in a showy kiss for the paparazzo. When he hauled her up, she looked off balance. Good. Trip wanted to be in control now. He walked her back to the car and ushered her inside. Once they got on the road, she turned to him.

"So, Trip, how has your week been?"

He thought they had come to an understanding over Valentine's Day. "Bambi, there's no point in pretending when we're all alone."

"Oh," she said, but she didn't bug him anymore, which was just fine with him.

Once they arrived at the bowling spot, though, Trip made another show for Jim, Jack, and Elizabeth, who were waiting there. He helped Bambi with her bowling shoes. It reminded him of their first date, back at the Frog Pond. God, if only he knew then what he knew now.

Once the bowling started, though, it was a convenient reason to keep his eyes and mind off Bambi. But she started talking about work again. Her evident enthusiasm for her research made her hard to ignore.

"I'm really excited about the conference in April," she was saying, "but worried at the same time. This is a major conference. The biggest in my discipline. There are all these rock stars of women's studies that will be there. I've always wanted to go to England. Or anywhere abroad."

"You've never been outside of the United States?" This revelation shocked Trip out of his planned silence. Maybe he shouldn't be surprised, but he was. His parents had been dragging him on trips to London, Paris, Athens, Rome, and even Kenya since he was about old enough to walk. And Trip had traveled on business to survey matchmaking techniques across the high societies of Japan, England, France, and Russia.

"No. I've traveled in the country a bit for conferences, but . . ." She shrugged as she picked up one of the small bowling balls and traded places with him to bowl her turn.

"What about spring break? Winter break? Summer break?"

"I worked my breaks. It was the best time to make money in college—I didn't have to worry about classes." She bent down to bowl, which gave Trip a great view of her butt, then straightened up. "I mean, not that I didn't work then, too."

"But c'mon. You must've been to Canada. Montreal's only five hours from Boston."

"Never been." She bowled and knocked down a measly two pins. "Which is why I'm dying to go to London. I got my passport last year after I learned the conference would be there. Just to travel to the home country of Jane Austen, the Brontes, Mary Shelley, Robert Browning . . ."

"'Oh to be in England, now that April's there.'" Trip said absently. When Bambi eyed him curiously, he explained, "My high school English teacher forced us to memorize a couple of poems. To tell the truth, I kind of liked doing it."

"Was that when you learned about Emerson?"

"It was a year before. We did European poets junior year. And American sophomore year. My English teacher that year was obsessed with the Transcendentalists. We took a field trip to Concord the fall of that year. It was my first ever visit to the cemetery."

"And you liked it that much?"

"Yeah, I guess I did." Trip smiled. "Although, at first, it wasn't about the literary minds that were buried there. It was about the ghosts."

"I should have guessed. Teenage boys are all the same."

"I feel like I should resent that, but it's probably true. A couple of my buddies and I were really into the dark Goth thing at the time, and we figured that it would be cool to hang out in a graveyard. I had just gotten my license, so Sleepy Hollow was perfect."

"Why not somewhere in Boston?"

"With all those tourists? No, that just didn't fit."

"And you're telling me the graveyard of Louisa May Alcott, Nathaniel Hawthorne, and Ralph Waldo Emerson doesn't get a lot of tourists?"

"You're right. It does. But it has the advantage of looking creepier. Plus, it was far enough away that we could sneak booze or cigarettes there without someone we knew catching us at it."

"Oh, that makes much more sense. You smoke?"

"Did. For about two years off and on, till I turned 18. Somehow, it lost its appeal after that. What about you?"

"Never."

"Not once? No one ever offered it to you and you did it just to be cool?"

"No. God, I hated the smell of it. I couldn't imagine what it would be like to inhale. My mom smoked like a chimney. She swore that she quit when she was pregnant with me, but I don't know if I believe her."

"Seems like she did. You're a pretty smart woman," Trip said. He avoided looking Bambi in the eye. "It's still your turn to bowl."

"Oh, yeah. Okay." She turned back to the bowling, but Trip could sense something had changed. His anger was dissolving and he couldn't explain why.

The next Monday, Trip sat in his office contemplating his latest date. Before, when she had been just a bimbo, babbling on, he had found it easy to ignore her even though he didn't want to. Now, when he wanted to ignore her, he couldn't. She was too interesting. And maybe he was a little curious. Just then, Pat walked in. The only interaction they had had since Trip learned of Pat's betrayal had been business-related.

"Trip." Pat nodded his head and gingerly placed a folder on his desk.

"Geez, man, I don't bite."

"I don't know. Sometimes I worry." Pat smiled, but it was a ghost of the smile he had used when they joked around before. He began to walk out, and then turned around. "I forgot. About a month ago, we talked about the Young Professionals wine event at the Museum of Fine Arts this weekend. You and Bambi were supposed to attend, but I wasn't sure if that was still the case."

"Yeah. We'll go. I'll make sure Elizabeth has the details."

"Okay. Good to hear. Well . . ." Pat began to turn around again. But again he turned back to Trip. "How are things going there? I mean . . . since . . ."

Trip looked at Pat. Clearly, his friend was extending the olive branch once more. Trip had gotten so used to rejecting it over the past several weeks that he almost didn't think before doing it again. But with his confusion around Bambi, Trip had no one to talk to.

Pat spoke again. "Listen, Trip, I know you're angry at me and I'm sorry. Maybe I should've done something different. In the name of solidarity or friendship or whatever. But I've been tiptoeing around you for the past several weeks, apologizing and getting nothing in return. I wanted you to know that I'm just about up to here with it."

"You done?"

"Yeah." Pat was angry.

"Okay. Well, I'm sorry, bud. I was wrong. This Bambi thing is still making my head spin, and I need your advice."

Pat warily sat down in the chair across from Trip's desk. "Okay. So tell me more about what's going on with Bambi."

Trip felt a little bit more grounded and ready to attack the problem now that his friend was back. "God. I don't know. One second, I'm so mad at her that I can barely manage to be around her. But there's something there. I mean, she's so pumped about her work. She gets so excited and it's fun to watch."

"That's interesting," Pat said.

"Don't give me that. It's bullshit. It's crazy. Why am I so interested? And why can't I just continue blowing her off to everyone except the camera? You would think it would be easy, make me happy even. But that seems to make me as miserable as it does her. Even when Connie practically offered herself on a platter, I couldn't follow through."

"Whoa. Hold on a sec. Connie?" Pat raised an eyebrow. He knew what trouble Connie could be.

"Yeah. My mom invited her and her mom to dinner with us. The weekend after the whole Maddy Hart debacle, actually."

"And?"

"And nothing. We talked. It was just refreshing to talk to a girl who doesn't have some sort of agenda, you know?"

"I know, Trip. But you're playing with fire there. Especially in this high-profile romance with Bambi."

"God, you sound just like my dad."

"Just be careful, Trip. But let's get back to Bambi."

"Glad the lecture's over. What do I do?"

"Listen, man, I don't think you have much to lose in giving friendship a shot with Bambi. To make the last couple months of your relationship bearable. Or at least believable to the press."

"They think we're doing better than ever!"

"That's because they're idiots. But sooner or later, they'll catch on. And you probably don't want that. I know your dad doesn't want that."

"Maybe."

"Plus, if the friends thing doesn't work out, you just cut her out of your life forever after your fake break-up. You wouldn't be the first couple to break up and never see each other again. Ask Elizabeth—you might even be able to play it off to your advantage. Like you're so grief-stricken that she broke your heart that you never want to see her again."

"I guess I see what you mean. But how do I know that she's

not setting me up again?" Trip wasn't sure he could trust Bambi so readily.

"I just don't think she is."

"No offense, but I can't base my decision about this on your gut feeling."

"It's not exactly a gut feeling." Pat seemed uneasy. He shifted in the chair under Trip's scrutiny.

"Then what is it?"

Pat looked down at his desk. "Allison likes her."

"Really? That's what you got?" Trip wondered if marriage had changed his friend more than he thought. Was Pat just adopting all of Ally's opinions? Trip cleared his throat and coughed "Whipped."

Pat snapped his head up. "What did you say?"

"Oh me? Nothing. Nothing at all." He coughed again, "Whipped." Then he couldn't help himself and he laughed.

"Oh, you think you're so funny. I am not whipped."

"Looks different to me. So when did you stop thinking for yourself? Right after the marriage vows? Or was it during honeymoon sex? Must've been pretty good. I didn't realize before. I would've forgiven you sooner."

"It's none of your business, but the honeymoon sex was great. Not my fault you're jealous."

"Jealous! That's ridiculous. And unlike you, I retain the use of my brain after sex."

"Like I believe that." Pat snorted. "Anyway, seriously. Bambi and Ally talked during the wedding."

"Clearly. Or we would have been speaking during the past couple weeks."

"What I mean is that Bambi asked Ally. About you. If what

she was doing would hurt you too much. Wasn't deserved. Something." Pat blushed.

"What?" Trip was floored. "And Ally said I would be okay? That I *deserved* it?"

"Uh . . . yes." Pat knew there was no way around it. "Listen, she didn't know it was going to be with Madison Hart. That may have put a different spin on it. Bambi didn't even know that much to tell her."

"And I thought she was my friend."

"Come on, Trip," Pat sighed. "I wasn't going to tell you about that, but I think it should make your decision easier."

"To know that Ally ganged up with Bambi on me?"

"No. To know that she cared enough to ask Ally how you would take it."

"Whatever that means."

"Trip, don't be a dumbass. She's not out to hurt you. Teach you a lesson, maybe. But she wasn't trying to hurt you then. Why would she be now?"

Trip let the question hang in the air. He had spent a lot of time thinking about how Bambi had meant to hurt him. Maybe that hadn't been true. Maybe humiliation had been the only goal. But part of him retained a deep distrust of her motives.

"Maybe," he said.

"Just think about it." Pat got up to leave.

"Listen, Pat. Thanks. For being my friend. Even if your wife is a backstabber."

Pat smiled. "She cares about you. Someday you'll understand, Trip. Now get your ass back to work."

CHAPTER THIRTEEN

"We're so excited to have you here, Mr. Whitley," said Kevin O'Shea, the director of the museum, as he extended his hand to Trip.

"Well, Belles and Beaux thinks this is a great opportunity for both of us. For you to encourage an enjoyment of art in young people and for us to garner the kind of clientele that makes our site so special."

"Sounds like Belles and Beaux couldn't have engineered a better match," Trip heard Bambi's voice saying from behind him. "Hello, darling," she said, winding an arm around his waist.

Trip noticed that the Bambi who had just twined herself around him was unlike any other incarnations he had seen. She looked every inch the young professional: brown suit that was clearly off the rack, pink collared shirt buttoned just one button below strictly professional, demure pearls fastened at her ears and around her neck. He smiled. "Mr. O'Shea, I don't believe you've met my girlfriend, Bambi Benson. Bambi, Kevin O'Shea is the museum's director."

"Such a pleasure, Miss Benson." O'Shea extended his hand, lingering on the handshake in a way that Trip didn't find completely professional. "I would pretend I didn't know you, but you have created quite a stir among some of the mature patrons on our board."

"It's a pleasure to meet you too, Mr. O'Shea." Bambi extracted her hand in a way that managed to be graceful, although Trip thought he had caught a flicker of distaste. "I hope that the Museum hasn't suffered because of it."

"On the contrary, completely. I think the registrations for this event doubled once we announced you and Mr. Whitley as guests. So many new people, it's wonderful!"

"Excellent. Well, Mr. O'Shea, we shouldn't keep you. I'm sure you must be incredibly busy preparing for such a large event. We wouldn't like to distract you, would we, Trip?"

She turned her face toward him and looked so innocent that Trip struggled not to laugh. He really disliked it when Bambi's deviousness was directed at him, but he could enjoy it if she directed it at someone else. Luckily for them both, Mr. O'Shea hadn't noticed that he'd been all but dismissed from their presence. He still stood smiling at Bambi, dropping the occasional gaze toward her generous breasts, even deemphasized as they were by the suit jacket.

"Of course, you're right." Mr. O'Shea returned his eyes to Trip for the first time since Bambi had entered. "I hope you'll enjoy yourselves."

Once the man was out of hearing distance, Trip laughed out loud.

"What's that for?" Bambi asked, pulling her arm from his waist.

"You. I wish I could be that smooth sometimes. Have you always been able to do that? Get rid of a guy without his knowing?"

"Probably not always. But by the end of sophomore year of high school, I had it down pat. Had to, or I would be bothered by horny teenage boys on the way home from school every day. And then my mother's boyfriends at night."

"Really?"

"Weren't you a teenage boy once? Obsessed with boobs and the whole thing?"

"Umm ... yeah ... but that's not what I was talking about. Your mom's boyfriend?"

"Boyfriends. Plural. Let's just say that they weren't quite the winners she swore they were. I just happened to find that fact out before she did."

Trip wondered what she wasn't telling him. But it was clear that Bambi wasn't going to give him any more details of her experience growing up. He moved on. "What are you up to these days? How's the interview process going?"

"Excellent, actually." Bambi smiled. "The girls have been really open with me. And they've brought friends in who work at places other than The Booby Trap."

"Have you talked to the owner yet?"

"Joe? About doing the research? Of course."

"No, I mean, have you given him the whole interview rigmarole?"

"No." Bambi looked at Trip like she thought he was the stupidest man ever. She spoke more slowly. "He's a man. I'm trying to figure out what the atmosphere there is like for women."

"Don't you think Joe has thoughts on that? Or that the way he chooses to conduct business might impact that atmosphere?"

"You know, I never thought about that."

"Maybe you should. I remember, as a kid, always thinking that my school teachers didn't live outside of school, that they existed just to teach me. Sounds to me like that's the way you're thinking of Joe."

"You're right. I guess I have been thinking of him that way. Even though I should know better than anyone that there's life to Joe beyond The Booby Trap."

"Why you, better than anyone?"

"Yeah. You know how I mentioned my mother's boyfriends? Well, Joe was one of them. One of the few good ones. Which meant that he didn't stick around too long. But we managed to keep up."

"So that's why he gave you the job."

"Yeah. Although I guess I ought to resent the implication."

"Which is?"

"That I couldn't get a job at The Booby Trap on my own."

"Sweetheart, I'm sure you can get a job at a place called The Booby Trap simply on your own . . . charms, we'll call them."

Bambi laughed, and Trip felt gratified. He had worried that she would somehow take offense at his comment. "Oh, you think so, Trip?" She put her hands on her hips and eyed him with a glint of humor.

"Well, it's not up to me. But I'm pretty sure that Mr. O'Shea would've given you a reference."

They both laughed.

"I guess we should go out and mingle with everyone," Trip said. He watched the bartenders open a few bottles of wine in preparation for the people who were beginning to come through the doors.

"Is there anything I can do to help?" Bambi asked. "I mean, would it be better if we do this separately or together?"

With that question, Trip understood that Bambi was giving him a way out of spending the evening with her. A week ago, he would have jumped at the chance, no matter what it made people think. But today, it seemed as though they had started over, or at least found some common ground.

"No. We're the draw when we're together, mostly. But you could do me a favor by talking up Belles and Beaux."

"Sure." Bambi smiled and Trip felt warmth course through his body. She wound her arm around his waist again, and it felt like it belonged there.

"Shall we?" He nodded toward a couple of girls lingering around the first wine table. They looked like they might be just out of college. Trip guided Bambi toward the girls. "Hello, ladies. I do hope you're enjoying the event so far."

"Ohmigosh! Trip Whitley. And Bambi," one of the girls said. Then, as if realizing she had reacted like a crazed teenage fan, she colored and said, "We just got here, but we're having a lovely time."

Her friend added, "You really should try this Chardonnay. It's quite good. I wonder if all of the rest of the wines are this good."

"I hope so. I helped pick them," Trip said.

"Trip, I didn't know that," Bambi turned to him.

"That's so cool," the second girl said. "You can never trust wine at events like this. Sometimes they just use the worst stuff."

"Well, just because we're young doesn't mean that we can't appreciate the finer things in life," Trip said.

"Cheers to that." The first girl raised her glass before realizing that neither he nor Bambi had a glass of their own. "Oh."

Trip smiled. "I'll take that as a rather gracious way of pointing out that I've been remiss as a date. Will you ladies excuse me while I pick up glasses for Bambi and myself? Then we'll make that toast." He made sure to smile at the girl and was glad to see that she brightened when he did.

Trip was delayed while waiting for the wine by a group of guys who recognized him and wanted to ask him about Bambi. They all wore Brooks Brothers suits in grays and blacks, and had the arrogance Trip associated with some young investment bankers.

"Must have been a rude awakening to start dating a girl from a strip joint only to find out she's a feminist!" one said.

"Yeah, girls like that take all the romance out of dating."

"I don't think so." Trip felt the need to defend Bambi. "She's just a modern woman. I mean, what's wrong with wanting everything that you and I want?"

"I don't know. Sometimes, I just want a girl to smile and grab me a beer without claiming that I'm keeping her from realizing her potential."

Trip resisted the urge to punch this Neanderthal in the face. He took the drinks from the bartender and looked over at Bambi. She seemed to be deep in discussion with the two girls. Even the girl who had blushed so much was talking animatedly. Bambi smiled and encouraged her, and then she looked up and caught Trip's eye. She directed a smile at him.

"You know, I thought that was me," Trip found himself responding. "But I want a girl who can keep up with me. Who can challenge me. Who can keep up with the other strong and smart women in my life. You're missing out, buddy, if you don't want that, too."

Trip turned and walked away, no doubt leaving a discussion in his wake. He realized things had changed. Once, he would have defended Bambi in order to keep up the pretense of their relationship; but just now, he had defended her because he believed every word. He liked having a smart conversation with Bambi. He liked knowing that the other strong women in his life, like Allison, would appreciate and get along with Bambi. He had laughed at Mrs. Bradford's consternation at meeting the bimbo version of Bambi, but he was confident that the real Bambi could go toe-to-toe with the matron any day of the week.

Trip lingered a couple of steps away from Bambi and the girls after he saw her give him a little shake of her head to warn him away. Wondering what was going on, he listened in to the conversation in progress.

"I don't know," said the more confident of the girls. "I feel like I haven't exhausted my avenues of meeting guys. I mean, it's harder now that we're not in college, but I still meet guys."

"At bars?" Bambi asked.

"Yeah. But that's not as bad as everyone says it is. I just don't think I'm really into the whole online dating thing."

"I just feel like it would be giving up, being desperate," another girl complained.

"Joining Belles and Beaux is not giving up, I promise," Bambi responded. Well, Trip thought, Bambi had jumped into the role of promoter for Belles and Beaux quickly. He wondered how she would convince these girls to check it out. He listened as she continued, "And it's not desperate to want someone to share your life with. That's what the guys are looking for, too. You have to realize that people come into your life in unexpected ways. Why not open yourself up to the possibility?"

"I guess."

"Besides, I'm sure that Trip would be happy to sign you up personally if you went into their offices." She looked from the girls to Trip, and he knew that was his cue. He made his way over. "Trip, do you have one of your cards? These ladies might be interested in signing up for Belles and Beaux."

"Of course, Bambi." Trip smiled at each girl as he handed her a card. "Be sure you ladies ask for me personally when you come in. I'd love to help you get set up."

They talked to the girls for a little while longer. On their way toward a larger group, Trip turned to Bambi.

"That was impressive."

"What?"

"How you convinced those girls to check out Belles and Beaux."

"Oh, that was nothing. They just needed to be reassured that signing up wouldn't make them some kind of freaks."

"You know, I never understand that. There are these gorgeous girls who come into my office every day. And I can tell they feel self-conscious about signing up."

"Gorgeous girls?" Bambi winked at Trip. "I do remember your speech at Pat's wedding."

Trip chuckled. "Those were good times. But back to those girls. I totally don't get it. Why are they nervous about it all? It's hard to meet someone if you don't run into singles as part of your job. People are busy. We make it much easier."

"I don't know for sure. But some of my friends at least take it more personally. Like joining a dating site means that you can't pick up guys from a random selection at a bar one night. Like you're not enough."

"That's absurd."

"I completely agree, Trip."

They didn't have the opportunity to continue the discussion as they dropped in on a group huddled around a Velazquez painting.

Trip watched Bambi charm this group as quickly as she had charmed the two girls. He noticed that the boys' eyes went straight to her cleavage, covered though it was. He had a sudden protective urge that he hadn't experienced before. He wanted to take them by the chins and force their eyes to Bambi's beautiful face. He wanted to remind them that she was a person, not just a set of boobs. He wanted to tell them to quit ogling his girlfriend.

Holy shit. Girlfriend? Trip knew he should do everything in his power to avoid feeling anything more for his beautiful date. But somehow, his brain wasn't winning out. After the twenty-somethings had trickled out, Trip and Bambi made their way over to Kevin O'Shea to pay their respects.

"Miss Benson." O'Shea detached himself from the clean-up crew he was directing and headed directly toward Bambi, kissing her on both cheeks. "And Mr. Whitley." Trip knew he wasn't imagining the coolness in the greeting he got compared to Bambi's.

"Mr. O'Shea. I'm so glad our two organizations could work so well together."

"Of course, of course." O'Shea tore his gaze away from Bambi long enough to be polite. "I hope you both had as wonderful a time as I did."

"Of course," Bambi gushed. "It was such fun to meet everyone, and what a beautiful setting!"

Kevin O'Shea blushed. Trip grumbled under his breath.

O'Shea put his hand on Bambi's arm. "Well, Miss Benson, if you ever need a *personal* tour of the museum, don't hesitate in the least to contact me. Sometimes, the best treasures are hidden in the darkest corners." He smiled and handed her his card.

Trip didn't doubt there was more than treasure to be found in dark corners, but he didn't give Bambi time to respond. He grabbed her free hand and dragged her away from the museum director and out of the museum. The whole interaction made him feel surprisingly primal, like a caveman dragging his prize back to his cave.

Bambi couldn't help laughing as Trip pulled her toward the car. The look on that little man's face when he gave her that whole spiel about treasures and corners—it was priceless. Who did he think he was fooling?

Bambi had enjoyed the whole evening and right now, she felt like a bubble floating on air. The glasses of wine Trip had kept placing in her hands had tasted divine, and the night had been going so well. The awkward truce between them had melted away into something that seemed almost like friendship. And if not yet friendship, at least partnership. And that she could handle for six more months.

Besides, Bambi couldn't help noticing how Trip stood out from that crowd of boys. They might as well have been a bunch of pimply high schoolers for all the competition they gave Trip.

Although Bambi had never thought of Trip as the sharpest tool in the shed, she watched him play the crowd and began to understand his unique talents. He managed to make everyone around feel comfortable and noticed.

She had watched as the girls' eyes took him in. That tousled hair, the long and lean body so at ease in the suit cut just right. His chest tapered down to a slim waist and a butt that Bambi had dreamed of touching.

"Whatcha thinking over there?" Trip asked.

Bambi started and blushed. She couldn't very well explain that she had been considering the tactile quality of his posterior. "Nothing. You, I guess. You're good in a crowd."

"You're not so bad yourself. You had everyone hanging on your every word. Plus I bet we'll have a bunch of new clients at Belles and Beaux tomorrow thanks to your sales pitch. I wouldn't have thought a feminist could be such an advocate for romance."

"I'm not against romance. I just don't think it should mean everything in a relationship. In fact, your site matches up people according to very measurable variables, I would assume. Like interests, professions, and plans for the future. Romance is something that they bring to it themselves."

"I guess you're right."

Trip stopped at a red light and turned the force of his gaze on Bambi. She could feel herself being pulled into those brown eyes, and a shiver ran down her spine. A delicious, promising shiver. And tonight, she didn't want to ignore it.

"Maybe we make a decent team."

"Yeah. Maybe we do."

Bambi spent the rest of the short car ride in silence, stealing an occasional glance at Trip, who drove with casual confidence through the dark streets of Boston and then Cambridge. By the time that they pulled up at her building, Bambi had almost fallen asleep.

"Bambi," Trip whispered close to her ear. The tickle of his breath on her neck woke her right up.

"I'm awake."

"Oh. We're here. Which, of course, you knew. Since you weren't asleep."

"Hey! Okay, maybe I did doze a little."

"Exactly. Want me to walk you up? I should. My mother would kill me otherwise."

"I'm fine. The door's just 20 feet away."

"I know you're fine. But my Southern gentlemanliness is kicking in. There's no stopping me. Just give in." Trip smiled, and Bambi's resistance melted.

"Fine."

Trip was out of the car and had circled to her side to open the door before she could force her sleepy mind into gear. He extended his hand to help her out, and Bambi figured she might as well forget being an independent woman for the time it would take to get from here to her door. And if she were honest, it felt pretty good to be tucked against Trip's side.

They reached the door of her building much too quickly. She was reluctant to leave Trip's arms and he seemed just as reluctant to let her go. Bambi searched in her purse for the keys hidden inside, and drew them out with a sigh. Trip's gloved hand closed over hers and she forfeited the keys to him. But as he turned the lock and opened the door, he failed to release his hold on her, as Bambi had expected him to. He still held her close when they entered the foyer and headed toward her apartment. Any sleepiness she had felt suddenly vanished, and her senses went on high alert. Electric, crackling tension filled the air and Bambi was afraid to speak and drive it away, but afraid to stay silent and let it mount.

Trip deftly inserted the key into the lock and opened the deadbolt, then the lock. The door swung open and he placed the keys in her hand.

"Here. You should take these."

"They are mine." Bambi found herself having trouble concentrating. The buzz she had gotten from the wine had been replaced by buzzing around her whole body, making her feel as if she were a live wire, tossing from side to side.

"Good night, Bambi."

"Good night, Trip." She looked up into his eyes, which set that live wire part of herself dancing even more frantically.

He stood there for an agonizing moment as Bambi debated whether she could face his leaving or avoid his staying. Then, with no warning, she found his lips on hers. His tongue dove into her mouth and tangled with hers. Desperate to be closer to him, she grabbed the lapels of his coat and pulled her body hard against his, damning the extra layers of fabric that separated them.

She wasn't sure how long they stood there, entangled in that kiss. It was as if the world were spinning on a different axis than it had been a mere five minutes ago. She had known that kissing Trip could be amazing—that had been settled by the kiss they had shared during Pat and Ally's wedding—but this was beyond what she had thought possible with any man, much less Trip Whitley.

Bambi felt her need grow to a chasm such that she wondered if it could ever be filled. As Trip reached down to grab her butt to pull her up against him, she knew with a sudden glimpse of clarity what she wanted.

"Trip," she reluctantly pulled her mouth away from his. He kissed a path down her neck, ripping away her scarf and finding the spot where her neck and shoulder met, rendering her incapable of coherent speech for a moment. She moaned. "Oh, God, Trip. Inside. Come inside."

Trip glanced up at her for only a moment before he reclaimed her mouth, and they stumbled inside the apartment. He kicked the door shut behind them. Bambi reached past him to secure the deadbolt and then moved her fingers back to his chest. She splayed her hands across the warm wool of his coat before realizing that she wanted more. Needed more. She moved her fingers to undo the large buttons. She pushed the coat off his shoulders, sending it to the floor in one smooth move and finding her own coat on the floor soon after.

She attacked the buttons on his shirt next, cursing them at the same time she thanked her lucky stars that he had taken off the tie between work and the wine tasting. She could barely concentrate as Trip grazed a finger across her nipple and began to toy with it through the fabric of her shirt and bra. Finally, willing to take no more, she pulled his shirt from his pants and forced him to pull it over his head.

In the meantime, he had opened her blouse and pulled down her skirt and hose. Seeing him, standing in front of her, shirtless with his muscular chest, Bambi felt shy for the first time. But Trip grabbed her back into his arms, pushed the cups of her bra down, and bowed her body back to begin suckling her nipples. Bambi felt herself bucking against him, the hardness in his pants so tantalizingly close.

Somehow, he understood what she wanted and gave up his ministrations on her breasts to shuck his pants and underwear. Bambi used the moment to undo her bra and throw it on the floor with her panties. "God, you're beautiful," he groaned. Bambi could say the same. She was amazed at how good the man looked in well-cut clothes. But out of them, it was even better. His broad shoulders tapered to a narrow waist and onto powerful legs dusted with light brown hair.

They came back together and stumbled past the tiny kitchen and bistro table to fall onto the bed, unwilling to take their mouths and hands from each other. Bambi explored the muscles of Trip's back and curved her palms around his tight butt.

As they rolled onto the bed, she reveled in the feel of all of his skin against all of hers. She found herself almost unwilling to delay the moment when he entered her. But a small part of her brain still worked, and as she kissed him and grabbed him with one hand, she searched blindly in her nightstand for the condoms she kept there.

"If you want to come in, you have to use the key." She held up the small package.

"Oh, I want in," Trip growled. He swiped the condom, opened the plastic wrapper with his teeth and rolled the thin sheath onto his swollen shaft. Bambi smiled once it was in place and leaned back on her pillows.

"Come on, Trip."

He needed no further invitation. As they kissed, he entered her in one smooth stroke. Simultaneously, Bambi felt something in herself calm and something else start dancing to a not yet identified rhythm. But as he began to move inside her, she felt their rhythm come together, and she felt herself responding, moving with him in that primal dance between man and woman.

Trip pushed her until she didn't think she could take it anymore. Then, with another thrust, the time bomb within her erupted in a drenching pleasure that weighted her limbs. Moments later, she heard his groan as he succumbed, too. He collapsed on her, nestled inside her, and together they breathed and waited for the world to stop spinning.

CHAPTER FOURTEEN

As soon as her brain began working again, Bambi wished it hadn't. What the hell had just happened, and how could she have let her guard down? Suddenly, Trip's weight, which had felt so cozy before, was pushing down on her chest so that she couldn't breathe, couldn't think clearly.

Bambi shifted uncomfortably. Trip yawned and lifted his face from her neck.

"Much as that was amazing, I don't think I can go again. You tired me out." He smiled that lazy smile that usually turned her resolve to jelly. But she commanded that resolve to straighten up and forget the wonderful way Trip had made her feel.

"I need you to get up."

"Sure. Okay." Trip looked a little confused and maybe hurt, but he complied, shifting himself off of her and to the other side of the bed. Bambi curled herself into a ball, wondering what she should do next. And then Trip did something completely unexpected. He pulled her folded form against his chest and threw an arm around her to keep her clasped tight to him.

Really? Just this once, she wanted, no, needed Trip to be an arrogant jerk. So that she could find that distance, get back to the safe place in their relationship that didn't blur the awkward lines between what shouldn't happen and what couldn't happen. But here he was, snuggling up to her, his body warmth creating a cocoon that she was powerless to resist. She forced that little niggling doubt to be quiet and fell asleep.

But when Bambi woke up, she found the doubt still hiding at the back of her mind. For goodness sakes, he was paying her to be his girlfriend! That fact forced her to look it in the face. She contemplated the fact that a good lawyer could make a case against her for prostitution. Hell, even a bad lawyer would have a decent shot. She had to get him out of her bed. She pulled herself out of Trip's embrace and tapped him on the shoulder. No use. He groaned and turned over. She moved to the other side of the bed and poked him with more force. Still nothing. So she grabbed him by the shoulders and put her face close to his.

"Wake up!"

"Huh?" Trip sat upright so fast that he knocked her onto the floor. As she gathered herself up, she watched him try to figure out where he was. Then his confusion turned to panic. Perfect. Now he was panicking, too.

"What time is it?" he asked. "Shit! Where's my phone?" He fumbled through the covers. Then, he caught sight of her clock.

"Geez. It's only seven thirty. Why didn't you say something?"

"Uh . . . I don't know." Bambi grabbed the sheet off the bed and wrapped it around her.

"Well, I should probably go." Trip began to get up slowly. "Get ready for work and all. Change clothes."

"Yes, you probably should." Bambi tried to avoid looking at his naked body.

"Unless . . ." Trip's voice trailed off and quirked a brow suggestively. He headed toward her and had crossed so quickly that Bambi failed to stop him until he was a breath away.

"No." She stepped back. "Last night was a mistake."

"But this morning could be just right," Trip said. "And if not, I always like to learn from my mistakes. You have to make mistakes to learn from them, you know." He stepped toward her again and trailed a finger down her jaw.

"I'm serious, Trip." Bambi grabbed his wrist with the hand that wasn't holding the sheet. "I was happy the evening had gone well. But this—I mean, we can't have sex." Bambi let him go and circled around the bed to pick up his clothes from the floor.

"Why not? I think we pretty well established that we're good at it." Trip followed, taking each piece of clothing as she hammered it at his chest.

"Has it escaped your memory that you *paid* me to go out with you?"

Trip looked blank. Then she saw understanding dawn on him. "You don't really think—I mean, you don't think that I think that this, the sex, was included in that deal?"

"No, Trip." Bambi sighed, "I honestly don't think that. But I can't escape what it *feels* like."

"That's ridiculous!" He shoved his leg into his pants. "Do you see Jim or Jack? Or Elizabeth Pinckney? No!" He stopped once he had his pants on, still shirtless, and reached to cup her face. "Bambi, this was just us."

"No." She pushed at his chest just enough to push him away. Bambi felt tears welling up, but she refused to cry. "Whatever it was, I still feel like a prostitute. And that's not who I am. And I am not my mother."

"What does your mother have to do with this?"

"Just go, please."

"Fine." Trip balled up his shirt in his hands and shrugged into his jacket. He left without another word. Bambi sat down on her bed and put her face in her hands, expecting tears now that he had gone. But all she felt was the dull thrumming of a worsening headache.

Trip bounced a ball off the wall of his office for the thousandth time that day. He ought to be working, refining the information he had gotten from the twenty-somethings that had been flowing in for days, thanks to his and Bambi's command performance at the museum. But he didn't want to think about that night. Not that he could stop thinking about it, even if he wanted to.

"You have got to stop that." Pat's voice in his doorway startled Trip enough that he failed to catch the ball and it rolled under the desk.

"What does it matter to you?" he asked, feeling peevish.

"My sanity, to be honest. Thump, thump, thump. All day long. But now that I think of it, no, not all day. At random intervals, it would stop. My brain would find relief for about 15 minutes. Only to be plunged into a worse hell than before when the thumping resumed."

"You're growing into the worst nag, you know," Trip said from under his desk. "Ally teach you that?"

"Very funny. And no. What's with the bouncing?"

Trip resumed the game. "Helps me to think."

"Bullshit. You didn't need it to think before now. So what's the problem?" Pat pushed himself out of the doorway and onto Trip's couch.

"Nothing's the problem."

"Sure. Which is why I've had to field a bunch of kids who came here to see you and sign up."

"Hey! We've been flooded. Sorry if I thought my teammate and friend might be able to help me out."

"Oh no. You're not getting off that easy. If you'd been so busy, I wouldn't have heard so much thumping. 'Cause your fingers would have been on those keys." Pat nodded at Trip's computer. "Something go wrong with the museum thing?"

"It went great," Trip said. Then, under his breath, "Maybe too great."

"What's that you said? Too great? Then what's the problem, bud? Why do you feel the need to drive your old pal crazy?"

Trip blushed. He was sure he hadn't blushed since he was about eight, and he had no idea why it had happened. He'd never felt embarrassed about his sexual activity in the past.

Pat was watching him closely. Trip knew there was no use in concealing the truth from his friend.

"We slept together."

"Well, that's just great! Ally and I took bets on—"

"Wait a second," Trip interrupted. "You took bets?"

"Yeah. And dammit, she's gonna win."

"Oh, I think she already had you beat long before this bet." Trip couldn't help laughing.

"Yeah." Pat chuckled a little himself. "But you said you slept together as if it were a bad thing."

"It was." No longer laughing, Trip pulled a hand through his hair and stilled the compulsive ball bouncing.

"Really? Hmmm . . . not what I would've thought, but I guess you never know. Well, it's behind you now—you've got it out of your system and now you can both just move on."

"Oh. It wasn't bad that way. It was great. Amazing. I mean, her breasts—"

"Hold on there. I'm a newly married man." Pat gestured at the ring on his finger. "Still, I don't see the problem. Unless . . . did you begin to feel something for her?"

"Begin? Hell, I was trying to talk myself out of it, but I think she's been crawling under my skin from the beginning. Or at least from the time of your wedding. And that's freaky enough, but it's not the problem, either."

"Then what?"

"It's the money thing."

"But that shouldn't bother her—wait, oh, I see. Not how much more money you have than her. The fact that you're paying her to be your girlfriend."

"You got it. I mean, believe me, I never thought of what we did, you know, in that context. Not at all."

"But the line is a little blurry."

"Yeah. When she said it, she hit me with it at the wrong time. I mean, we had just spent the night together and I was having these feelings . . . man, I don't know. But when I got home, got cool, I realized she might not be totally unjustified."

"That's a rough one."

"Yeah, tell me about it." Trip got up from his chair and circled around the desk to flop on the couch next to Pat.

"Well, I can think of one solution. Stop paying her."

"I guess I could do that. But then, what if she doesn't want to see me?" Trip felt childish and small when he admitted that fear. Something had changed that night at the museum, even before the sex.

"Then you'll just have to work that out. Man," Pat clapped Trip on the shoulder, "I don't envy you. But you should try it out. You never know how far something will go unless you test its limits."

Bambi got out of class late and thrust on her coat to protect herself against the cold March winds. Which was fine by her these days. The cold helped her keep her mind off the incredible heat she and Trip had generated together.

But she wouldn't be able to keep her mind off him for much longer. She had agreed to meet Trip at John Harvard's, a restaurant in the square. He had originally suggested they meet at her apartment, but there was no way that was going to happen. John Harvard's was sufficiently bright, and there were enough precocious and celebrity-crazy undergrads that hung out there to ensure their meal wouldn't go uninterrupted. Which was good. Because Bambi couldn't talk about that morning again.

She wished fervently that she could have the reassuring protection of Elizabeth, Jim, Jack, and the cameras. Although she wasn't sure if she could face Elizabeth, having not had the guts to call her friend and tell her what had happened.

Bambi pushed through the door and took the steps down into the restaurant. Already buzzing with activity although it was relatively early for dinner, it embodied what visitors wanted when they thought of a place like Harvard. Old brick, stained-glass panels, warm wood bar.

She made her way to the bar, stripping off her heavy coat. Even though she had known she'd be meeting Trip that evening, she'd intentionally skipped make-up and forced herself to wear a ratty wool turtleneck in an unflattering brown and a long, schoolmarm-type skirt that she usually reserved for much colder days. Bambi's gaze traveled to Trip. She viciously told her heart to quit squeezing at the sight of him nursing a beer but it ignored her as usual. He looked handsome as usual: perfectly pressed pants, crisp white shirt, and a jacket thrown casually over the back of the chair.

"Hi," she said. When Bambi sat down next to him, she felt the surreptitious stares and heard lowered voices around them.

"Bambi. I didn't see you come in. Hi. Thanks for coming." He paused. "I guess I wanted to talk about . . . what happened," he said.

"At the museum gala?"

"And after."

"Did you end up getting new clients after that? I was curious about how many people would follow through and show up." Bambi knew she was ignoring the subject at hand, but she couldn't help it.

"Several of them turned up. But that wasn't what I meant." His look seemed to add "and you know it."

"Trip, there's nothing more to discuss. I'm pretty sure I made myself clear. And my feelings haven't changed."

"Yes, well, I think there's more. I think we need to work this out." Bambi felt herself shaking her head in rejection. But he continued, "First," Trip kept his eyes on hers and reached out to pull her hands into his. "I need you to know that that night wasn't what you felt like it was." He lowered his voice. "I never thought you owed me sex for the money I was paying you."

Bambi started to pull back. He would never understand how their night together made her sick inside. But he wouldn't allow her hands or eyes to retreat from his.

"But I do understand the way you feel," he continued. "The money makes things different. Which is why I suggest that . . ." Trip paused and drew a deep breath. Bambi could feel his hands shaking a little. "We take it away. Give this thing a real shot."

Bambi sucked in her breath. This wasn't expected. But part of her wanted badly for it to work out. When she pulled her hands away this time, he didn't try to stop her. She crossed her arms under her breasts. There were so many questions to answer. "What about the sex?" she challenged him.

"It was great. If it happens again, great. But there's no pressure either way. This would be a real relationship."

"Well, then there would be pressure."

Trip rolled his eyes. "I mean I have no assumptions. Don't make this any more difficult than it is. The relationship would be the two of us, getting to know each other for real. No scams, no ulterior motives."

"What about the cameras?"

"Unfortunately, they have to stick around. At least for the nine months."

"And what if we break up before then?"

"Then we really break up. I wouldn't try to keep up the charade once real feelings were involved. Don't worry. I can handle Ms. Pinckney and my father."

Something in Trip's face, the determination or the vulnerability, spoke to Bambi's heart. She felt a spark of hopefulness light within her. "Okay."

"Okay? Does that mean you're in?"

"To be honest, Trip, I don't know. I'm willing to try it out. Clearly we have something together—chemistry at least."

"I don't know if I would call that 'least.'" Trip smiled. "But there's more. I know it. We just need to give things a chance."

"Okay. One more date. In public." Bambi wasn't sure if she was allowing her body or her head to do the talking.

"Great." Trip let out a breath. "Name the time and place and I'll be there."

Bambi thought for a moment. "Beacon. Saturday, seven o'clock."

"Is that a challenge? Beacon is the hardest restaurant to get a reservation at in the city."

"No. I just want to go there, and what's the point of celebrity if you can't take advantage of it once in a while?" Bambi grabbed her coat and stood. "I'll see you on Saturday."

Trip stood, too. "You can't get away that easy." She stopped and turned toward him. He pulled her toward him and kissed her. His tongue darted into her mouth and caressed it. Bambi could feel the warmth that it carried all the way to her toes. Trip pulled away. "Come for the chemistry. We'll see where it goes after that."

Bambi nodded and turned around. As she walked away, she recognized the curiosity she had so often felt in academia that had caused her to want to delve into subjects and learn more, to take a journey toward truth. But now, that curiosity was directed toward Trip Whitley.

CHAPTER FIFTEEN

Trip followed Bambi as they made their way into Beacon. The red brick path led into a dining room with dark wood floors that looked worn and polished. Square tables of varying sizes were laid with white sailcloth and twinkling nautical lanterns. The tables also held sturdy red dishes and the signature thick black-and-white striped napkins, rolled and held together with rope napkin rings fashioned into sailor's knots.

"You met the challenge." She smiled across the table at him. "Thanks for getting us in here."

"I would tell you it was easy, but that would be lying. It took every bit of our collective star power and Teena's considerable persuasiveness to get us in here. But I'm glad we made it."

"We would have still been able to have our date. I wasn't serious about the challenge." Bambi placed a tentative hand over his. It felt pretty good.

"Oh, you think I'm glad because of that?" Trip feigned lack of awareness. "No. It's definitely because I heard that the fried scrod is out of this world."

"Aha." Bambi laughed. "Sounds like you have your priorities straight."

"You bet." Trip tucked his napkin into his collar, which made Bambi laugh even more. "So, now that I'm ready to order, why'd you suggest this place? It doesn't seem like your type of place. Was this her idea?" He jerked a hand back to indicate Elizabeth Pinckney, who stood in a corner with Jim and Jack. The trio was trying to be as discreet as possible. That was not very discreet, however, since Jim—or was it Jack—was carrying a giant video camera.

"No. Actually, I heard about it from Lainie."

"Friend from school?" he asked.

"No. The Booby Trap."

"Huh. Wouldn't have guessed that." The moment the words were out of Trip's mouth, he wondered whether he should have said them. But Bambi didn't seem to notice.

"Me either. She isn't into the Boston scene. But it turns out that, 10 years ago, she was in love with Shaun Parker."

"The executive chef? The guy who made it okay for Boston socialites to eat fried food again?"

"The same. Apparently, he wanted to start a restaurant back then, too. And Lainie was helping him save for it. That's why I wanted to come. I was immensely curious."

"Well, I'll see what I can do to satisfy you." Trip watched Bambi blush. "Get your head out of the gutter, Benson."

"Hey, I know what you meant." She smiled.

"Sure, sure." Trip was still nervous and now a little aroused.

"How about we change the subject?" He wracked his brain for what little he knew about her. "How are the interviews going?" Trip sipped some iced tea that the waiter had brought and watched Bambi light up, as she always did when talking about work.

"It was great. I think that the women will end up being a wealth of information. Right now, I'm particularly interested in how they draw the line between how strippers use their bodies and how they do. The women I've spoken with seem to run the gamut—some see the job as pretty sexualized, while others don't at all."

"Interesting. And what are you going to do with all this information once you've gathered it?"

Bambi shrugged. "My dissertation. Hopefully, I'll get to publish an article or book based on what I learn, too. But that's pretty far into the future. I've been working on a presentation to take to conferences in the fall based on my firsthand knowledge and book research. I hope to show that to my advisor soon, but the dissertation won't be finished till at least next spring."

"That's quite a long-term project. I wish I knew more about your subject."

"I'll give you a couple books. I promise they won't be too dense."

"That would be great." Trip smiled at Bambi. They both looked at each other, Bambi waiting expectantly. Trip didn't know what to say. Was their date already bombing?

Thankfully, Bambi saved him. "How about work for you?"

"Actually, things are great at work. This PR stunt is really doing wonders for the company. We've gotten so much new business that Pat and I are having trouble handling it all. Dad is thinking about bringing on a new associate."

"Is that so?"

"Yeah. And I think that maybe we should bring in a woman. Pat and I pretty much have some angles covered, but watching you at the museum gala the other night made me think we could benefit from having a woman on the team. I'm going to run some figures on it before I talk to my Dad."

"That's great. Do you think he'll go along with it?"

"I hope so. Although he hasn't always wanted to see me taking over more of the business, so I'm not sure. Sometimes, I think that he doesn't see me as capable of helping out with anything beyond publicity."

"Do you want to take on a bigger role than that?" Bambi remembered him mentioning it right before they were about to tape Madison Hart's show.

"Yeah. Of course. I want to learn how he does what he does, but he shuts me out."

"I didn't know that. Maybe he doesn't think you're serious. But that's just my Lucy van Pelt analysis."

"Lucy van Pelt?"

"Sure. From 'Peanuts.' You know—psychiatric help, five cents. So pay up, buster." She smiled. "But seriously. You should show him you're committed to Belles and Beaux. Talk to him about your idea for a female associate. Also, maybe you should plan an event for us. A big thing. Surely that wouldn't be stepping on his toes."

Trip thought about what Bambi said. Maybe he could do something that would earn more of his father's respect. He also picked up on something else she had said. "So we're going to have more dates?"

"Looks like it right now. But we haven't even gotten our

dinner yet." As she said that, their waiter appeared with their order. She turned to Trip, "Did you choreograph that ahead of time?"

"Of course not. You'll back me up, right buddy?" he turned to the waiter, who just smiled and walked away. He turned back to Bambi. "So, if we're going to have more dates, I need you to tell me more."

"About what?"

"Yourself, of course. You grew up in Charlestown, right?"

Bambi looked taken aback and Trip wondered what he had said. But soon, she had recovered herself. "I did."

"Well, tell me about your family. You know all about mine. Mom, Dad, sisters, brothers?"

"I lived with my mom. No siblings. Just the two of us."

"Only child, like me. What about your dad? Divorce?"

"Frankly, I don't know much about him. He was gone by the time I was old enough to remember anything."

"Well, it must have been cozy, just you and your mom," Trip said, trying to lighten the tone.

"I don't know if that's the word I'd use for it. My mom and I never exactly saw eye-to-eye on a lot of things."

"I'm sorry. My mom is the best—once you get past a little bit of a prickly exterior. I know she feels pretty bad for coming down so hard on you when she first met you. My dad, he's a lot harder to read sometimes. And a lot harder to talk to. So your mom dated Joe?"

"She did." Trip noticed that Joe's name brought the first smile to Bambi's lips since they had begun speaking about her family. "He dated my mom for about a year when I was seven or eight. We had such a great relationship that we kept it up after they broke up." She paused. "Well, I guess I didn't so much keep it up as he did. He was great."

"Well, I'll have to meet Joe."

"That would be great." Bambi smiled again.

"And your mother, too."

"I don't know about that. I'm not sure if she's even in Boston anymore."

"Okay. You two don't talk?" Trip had sensed a rift between mother and daughter, but he had no idea it went that deep.

"No."

"Any reason?"

"I'd rather not talk about it." Bambi put down her forkful of fish. "I'm not hungry any more." She pushed her plate toward him. "You should finish this."

Trip looked at her with concern. He hated that he had unwittingly made Bambi so uncomfortable. He tried to make it up to her by distracting her from whatever was bothering her. "So, what did you do for fun as a kid?"

"Read, mostly. I love books."

"So you did read *Little Women*, despite what you said."

Bambi nodded. "All of it. Probably 10 times. It was one of my favorites as a kid. I was dying to visit Orchard House that day, but I couldn't tell you why."

"I see." Trip narrowed his eyes at Bambi. "It did seem at the time that you remembered an awful lot from the movie." He was rewarded with a shy smile, which encouraged him to continue. "Any other favorites?"

"Oh, countless. *Jane Eyre, Beloved, Pride and Prejudice, The Handmaid's Tale*. Those are just a few. What about you?"

"*The Amazing Adventures of Kavalier and Klay*. Recently, I've gotten into books by Sarah Vowell. And as a kid, I was crazy about *The Catcher in the Rye*."

"Of course you were," Bambi teased.

"What does that mean?" Trip laughed.

"It's such a boy's book. I never really got what all the fuss was about. Too much angst. Grow up."

"Says the woman whose favorite book is *Little Women*."

"What are you saying?"

"I'm saying it's a girl's book."

"It's a classic!"

"Okay, well if you're so confident that it's a better book, can you handle a small wager?"

"Of course. Jo March could beat Holden Caulfield in his sleep. What's the plan?"

"We each reread the other's favorite book. Then we sit down and have an honest discussion about which one is better. We both get to make a plea for our book at the beginning of the reading and at the end of the discussion. Whoever loses owes the winner dinner here at Beacon."

"It's a deal. If we can ever get back in here." Bambi stretched out her hand and they shook.

Trip smiled. More plans for future dates. He had been worried that everything in their past together would somehow prevent them from enjoying this date. And he didn't want to let Bambi go without exploring the something he knew was there. He couldn't quite put his finger on it yet, but it was definitely important.

They continued talking for another hour. Then, Trip noticed Bambi yawning. "Should we get the check?" he asked.

She nodded. He signaled their waiter, a little sad that their evening was ending.

Bambi felt like she had discovered a whole new person. She looked across the table at Trip as he scrawled his name on the receipt and almost didn't recognize him. There was that mischievous glint in his brown eyes, but somehow the way she understood that glint had changed. No longer was he having fun at her expense; instead, they were working together. She'd had real fun on the date tonight. Well, except for the discussion of her mother. She wasn't quite ready to tell him the whole truth about that. He wouldn't understand.

Screw that. Bambi thought to herself. She knew that he might understand just fine. She just didn't want him to know. Not yet. Their relationship seemed too fragile right now to bear the weight of what the whole story of her mother would involve.

She shook her head to clear it and saw that Trip stood behind her with her coat. She allowed him to help her shrug into it and used the tingle his hands sent through her body to distract her from thoughts of her mother. She would deal with those later.

He ushered her to the car and they began the 10-minute drive to her apartment. But Bambi didn't want the night to end. She wanted to learn more about Trip.

"Would you want to get drinks?" she asked.

"Umm. No. Early morning tomorrow. Got to get to sleep." He seemed suddenly more nervous, and Bambi stung with his rejection. He had just given her the flimsiest excuse in the book. Apparently their date hadn't gone as well as she thought.

"I see."

"No. Wait. I promised myself that I would stop lying. I thought the date was great. I want to spend more time with you, I do. But I can't."

"And what's the real reason?"

He paused. "This is going to sound ridiculous."

"That should be par for the course for you." She smiled to show him she was joking.

"I just can't handle being this close to you. I'm afraid you turn my self-control into rubble. And I don't want to mess this up. Just a short time ago, we had sex with disastrous consequences. Or nearly disastrous. And two weeks before that, we were lying to everyone, including ourselves. I just feel like we should take it slow." He waited a beat. "I sound crazy, huh?"

Bambi had never had a man profess such a lack of self-control around her. Her academic brain thought about it feeling empowering, just like some of the women at The Booby Trap felt by using their bodies to elicit higher tips. But then her emotional brain took over. *You're analyzing this in order to avoid looking into the feelings that he evokes in you.*

"I see." She was quiet, and he didn't say anything more as he navigated across the bridge and into Cambridge. Bambi knew Trip was right; they shouldn't be having sex. It would be a terrible idea. But they had known each other quite awhile, even if they hadn't really *known* each other. And they had had sex before. Maybe she owed it to herself to explore that chemistry again? To see if the first time was a fluke?

No.

He pulled up in front of her apartment building. He stopped, unbuckled his seatbelt, and got out of the car. Bambi watched him as if he were in slow motion. He walked around to her side of the car, opened the door, and helped her out. Together, they walked to the front stoop of her building. Then, he kissed her.

She knew it was supposed to be a chaste peck on the lips, but she wanted more. She pulled him close and tangled his tongue with hers until she could feel him leaning hard into her.

Yes.

"Maybe we should have a drink upstairs?" she asked when she finally broke the kiss.

Trip closed his eyes, and she watched him breathe in and out twice. "Are you sure?" he asked when he opened them again. She knew he wasn't just talking about the drink.

"Yes."

She unlocked the door and stretched out her hand for his. He grabbed it and followed her inside. Together, they walked up the stairs to her apartment, where she opened it deliberately, surprised her hands weren't shaking.

They took off their coats in the small foyer and hung them on her coat tree. She took his hand again and led him toward the bed. There, she kissed him. Softly, at first, she explored his mouth with her lips and her tongue. She felt the ridges of his teeth and the soft inside of his cheek. She deepened the kiss and he seemed ready to take the ride with her. His hands moved down her back to her bottom and she could feel him press her against himself. She could feel his erection, and her body answered with delicious warmth deep inside.

She reached up and peeled off his suit jacket. He took the moment their lips were apart to grab the hem of her dress and pull it over her head.

"Wow," he said. She watched his eyes go to her breasts and she reached around to undo the clasp on her bra. With her breasts free, she invited him back into her arms. He kissed her mouth hungrily, then traced a path down her neck to her breast. There, he set to teasing her nipple with his mouth, using lips, teeth, and tongue. Bambi felt herself bucking against him as the sensations came upon each other, hard and fast. When he took her other nipple between his fingers and worked on both at the same time, she couldn't take it any longer and felt the release of her first orgasm.

As soon as she regained her breath, she said, "I need to touch you." He stepped away from her and they both stripped naked as quickly as possible. She couldn't bear to be without him for much longer. As he approached her again, she thought to herself how gorgeous he was. Long, toned arms, long legs. His broad chest was bare, and she reached out to feel the hair there and trace its path downward over his flat stomach. She wrapped her hand around him, warm and hard.

"Oh, God, Bambi. I can't handle it. Just let me be inside you." He tumbled her onto the bed and sank into her. He started a driving rhythm and Bambi's body responded immediately. She cried out as she felt the pressure building and building again. Then, he stopped. *What was the problem?*

"Condoms," he breathed.

She did what she could to scoot her body toward the nightstand without dislodging him, feeling the glorious friction of their two bodies. She could barely contain her body's urge to move against him. Finally, after a few moments of blind searching, she came up with the small box. Trip snatched it from her hand, grabbed one square, tore open the wrapping, and pulled out of her.

"No!" Bambi couldn't stop herself from yelling at the indignity of his body being gone from hers. She bucked as he rolled the condom onto his shaft. Then, he was back inside and they were moving. Bambi couldn't decide whether to close her eyes and feel like she was being propelled through the stars or watch his face. But when her climax came, she closed her eyes in order to keep that exquisite feeling in place just a second longer. Trip collapsed on her with a groan.

"Amazing," he said, minutes later, having not moved. "Good idea."

"It was my idea, don't forget," she said from beneath him.

"I won't. You're the brains in this relationship." She could feel his smile against her forehead.

"Does that make you the brawn?" she asked.

"Hell, yes. And don't sound so skeptical."

"You haven't moved an inch in 10 minutes. That doesn't seem very brawny."

"I'm comfortable."

"Well, I'm going to get up and get something to drink."

"No, you're not. I like you like this."

"I don't think you can stop me."

"You're challenging my brawniness?"

"I am." Bambi smiled. She tried to thrust a leg past his, but only got pulled back in. She reached a hand out and he grabbed her wrist and replaced it on his butt. She spread her legs and then brought her knees into a tuck to try to shove off his weight. She made it to the edge of the bed before he grabbed her from behind and wrestled her back onto the bed. She collapsed into a fit of giggles.

"Is there something you'd like to say?" he asked, nuzzling her back and trying to spoon her.

"I was wrong. You are the brawn."

"You bet." He let her go. "Now, can you grab me a water while you're up?"

She did, and when she got back into bed, he took a sip then snuggled up to her back, playing big spoon. She sighed and felt strangely comforted and calm.

When she woke up the next morning, Trip was already out of the bed. She heard the shower running and knew that he hadn't left. She analyzed her feelings, looking for some trace of the fear and disgust she had felt the last time this had happened. But nothing was there. Just contentment. She smiled to herself and got up to put on some clothes and make coffee.

When Trip came out of the shower, she realized he wasn't the only one with control problems. She had his towel off and he was back inside her within minutes. The second time Bambi managed to get up and dressed was more successful.

"I've got a racquetball game with Pat," Trip said. "I've got to get home and changed."

"Okay. Walk you to the door?"

Trip nodded and Bambi found some slippers. They stopped on the front stoop and Trip kissed Bambi. It felt like a promise. She heard the click of a camera and looked across the street to see the paparazzo hanging there.

"Don't worry about him," Trip said. "A couple weeks, this'll get boring for him." He kissed her once more. "See you later."

"Tonight," she said.

"Tonight," he agreed.

Bambi looked back at the paparazzo with his camera. Yes, this was something he was going to get bored by because she hoped that it would be a regular scene. She turned back to her apartment to continue working on her dissertation.

Trip sat in his familiar spot in Clink. He hadn't been there in weeks, but Pat had suggested they return for old times' sake. The girls were working late—Ally at the hospital and Bambi at The Booby Trap—so it would just be a guys' night. But Ally's night had ended earlier than planned and Trip now sat alone on his stool. He thought about moving to a quiet corner and pulling out the book in his pocket—*Little Women*.

"Why, Trip Whitley, I haven't seen you here in a while," Connie Bradford disrupted Trip's thoughts as she approached and slid onto the stool next to him.

"Nice to see you, Connie. And you're right; I haven't been here much recently. But I didn't realize you came here often enough to know."

"Well, I didn't used to. But it's close to the office, and I find I sometimes need to wind down after work." She turned from him and caught the bartender's attention. "Knob Creek on the rocks."

Trip's ears perked up at her order. "I didn't realize you were a bourbon fan, either."

"I am." She accepted the drink from the bartender and swirled the ice in the glass before taking a sip. "It's funny, actually, how I became a bourbon fan." She laughed low and mirthlessly. "In fact, it's because of you."

"Me?"

"Yeah." She looked away from him. "It was in college. About halfway through first semester, I realized I'd made a horrible mistake." She looked up from the drink and into his eyes. "I guess I started drinking bourbon because it made me feel closer to you." She looked back at her glass. "Silly, I know."

Trip looked at Connie. For years after their break-up, he had imagined various scenarios like this, with her expressing regret and his either taking her back or laughing at her. But at this moment, Trip couldn't summon up any of the intense feelings that he thought he would have felt now that one of those scenarios was actually playing out. He looked back on that time and responded truthfully, "That was a long time ago, and we both acted pretty silly."

"Yeah." She smiled a sad smile. "But you want to know something?"

Trip didn't want to ask, but he didn't know what else to say. "What?"

"It is still the biggest regret of my life." Before Trip could respond, she had leaned in and was kissing him. And what seemed like nanoseconds later, the bright flash of a camera went off in Trip's face.

He wrenched himself from Connie. "I have to go." He bolted off the stool toward the entrance, desperate to get away. When he got outside, he cursed the fact that he had left his car with a valet. He was waiting for it to arrive when Connie rushed up.

"I'm so sorry, Trip. I shouldn't have done that in public," she breathed.

"No kidding." Trip couldn't look at her.

"I had to let you know, though. Trip, look at me." She grabbed his arm to turn him toward her. "I never got over you. I think we might still have a chance—"

"I'm dating Bambi." Trip pulled his arm away.

"Come on. You know I know that's a sham. And we don't have to mess that up. We can keep this private until things are up with her. I understand how it works."

"No, you don't. See, I'm in love with Bambi!" he shouted.

Connie recoiled as if she'd been slapped. "Oh. I see." Trip could see her trying to stanch the flow of tears. "I have to go." She turned and walked quickly back into the bar. Trip wasn't sure whether he should go after her to see if she was okay, or whether he should get as far away as quickly as possible. Then, as he was making his decision, he looked up and saw Elizabeth Pinckney, transfixed. He had no idea what she had seen, heard, or inferred. He was trying to make his mind work when the valet pulled the car around. Trip had no idea what to do, so he jumped in the car and sped home.

The next morning, Trip knew exactly what he had to do. He called Elizabeth and she met him at his office just after nine. Normally, she would be the last person he would want to talk to in this frame of mind, but he knew that she was the only one who could fix the paparazzi problem.

When she arrived, she took a seat and looked at him. Then, she spoke.

"Listen, Trip, we got off on the wrong foot. I wanted to say I'm sorry for that."

"We did. You tried to control my private life." Trip regretted the line the moment he'd said it. He was here to ask for Elizabeth's help, but now he had her on the defensive. He watched her nostrils flare as she struggled to keep control. "Sorry. I didn't mean that."

"No, you're right. Maybe I did." Elizabeth took a controlled breath. "But you tried to sabotage me."

"I don't know what you're talking about."

"Come on, Trip. I knew all along that Bambi was a plant. That she was some kind of way for you to get around the plans that I had—that this company had—for you. You wanted to ruffle some feathers enough that I would get fired or at least that you wouldn't have to put up with my dating scheme."

"I don't know what you're talking about," Trip repeated. Inside, his mind was racing. *Was she telling the truth? Had she really known all along?*

"Whatever." She shook her head. "The point is I like Bambi. She has become my friend through this ridiculous process. So if you hurt her, I am coming after you. With everything I have."

"Whoa. I got it. You're her white knight."

"Yes, I guess. Think of me like that if you want. But I am the better female version. If there is anything Bambi's taught me, it is that heroes do not have to be men."

Trip chuckled in spite of himself at that. "You're right about that. Coincidentally, she and I might both need your services as a white knight now." He took a breath. "I messed up."

"Okay." Elizabeth drew out the word. Then she seemed to brace herself. "What's the problem?"

"Well, you know I was at Clink last night."

"Yeah." Elizabeth colored. "But I don't understand."

"A paparazzo caught Connie Bradford kissing me."

"WHAT?" Elizabeth exploded. Whatever she had been expecting, it hadn't been this.

"I need you to figure out who the guy was and make sure those pictures never see the light of day. I know he usually hangs out at Bambi's house. I've seen him there before." Trip glanced at Elizabeth, but it seemed like she hadn't heard him. "Do you think you can do it?"

A moment of silence passed. Then, Elizabeth lowered her voice to a harsh whisper. "What were you thinking?"

"Thinking about what?"

"About Connie Bradford! I thought you loved Bambi! That's what you said outside, anyway." Trip tried to interrupt but Elizabeth plowed onward, almost as if she were speaking to herself. "I should never have let Bambi get roped into this, into putting her heart on the line. I should have said something when she said that you guys were going to give your relationship a real try. But no. Stupid me. I thought I needed to take a step back and let her make her own mistakes. But by God, Trip—"

"Hold on, Elizabeth." Trip finally got a word in. "Connie kissed me! Out of the blue. And I do love Bambi. I don't know if I even knew it before I told Connie, but I do now." Then it was Trip's turn to blush. "But I think it gets worse."

"Worse?" Elizabeth closed her eyes and took a breath. "I am trying to give you the benefit of the doubt, but what's worse?"

"I think he was there before. When Connie and I had been out before at Clink."

"Before? Are you kidding me? And you took her to Clink, of all places? Bright idea! All of Boston knows that is your bar."

Trip sighed. "It was after the interview with Madison Hart. I was feeling bad and my parents invited Connie and her mother to dinner. Then I went out for drinks with Connie." Trip paused. "I know it looks bad. But what they would say about Connie and me wouldn't be true. I'm in love with Bambi."

Elizabeth studied Trip for a long moment. Trip looked her in the eye, knowing that she had to believe him in order for this to work out.

"Okay," she said finally. "I'll deal with it."

"Thank you so much, Elizabeth." Trip heaved a sigh of relief. Hopefully, Bambi would never have to know what had happened at Clink.

Bambi ducked into the cozy interior of Burdick's Chocolates and searched for Lois Williams. Her advisor had not arrived for their scheduled meeting yet, so Bambi ordered one of the store's famous hot chocolates and sat down at one of the small tables. She pulled her computer out of her bag and paged over to the new document of comments she had begun since she started interviews at The Booby Trap. Although she hadn't yet transcribed all of the interviews, she was using this document to record particular observations that she wanted to incorporate into a potential presentation for conferences in the fall.

She marveled at how much progress she had been able to make, despite the fact that her life was busier than ever. But somehow, Trip inspired her. They had spent nearly every night together since their dinner at Beacon. Coming home at night and being able to discuss her day and her thoughts with him had truly helped her. She smiled and began typing.

"Bambi." Lois stood in front of her a few minutes later. "Sorry for being late."

"No problem, Lois. I was just getting some work done." She closed her laptop and watched as Lois Williams took off her giant red coat. "What did you want to discuss?"

"Well, Bambi, I don't really know how to broach the subject. But I wanted to talk to you about your dissertation—broadly— and whether you thought you were going to continue making the required progress on it."

Bambi wrinkled her brow. "Of course. Why wouldn't I?"

"I see that you've been quite busy lately. With Trip Whitley." Lois shrugged. "Normally, I don't follow that type of news, but my daughter does. She's a little obsessed with the two of you."

"Oh." Bambi laughed. "You don't have to worry about me."

"I'm sorry," Lois said. "I don't normally get involved in the personal lives of graduate students."

"It's fine, Lois. I appreciate your concern."

"So are you still planning on heading to London?" Lois asked.

"I am." Bambi smiled. "In fact, since I've started interviews with the women at The Booby Trap, I'm more convinced than ever that the conference will be a wonderful experience for me."

"You've started interviews? I didn't realize that."

"Well, I did get my approval from the review board. And I only started a few weeks ago. But I've been able to compile quite a bit of information. In fact, I'm already working on a presentation for the fall conferences."

"Well, you are much farther along than I thought. That's wonderful."

"Thanks. Would you like to see a draft of what I have so far? I'm sure I could use your expertise."

"I would be very interested in seeing your work so far," Lois said.

"But you'll have to be kind! It's nowhere near finished." Bambi thought her advisor might be eager to read the presentation because she wanted to make sure that Bambi wasn't lying.

"I will be. Just email it on to me." She looked at the clock on the wall. "Oh goodness, I'm sorry but I have to run to pick my daughter up from lacrosse practice."

"I'll send it on. Go ahead. And tell her hi from Trip and me." Bambi smiled.

"Won't that just make her day." She threw up her hands. "Teenagers." She waved goodbye and flew out the door. Bambi thought about following her, but decided that she was pretty cozy sitting right there with her hot chocolate. She opened up her laptop and decided she would clean up her draft presentation before she sent it to Lois.

CHAPTER SIXTEEN

A week later, Trip picked up Bambi from The Booby Trap. He had been holding his breath for the pictures to come out, but nothing had surfaced. He had begun to relax and had come up with a great idea for their next public date. Trip was bursting to know Bambi's opinion. In fact, this new idea wasn't all he wanted her opinion on. In the short period of time since they had begun their real relationship, he had found he wanted to know her opinion on a million things. Big or small. They didn't have to agree, he just wanted to know, wanted to watch her mind work.

"Hi." Bambi grinned when she hopped in the car.

Trip watched her smiling at him and couldn't resist a simple kiss. But he was finding that nothing with her was ever enough. Just like her opinions, he couldn't get enough of her kisses, the feel of her lips against his. He wanted more. Of everything.

He somehow found the will to pull away from her. "We need to talk. I want your opinion on something. You see, I had this great idea for another one of our public dates."

"Don't you think we're past all that? I mean, I think we've been out enough to give the paparazzi plenty of chances to catch us together."

It was true. Since that night at John Harvard's, the celebrity stalkers had had many more opportunities to find them together, whether out to take in the Boston Pops or just enjoying a stroll down Cambridge Street for lunch on one of the few sunny days.

"I know. But this is different. We'll get the chance to do more with our celebrity. For Belles and Beaux and for something I threw in for you."

"Okay then. Let's hear it."

"Well, you know St. Patrick's Day is coming up, right?"

"Mmmhmmm. Just a week away, so you're a little behind on planning something already."

"I know, I know. But I'm pretty sure even I can pull this off. I think we should do a pub crawl."

"Okay."

Trip could tell Bambi wasn't convinced. "Yeah. We'll hit some of the classic bars in Boston. Places in Southie, probably. Maybe famous movie locations? We'll sell tickets exclusively to Belles and Beaux clientele for the opportunity to join us. Singles only. A mixer kind of event. We'll charge people about 20 bucks a pop. Everyone gets a T-shirt. Something green, obviously."

"Obviously." Trip could see her smile.

"But—and here's the piece for you—the extra money goes to a rape crisis center. It's a singles pub crawl for charity!" He glanced at Bambi to catch her reaction.

"Trip, that sounds wonderful! Of course you'll be able to drink me under the table. But it sounds like fun. Do you really think people will pay 20 bucks just to drink with us?"

"I'm sure they will." Trip puffed up with pride. "And I'm glad you like the idea. I've already reserved the conference room and everyone's schedules tomorrow to get the ball rolling. It would be great if you'd come along. Lend a voice. I'm not sure my father will think a pub crawl is such a good idea."

"Well then, he'd be crazy. You're always saying that he's trying to be old Boston, right? Well, what's more 'old Boston' than celebrating St. Patrick's Day and enjoying a pint? You can count me in, so long as I don't have class."

"Honey, you've got plenty of class," Trip teased. "But I checked your class schedule, too. It's posted in your apartment. You should be free."

Trip headed into the conference room about 10 minutes before his meeting was to start. He laid out the documents he would need to reference in his pitch. It shouldn't be too hard to convince this group that it was a good idea, but he was nervous for some reason.

He waited for the others to arrive. He glanced out the window every few seconds to see if he could catch a glimpse of Bambi coming in from the T. It would be a tight squeeze for her to get here on time from class, but he couldn't start the meeting much later. Elizabeth came in and shook her head when he looked up expectantly. Apparently, she hadn't been able to track down the pictures yet. But since they hadn't come out so far, Trip put that worry out of his mind. Maybe no one wanted them. He was in the middle of rehearsing the pitch in his head for the tenth time that morning when his father walked in the room.

"Are we going to start this meeting?"

Trip checked the clock. It was 10 a.m. on the dot. Leave it to his father not to waste any time. He checked the door once more for Bambi. "Yes, Dad. Let's get started."

Just as he pulled out the first piece of his presentation, Bambi tiptoed in. Trip relaxed his shoulders. He hadn't realized that he'd been tensing them until she arrived. But just being in the same room with her made him feel calmer.

"I hope I'm not late. I'm terribly sorry, Mr. Whitley. I had to rush over from class."

"Of course, Bambi." His father smiled indulgently.

Trip saw that somewhere along the line, she had managed to charm his father, too.

"Well, now that everyone's here, let's get started," he said. He repeated the plan for the St. Patrick's Day date and could see that Elizabeth was on board from the beginning.

"I love it," she said. "Great opportunity to promote the business and engage in a little charity work. Plus, we have been doing so many responsible, mature events. It might be good to remind all those potential customers that you and Bambi are young people, and that young people are welcome on the site as well."

"I don't know about that," Trip's father said. "Public drunkenness? Is that really the image that we want to project?"

"Come on, Dad, it's St. Patrick's Day! Plus, I think it's good that we support the local culture here in Boston. It helps these Yankees forget that we're a bunch of rebels from down south."

"No one thinks of us that way," his dad said.

"Even so Mr. Whitley," Bambi countered, "What's more

Boston-like than taking part in a St. Patrick's Day event? Plus, I'll keep an eye on Trip."

"Well, if you're all convinced . . ." Alex said.

"We are, Dad," Trip said.

"Elizabeth, I'll expect you to keep a firm eye on my son, too."

"I will, Mr. Whitley. Now, Trip, I think we need to get moving fast on those shirts, and on contacting the bar owners to see if we can get some kind of discount for the crawlers."

"Already ahead of you, Elizabeth. I had our graphics people draw something up for the T-shirts, and it's ready to go for printing once I give the go-ahead. And I've made a list of Irish pubs that we've worked with in the past. I think they'll be more than happy to have our business again."

"Well, I must admit I am impressed," Elizabeth said.

"I am, too," his father said. Trip smiled. Everything was coming together.

On St. Patrick's Day, Bambi met Trip at the offices of Belles and Beaux. When she arrived, Trip dipped her in a deep kiss.

"What was that for?" she asked.

"You're Irish." Trip said, as if it were the clearest thing in the world. "And the motto of St. Patrick's Day is 'Kiss me, I'm Irish.'"

"Ah, but you have one problem there, bud." Bambi poked a finger in his chest.

"What's that?"

"I'm not Irish."

"Not even a little bit?"

"Nope. My people are mostly the people that persecuted the Irish."

"Hmmm." Trip placed a finger to his head in mock concentration. Then he lifted it as if he had just come up with an idea. "Doesn't matter one bit. I saw a sign today in Southie that said, 'Everyone is Irish on St. Patrick's Day.'"

"Is that so?"

"It is." Trip nodded seriously.

"Good to know." Bambi moved in and kissed him on the lips. When she pulled back, she saw the surprise written all over his face. "I wouldn't want to be accused of not getting into the spirit of St. Patrick's Day," she said.

Soon, Elizabeth, Jim, and Jack arrived. The two cameramen seemed to have caught on to the spirit of the day and were much more talkative than usual. Bambi thought she could spy the glint of a silver flask peeking out of Jack's back pocket.

They went over the locations of the pub crawl and the approximate schedule for making it to each location. Bambi's happiness deflated a little when she saw the name of the last pub on the list. But things had to have changed in the past 10 years, right? And even if they hadn't, Bambi's group might not even make it that far. She'd be lucky if she could make it through half the spots on the list.

"Everything okay?" Elizabeth asked. Sometimes, Elizabeth was just a little bit too perceptive for Bambi.

"Yeah. Yeah." She decided to put her worries behind her and focus on enjoying the day.

"Let's get started!" Trip was excited, she could tell. This was his idea, after all.

"Lead the way," Bambi said, linking her arm through Elizabeth's. "Where's the first bar?"

Trip sat back against the stool of the third, or maybe fourth, bar of the evening. He had finally begun to relax. When they had started out at the Black Rose near Faneuil Hall, he had been worried about how the event would turn out. But everything had gone smoothly. The kids who had come along had arrived tipsy and were game for just about anything. He had played a game of darts in one pub and a battle of the sexes in another, which the men lost. But he didn't mind paying for the round of beer that the ladies had won, and he also sprang for one for the guys. Bambi charmed everyone, just as she had done at the museum gala. Now, she had turned her attention to Elizabeth, trying to convince her to have just one drink. Boy, that would be something if she could convince the buttoned-up Miss Pinckney to sip something other than water.

"Come on, Elizabeth. Just relax and have a drink," Bambi said.

"Yeah. I won't tell my dad or Mr. Weldon anything." Trip lent his voice to the campaign.

"I can't. I promised your father," Elizabeth inclined her head toward Trip. "And I promised you, Bambi, that I would keep you on schedule. And after about 10 minutes, we have to head out." She pointed at her watch.

"But that doesn't mean you can't have a drink in the meantime," Trip said.

"Yeah, and who says we need to head out?" Bambi said. "New bar schmar. I like this bar. It's so cozy!" Bambi flung her arms around to encompass the bar, nearly hitting Trip in the process.

"I figured that you would like this bar. I picked it out just for you, you know. They have bookcases."

"Aww, you're so sweet." Bambi nuzzled him, just the response Trip had been looking for. "I love bookcases. And books. And you." She grabbed Trip's hand but those words made it feel like she'd punched him in the gut. "And you." She grabbed Elizabeth's hand, too. Trip felt cheated somehow.

"Well isn't that sweet," Elizabeth said. "Bartender, I think we need some water over here. Trip, we might need to pour her into a cab to get her to the next bar."

"But I don't want to go to the next bar. I want to stay here, with the bookcases."

"Would you go if I gave into a drink?" Elizabeth asked.

"Ooh, maybe."

Elizabeth ordered a tequila shot from the bar and downed it without flinching. "Okay, time to go," she said.

"Do we have to?" At this plea, Trip caught Elizabeth glancing over Bambi's head with a look that asked for help.

"Bambi, we have to go," he said. "I promised them we'd get there before the evening was over. Come on." He hoisted her out of her chair and made sure everyone had settled their tabs with the bartender. He put some cash on the bar, a hefty tip to thank the already busy place for letting his group come in and treating them well.

Between Trip and Elizabeth, they managed to get all of the revelers into cabs and headed toward their last destination in the trendy Back Bay area. When they pulled up to the bar, Bambi curled into him, making it difficult to leave the cab. Trip made a mental note to order her a water, because she had clearly had more than enough to drink. When he finally got her out of the cab, he could feel her muscles tense the closer they got to the door.

"Everything okay, Bambi?"

"Yeah. Of course. Maybe we could just skip this one? I'm pretty tired."

"Like I said, I promised the owner we would stop by. We don't have to stay long, I promise."

"Okay." Trip watched her swallow once and then wiggle out of the arm he had wrapped around her waist. She threw her shoulders back and did the best he assumed she could to keep the wobble out of her gait as she made her way into Nanny O'Brien's.

What was going on? Trip wondered. Before, when Bambi had been worried, she said it was about getting to every place. But now they'd done it, what was there to stress about?

"Is there something about this bar?" he asked as he watched her look around.

"Hmmm? No. Nothing. There's nothing about this bar." He watched her shoulders sag with relief as she repeated herself, as if trying to convince herself of what she was saying.

"Are you sure?"

"Absolutely positive."

Trip wasn't sure he believed her, and he couldn't explain it, but he didn't trust her in this place. He looked around for Elizabeth and called her name. When she turned around, he pointed at Bambi, hoping that Elizabeth would understand that she needed to be watched. Elizabeth cut through the crowd to Bambi's side and relieved Trip to turn around and order drinks.

When he returned to Bambi's side, he found her chattering away with Elizabeth, as if their first five minutes in the place hadn't happened at all. Trip took a big swig of his bourbon, wondering if he had been imagining things.

A half hour later and into his second drink, he turned to Bambi. "You want to go? I think we can head out now, and no one would care."

"No! This is so much fun! I never thought this bar could be so much fun. I want to stay."

"Fine." Trip watched Bambi head off to join a group of girls clustered in a booth talking and pointing at some guy in their group. No doubt she was sorting everything out and earning their trust like she always could. Like she had earned his.

Trip sipped his drink. His world had begun a lazy spin that seemed to throw everything off balance. The one anchor in his life was the blonde girl sitting 20 feet away. He hadn't realized how attached he had gotten to her.

"Heya, big man," he heard a raspy female voice say. The voice reached out a hand down the bar to touch his. Well, not the voice, but the person attached to it. His eyes slid up the arm to the face and body of the woman. She was older. Probably as old as his mother. But boy, she didn't look like his mother. Her hair had been bleached blonde and she wore so much makeup that it aged her rather than making her prettier. She wore a skimpy green camisole of far too little fabric to adequately cover her large breasts.

"Hi." Trip blinked to make his world stop spinning. "Do I know you?"

"Not yet," the fake blonde purred. "But you're going to get to know me after you buy me a drink."

What the hell, Trip figured. He signaled the bartender. "What do you want, ma'am?"

The woman laughed a smoker's laugh. "You don't need to call me 'ma'am.' Just call me Vicky. And I'll have a dirty martini."

"Martini for Vicky."

Bambi sat with a group of girls discussing whether one of them should ask one of the guys in the group out on a more formal date. According to the girl, they had made out at the first bar, but he had been ignoring her ever since. Midway through the discussion, Bambi wondered why she had been so scared of this place. It was a great bar! And everyone in the group was having fun as far as she could tell. Drunkenness had probably allowed her to imagine something that just wasn't true. At least not any longer. Now that she was almost sober, she could see that. And Trip had realized how out of it she was and helped her sober up. He was turning out to be so many things she hadn't anticipated. A caretaker, for one. She couldn't resist a glance in his direction. Sometimes just looking at him made her smile.

But this glance made her gasp in horror. She would recognize the back of that woman sitting next to Trip anywhere, even if she hadn't seen her for 10 years. Bambi hauled herself up and left the table of girls without a word. She stalked over to the bar and grabbed the wrist of the hand that covered Trip's.

"Keep your hands off him." Bambi noticed Trip's eyes widen, but she didn't have time to bother with his reaction right now. The one thing she had learned from Vicky was that you couldn't get distracted if you hoped to win against her.

"Darling, no need." Vicky extracted her wrist from Bambi's grip. "Your *boyfriend* and I were just getting to know each other. Why, practically the whole world knows you're dating, and you haven't even introduced him to your own mother."

"Your mother?" Trip slurred his words. Bambi kept her eyes locked on Vicky's.

"I should've known you'd be here. Never could resist the dirty martinis, could you? Or the men you could con into bed and then demand money from."

"It's so tawdry to bring up the past. Especially when you've landed such a big fish of your own. Or aren't you going to share the wealth?"

"It's not like that," Bambi said to her mother. Then she turned to Trip in case he didn't believe her. "It's not like that."

"Always been too good for your mother, huh? Always thought you were so damn pretty and so damn smart," Vicky shot back.

Bambi turned around. "You need to go."

But Vicky wasn't finished. "Poor, innocent little Bambi. You're a whore. Such a little whore. You charmed my husband away from me with your perky little breasts."

"I did not! You know he took advantage of me." But Bambi might as well have been talking to a brick wall. Her mother had gone into full actress mode and spoke directly to a wide-eyed Trip.

"Trip, I just want you to know what you're getting yourself into. I came home one day to find my husband—that's right, my husband—in bed with this little slut before you. In fa-fucking-glantre delicto, if you know what I mean!" She lapsed into tears Bambi knew had been practiced in front of the mirror.

Bambi colored with the shame of remembering that night. She turned to look at Trip, to convince him that it hadn't been her fault. He stared stone-faced at mother and daughter. Bambi could tell he was horrified. By her mother. By her. By the whole exchange. Before she could give Vicky the satisfaction of seeing her tears, she ran out of the bar.

CHAPTER SEVENTEEN

The next morning Bambi woke up with a horrible headache and the determination to put that night behind her. She couldn't face Trip. Not after that look he had given her. He seemed to have bought her mother's entire sob story. Besides, there were only a few short weeks until her trip to England. That trip would help her remember that she had not become her mother. She had found her worth not through a man but in fulfilling work.

She began compiling the notes from her interviews at The Booby Trap and spent the rest of the weekend doing the painstaking work of transcription from the audio files she had created. Elizabeth and Trip both called and texted, but she didn't pick up the phone or listen to their voicemails. She shut her phone off after texting Elizabeth that she had made it home safely but needed to spend the entire week working. And she did need to work. She wasn't hiding.

Maybe if she told herself that enough, she would believe it.

On Monday, she headed into work, dreading the hours she would have to spend in high heels but thankful for yet another opportunity to distract herself from thinking about that disastrous night.

But distraction was hard to come by, even at The Booby Trap. As she crammed her feet into the red heels, Bambi saw Lainie come in to the breakroom at the end of her shift.

"How's it going?" she asked Bambi.

"Fine. Whatever. I just wish that I could go to work in slippers some days."

"I hear you. You look pretty beat up, Bambi. St. Pat's weekend take that much out of you?"

"Nah," Bambi lied, "it was a pretty tame weekend."

"That's not what I heard. Jeanine said she was dying to join that pub crawl of yours, but by the time she found out about it, all the spots were taken."

"Oh, that. Yeah. Why did Jeanine care? She can see me any time she wants to at work."

"I don't know. But I suspect it has something to do with your other half. So how was it anyways?"

"It was fine. Went to a lot of bars, had a lot of drinks. Whatever."

"Well, you're not exactly a wealth of information. What bars did you go to?"

"Black Rose, Kinsale, Lir, the Purple Shamrock. Oh, and Nanny O'Brien's."

Lainie stopped stuffing things into her locker and turned to look at Bambi. "Nanny's?"

"Yeah." *Dammit.* Bambi had forgotten that she had told Lainie her whole sordid history with her mother.

"And was it like old times?" Lainie kept her eyes glued on Bambi while Bambi tried to look in every direction but at her friend.

"More than ever."

"You want to talk about it?"

"Hell no. I just want to serve some drinks to an asshole who will forget my name."

"Okay." Bambi heard the skepticism in Lainie's voice and ignored it. "See ya," she said, tying on her tiny apron and sailing past her friend.

It was surprisingly busy for a Monday night. In addition to the regulars like Looky Lou, the bar was hosting a viewing for the Monday night basketball game, Celtics versus the New York Knicks. It had brought in a big crowd of Bostonians eager to cheer against any team from New York. Bambi was able to lose herself in the rhythm of waitressing and the comfortable back-and-forth she developed with the guys who were mostly there just to watch the game. Ogling the girls was just a bonus to them.

She didn't waste time in the locker room after her shift, throwing on her coat and Uggs, slamming her shoes into the locker. She walked briskly down the hall and would have made it out quickly if Joe hadn't stopped her.

"Hey Bambi!" he called from his office. "I want to talk to you."

Bambi turned around and leaned in his doorway. "Does it have to be tonight? I'm pretty beat." She rubbed her eyes.

"Yeah. Tonight. Take a seat, kiddo."

"What do you want? I can't take another shift next week because I've got a lot to do."

"I'm not looking for you to take another shift. I know you're excited about your conference. Got everything you need from the girls? And from me?"

"I do. But much as I appreciate the check-in, Joe, like I said, I'm super tired. I'm close to being a road risk if I have to stay up much longer." Bambi stood up.

"Sit down," he said. Bambi obeyed. "Now, I didn't just want to dive into this because I know you've been busy building walls all night."

"What are you talking about? Did one of the customers complain?"

"No. No one complained. But I know how you get after you've seen your mother."

"What? How did you know that?" Before he could answer, it dawned on her. "Lainie told you. I told her I didn't want to talk about it."

"Well, Bambi, you may be able to say that to her, but you can't say it to me. We're going to talk, kid." He leaned forward and rested his elbows on the desk. "Tell me about it."

Bambi knew it was no use to say no to Joe. And he looked so kind and ready to listen. So she poured out the whole story, the night from beginning to horrible end.

"And that young man of yours, he was there?"

"Joe, I just said she hit on him!" Joe gave her a look Bambi knew she would have gotten from a father had she had one. "Fine. Yes. He was there. The whole time."

"And what did he say to all this?"

"Nothing. Or nothing that I remember. And you should have seen the look on his face, Joe. It was horror."

"Did you talk to him about that? After your mother left?"

"Are you kidding me? No. I left them. I had to get out of

there, Joe. I couldn't be with her any longer. And I couldn't face him."

"Seems to me like you didn't give him much of a chance to see what he would do. Maybe you should give him a chance to explain. Is he worth it?"

"I don't know. Maybe I should."

"Just remember one thing if you do decide to talk to him. You are not now nor have you ever been responsible for what happened with that creep all those years ago. And your mother got you totally wrong. Sometimes I ask myself what possessed me to date her as long as I did, much less at all. But I think it's because of you. You needed me then. But you've grown up into a strong, smart, wonderful woman. You are one of the best women I know, and kid, I know a lot of them. Don't let someone who doesn't matter ruin your life."

"Thanks, Joe." Bambi circled around the desk and put her arms around Joe. Somehow, after getting this out, she felt a whole lot better.

On the drive home, Bambi turned on her cell phone for the first time since the weekend. She saw dozens of missed calls from Trip and Elizabeth. She ignored the voicemails and dialed Trip's number. Joe was right; she should give him a chance. She should at least tell him her side of the story. But instead of his voice on the other end, she got his voicemail. She didn't bother leaving a message, sure he would call as soon as he saw that he had missed her call.

She drove home and miraculously found a parking spot a hundred feet from her apartment building. Apparently, the paparazzo who hung out in the tree across the street had decided he wasn't waiting up for her, because she saw no telltale flash as she darted up the steps to the front door.

Feeling so much happier than she had when she'd left, Bambi put on the kettle to make hot chocolate and slipped into her most comfortable pajamas. She flipped on the TV to some kind of entertainment news show. Since she'd started dating Trip, she had stopped watching them because the coverage hit too close to home. But tonight, she was in the mood for something light and fluffy. Maybe she would get lucky and there would be an interview with Julia Roberts or Anne Hathaway or some gorgeous male celebrity.

She was plopping the marshmallows into the steaming mug of hot chocolate when she heard the reporter mention Trip's name.

"In our couples news tonight, the fairy tale Boston romance we've all been watching since January might just be over. Despite footage showing Trip Whitley and Bambi Benson joining merrymakers for Boston's St. Patrick's Day festivities, this program has obtained photographs that indicate there may be trouble in paradise. The pictures on screen now clearly show Trip Whitley getting close with another woman! In fact, an anonymous source identified by local Boston show host Madison Hart suggests that Trip and Bambi's blissful relationship may have been cooked up for the tabloids and that the woman in the picture, whom we've identified as Boston Brahmin daughter Constance Bradford, is the real love of Trip's life. That's right, ladies. They were high school sweethearts, and it looks like they're rekindling the flame. We hope to be talking to Madison later on in the program. Stay tuned as we continue to cover this developing story."

Bambi realized she had frozen in place, standing in front of the TV, hot chocolate halfway to her mouth.

Just then, the phone rang. Bambi picked it up and looked down and saw Trip's name and number staring back at her. She held the phone as it vibrated in her palm, unable or unwilling to do anything. When the ringing finally stopped, she threw it down on the floor. It didn't shatter into a million pieces, like she had hoped. But the back cover flew off and the battery popped out. She left the pieces where they landed and crawled into bed.

Trip sat in his office Tuesday morning, but he wasn't getting any work done. He had commandeered Teena's time and had her calling Bambi every half hour. No luck. He hadn't spoken to her since the night of the pub crawl. The alcohol had worn off days ago, but he couldn't shake the pounding headache that had resulted from that night. Partially from the booze, partially from the fact that tearing his hair out had seemed the only logical response to Bambi's refusal to respond to his calls. Suddenly, the phone rang.

"Elizabeth?" Trip picked up the phone. "Any word from Bambi?"

"No." Something in her tone made Trip pause.

"What's the problem then?"

"Check out the *Hart of Boston* website."

Trip navigated to Maddy's page. There, splashed across the top of the site were pictures of him and Connie at Clink. The captions read "High school sweethearts reunite" and "Rekindling an old flame?" There was one picture of Trip with Bambi, too. It was taken on Valentine's Day, but he hadn't noticed the paparazzo hanging out in her neighborhood. He was glaring at her. This caption read "Fictional romance?"

"I thought you were going to handle this!" he yelled into the phone. He knew he shouldn't have, that this was partly his fault, but he couldn't keep the emotion out of his voice.

"I tried, Trip. I did."

"You didn't think I was good enough for her."

"That's not true!" Elizabeth took a breath. "Okay, okay. Maybe it was true before, but it's not true now. And Trip, I did try to get to the paparazzi. But Maddy was just faster. I didn't realize what had happened until today."

"Bambi won't take my calls. No wonder." Trip shook his head.

"I'm so sorry."

"Whatever." He hung up. Then he dropped his face into his hands. What was he going to do? While he closed his eyes and tried to wish the problem away, he heard a soft rapping at the door.

"Come on in," he said to Teena, who stood outside. She seemed unusually nervous.

"Bambi's here."

Trip felt his body jerk involuntarily. "Here? Okay." His mind was racing. "I'll be right there."

He jumped up and followed Teena up to reception. When he got there, he saw Bambi sitting in a chair, dressed in jeans and her short black coat, with her hair pulled up in a messy bun. He had a flashback to her sitting in those chairs the first time she had visited Belles and Beaux. She stood up as he approached.

"Trip. Thanks for taking the time." She was quiet, and her eyes were red and swollen, as if she'd been crying. He cursed himself for being the cause of her tears. He hurried over to envelop her in his arms, eager to console.

"Bambi. I didn't think you'd come," he said. But when he went to pull her into his embrace, she took a step back. Not a good sign.

"Can we go into your office?"

"Sure. Of course." He reached out his arm to place it at the small of her back and escort her there. At least she allowed him to do that much.

When they got to his office, he pulled the door shut behind them. He led her to the couch and sat down next to her. He took her hands and squeezed them, but she didn't squeeze back like she normally did.

"I'm so sorry," he began. "About what happened with your mother."

"Stop," she said, trying to pull her hands away. But he wouldn't let her.

"No. You have to hear this. I was frozen because I was horrified by her. How could she allow that to happen to her only daughter?" He shook his head, still not sure of the answer to that question.

"Thanks. Joe talked me out of reading anything into your reaction."

"Are you sure?" Trip searched her eyes, which had begun to well up. "Because I could go out there and pound the guy if you tell me his name. He deserves a good punch—several, in fact—for how he treated you. And your mother, well, I don't know if I'd feel quite as comfortable punching her, but just say the word and I will."

Bambi laughed a little and the tears cleared out from her eyes. Trip felt some of his stress ease. "No. No punches. It was so long ago that it's not worth it to me today." She shrugged, and then took a deep breath. "But I didn't come here to talk about my mother. I want to talk about Connie."

"Bambi, there is absolutely nothing going on between us. *She* kissed *me*. I pushed her away."

"Okay." Bambi still seemed anxious.

Trip continued, "Elizabeth saw—she can tell you. In fact, I told her about the pictures the paparazzo had gotten. I was hoping she could get to the guy before something like this happened."

"What? You told her about what happened with Connie?"

"Of course I did." Trip felt wary again. "I didn't want all of our hard work to go down the drain because of some pictures that don't tell the true story. Which is that I love you."

"But why didn't you tell me about them?" she asked.

"Because I didn't want you to worry." *Wasn't that clear?*

"You lied to me," she said. Trip felt as if she had shot him, and she looked just as startled.

"I didn't lie!"

"You did. Trip, I came here to clear things up. I thought this might be a misunderstanding. But I also thought we had restarted this relationship based on no lies. That is the one reason I've allowed myself to trust you. And maybe you didn't lie, per se, but you didn't tell me something I needed to know. Instead, you asked Elizabeth to sweep it under the rug." She paused and shook her head. "I can't handle that. I can't—I can't have a relationship with that person." She gulped. "With you. I'm so sorry. I've got to go." She stood up and turned toward the door.

"Wait," Trip said, standing. But when she turned toward him, he had nothing to say. What could he say? He felt miserable.

"Goodbye, Trip." She turned around and walked out of his office. He didn't follow because he couldn't. He collapsed onto the couch. The longer he sat, the more he realized that he had just let the best thing in his life walk right out of it.

CHAPTER EIGHTEEN

Bambi took the short walk across campus from her classroom to the Women's Studies Department to check her mailbox. Although still pretty chilly, the cold weather had lost its bite. Students wore their coats unbuttoned and lingered longer than usual outdoors. Bambi turned her head from a couple making out around the corner of the library.

She put her head down and continued onto the old campus of Radcliffe College. For nearly one hundred years, it had been the closest that women could get to Harvard University, so perhaps it was fitting that the department stayed on that campus. The department office also housed the mailboxes for graduate students, a relic of a past without email and the internet. Bambi almost never had mail there, but she checked it once a week anyway.

On her way in, Bambi waved at Wendy, the secretary who

had organized the department since its inception nearly 20 years ago. She was efficient and wonderfully nice.

"Oh, Bambi," Wendy said, "I was just about to email you."

"Me? Is there a kink in the schedule for next semester? Because I thought we had it all ironed out."

"Oh no, dear. I was just speaking with Martha Cheever and she mentioned that she wanted to get in touch with you. She's interested in scheduling a meeting very soon. I would recommend you go up and talk to her about it today."

Bambi worried that Martha might be pulling the miniscule funds that Harvard had given her to attend the conference, now just two weeks away. That would be only the latest in a string of miserable things. But she managed a smile for Wendy. "Of course. I'll stop by on my way out."

Grabbing the multicolored sheets of paper advertising brown bag lunches and speakers across campus from her mailbox, Bambi headed toward the chair's office. She detoured by the ladies' room to survey herself in the mirror. What looked back at her was pretty bad. She wore a drab green sweater with black pants and navy shoes. Back in her apartment she had thought the shoes were black and only discovered their true color after she walked outside. She hadn't cared enough to change.

In fact, "hadn't cared" could be to blame for everything. Her hair was a knotted mess. Bambi grabbed some tinted lip balm for her lips, but there was nothing she could do about the dark circles underneath her eyes. *Damn Trip Whitley.* Bambi resolved to take a shower and wrench herself out of the doldrums the moment she got home. No man, much less Trip Whitley, was going to make her feel this way. She was confident, powerful, smart, and satisfied before she had met him. And she could be now, too. She splashed cold water on her face and decided she had done all that she could.

Outside Martha Cheever's office, Bambi smoothed her hair back. She knocked softly, then entered the office, which looked the same as the last time she had been there. Oriental rug, fern climbing over stacks of books, Martha stationed behind her giant desk.

"Bambi," she said, "thank you for coming to see me today."

"No problem," Bambi was unaccustomed to the warmth Martha showed.

"You see, something rather unfortunate has occurred. One of our presenters for the London conference had a death in the family. She has to return home and won't be able to travel to the conference next week."

"That's so sad," Bambi said. *But what does it have to do with me?* she wondered.

"Yes, of course. We really would prefer not to let that spot go. But I was speaking with your advisor, Dr. Williams, the other day, and she said you had done some wonderful research since we last talked. She mentioned that your initial ideas were very thought provoking and that you might be a strong candidate for that open slot."

Bambi thought back to when she had sent the presentation to her advisor. Lois had emailed with comments and encouragement but hadn't mentioned anything about this. "Do you mean I would be able to present at the conference?"

"You were already planning on traveling, weren't you?"

"I was. I mean I am. I mean yes." Bambi felt her head swimming.

"Excellent. Now, I know that this could be a considerable

amount of work for you to do in the little time that we have. And I don't want you to attend the conference with an incomplete presentation. So do you think you could pull something together of the appropriate caliber? I know your social schedule of late has become . . . ahem . . . demanding."

"I can do it, I promise. Although I am continuing to interview, I have several initial conclusions that my research will firmly back up. And my social schedule, as you say, has gotten much less demanding very recently."

"Ah, well, I'm sorry to hear that but I am happy that you will be able to help the University."

"I can't say how much this means to me, Martha. Thank you so much."

"Well, I'm glad it's worked out. I'll see you in London." Martha extended her hand across the desk. Bambi shook it.

"See you in London, Martha. I can't wait."

Trip knocked on the door to his father's office. He had decided that he couldn't keep worrying over Bambi. Better to just take a break for a moment, keep his mind off her.

"Come on in," his dad said. Trip saw pity in his father's eyes, and that wasn't what he wanted.

"Dad, I wanted to discuss a business idea with you." He came in and sat down in the chair across from his father's desk.

"Sure, sure." His father cleared some papers off of the desk. "Listen, before we get going, I wanted to say I'm sorry about how this whole Bambi business is turning out."

"Thanks, Dad," Trip said quickly, hoping to stop his father from saying more. But his father went on. "I know you weren't too keen on this fix-up in the first place. And I wasn't too keen on Bambi when I first met her. But I think she grew on both of us. I'm sorry to see her go, too."

"I appreciate your saying that." Trip was now wondering about the wisdom of coming to see his father to get his mind off Bambi.

"Plus, she was great for the business," his father said with a gruff laugh.

Trip saw his opportunity. "That's what I wanted to discuss. We've seen an uptick in interest, and I think it's time to bring on a new associate."

"Do you think that we will continue to grow even after—"

Trip cut him off. "I do. I've been looking at projections and I think this might also be a great time to grow our brand—perhaps by doing more events."

"Interesting thought." Trip's father leaned back in his chair.

Trip pulled out some sales projections and copies of various event opportunities he had been working on. He had intended for them to be future public dates for himself and Bambi, but he figured they might work even without her. He handed the papers to his father. "Look these over, Dad, and I'm sure you'll agree about the need for a new associate."

His father took the documents, clearly surprised that Trip was so prepared. He grabbed his glasses to peruse them, and Trip sat back a little in his chair.

A few moments passed. Then his father spoke again. "At first glance, Trip, this seems pretty convincing. I'm impressed. I didn't realize you knew this much about Belles and Beaux."

"Well, I do have an MBA. And I'm learning more from being here every day."

"Very impressive," his father mumbled, then looked up. "Do you have anyone in mind for the job?"

"As a matter of fact, I do. I already did a screening interview last week." He put up his hand to stall the comments he was sure his father wanted to make. "I didn't let on that the position was definite, of course."

"Oh, of course." His father smiled.

"She can come in tomorrow if you'd like," Trip offered. He knew that the quicker he moved, the more likely he would get his first choice for the new position.

"Well, why not? I can't guarantee I will hire her or anybody, for that matter, but what's the harm?"

"Great, Dad. I'll go set it up now. 11 okay?"

"Sounds perfect." His father looked past him and Trip saw that Teena was waiting outside the office. She came in at his father's gesture. "Teena, what can we do for you?"

"It's actually Trip I need," she said. "There's someone here to see you. He says his name is Joe."

"No last name?"

"He didn't give one. I should've gotten it. Just wait a second, I'll go get it."

"No, that's okay, Teena." He turned to his father. "We're done here, right?"

"We're done." His father nodded.

Trip stood up and sighed. "Just send him to my office."

He got to his office just as Joe entered. He watched the older man sit down. Dressed in a relatively cheap gray suit and blue shirt, he didn't resemble Belles and Beaux's normal young and wealthy clientele. But Trip didn't want to judge. They were trying to expand. Still, something about this guy seemed classier than his suit. He had packed on some extra weight as he had aged, Trip assumed, but it mostly made him look more substantial. His gray hair was clipped in a neat, almost military fashion.

"Nice to meet you, Joe. Now, how can I help you in getting set up on Belles and Beaux?"

Joe laughed. It was deep and raspy, but somehow pleasant. "Trip Whitley. Nice to finally meet the man I've heard so much about."

"Aren't you here to sign up for the service?"

"No, no, son. Well, I came in here figuring that you would just know me. I don't know why I thought that, but I did. Maybe because your face is so familiar to me, from all those TV ads and stuff. No, Trip, I'm Joe Luna. From The Booby Trap."

"Wow. Joe. I've heard so much about you, too. And I should have recognized you. From Bambi's descriptions, that is." Trip felt like he'd been caught flat-footed. At once he wondered whether this man would be his one link to Bambi or whether he would be a confirmation that everything was over between them.

"Trip, I think we've got some business to discuss."

"Go ahead."

Joe unbuttoned his jacket and rubbed his hands across his thighs before leaning back. "Listen, I'm not going to beat around the bush here. Bambi came to work on Monday and she seemed real messed up. I didn't catch it myself until one of the other girls mentioned it to me. But when I called her into my office, she said she'd had a run in with her mother."

"I was there. I've never seen anything like that woman. And I was too drunk and too stupid to do anything but sit there in silence."

"Yeah, I thought I got Bambi straightened out at least enough to hear what you had to say. But you went off and did just about the most bone-headed thing you could. You couldn't wait to go out with another girl, could you? What do you think that did to her?"

"Joe, I swear it was nothing." Trip felt Joe's eyes boring into him and realized that he needed this man on his side if he wanted Bambi back in his life. He needed to tell Joe the whole truth. "That's not entirely true. I did go out with Constance, but it was months ago. Those pictures are months old. Then, she ambushed me the other night."

"Okay, let's say I give you that it was months ago. What were you doing running around on Bambi then?"

"Again, things aren't exactly what they seem." Trip laid out the history of his and Bambi's relationship from the night of the bachelor party up to the beginning of their true relationship. "You see, Joe, I realized then that I cared about her. And in the time since, I've realized that it's not just care, it's love. She's it for me, Joe."

"And what about that other girl?"

"Connie? Dead. Over. Kaput. It was over in high school, a million years ago. Joe, I told Bambi all that and she still walked out on me. Because I didn't tell her about the pictures."

"Well, that's the second boneheaded thing you've done. If I weren't convinced she loves you . . ." his voice trailed off.

"You think she still loves me?" Trip felt hopeful for the first time in a week.

"I do. And call me crazy, but I want it to work out. Lately, before this of course, she was pretty happy."

"Joe, I want to make her happy. That's my goal. But I can't do it if she's not a part of my life. Will you help me?"

Joe leaned forward. "Okay, Trip, I'm in."

Bambi slipped out of her heels after her last shift at The Booby Trap before the conference in London. Thankfully, everything was ready to go—even her luggage was packed with a new navy suit, courtesy of Trip's $5,000 date money. She had tried to stop thinking about him, stop wondering what he might have to say about this idea or that, stop missing the feel of falling asleep in his arms. But it had been in vain. So she resigned herself to the knowledge that the ache in her heart would be a constant presence, probably for a long time.

"Bambi!" Lainie burst into the breakroom, clad in jeans and a sparkly black shirt. "I am so glad you're here. I wanted to catch you before you left. Joe said you'd be working tonight."

"Well, you caught me on my way out. I need to get a good night's sleep. I leave for the conference early tomorrow morning."

"From the looks of it, you could definitely use at least one good night's sleep. You should quit worrying, honey. You'll do great."

"Thanks to you, mostly. The other girls wouldn't have been half so willing without your endorsement. And I wouldn't have gotten so far along that my advisor would have recommended me for the open spot."

"Oh, it was nothing." Lainie sat down next to Bambi. "And I'm the one who ought to be thanking you."

"Me?" Bambi wondered what Lainie might be talking about.

She didn't have any clue. "What did I do?"

Lainie leaned in. "I got the job," she said quietly. Then she smiled broadly.

"Congratulations!" Bambi was excited for her friend, but more confused than ever. Had Lainie discussed job interviews with her that she'd forgotten? Things had been such a blur in the past couple weeks. "Umm . . . which job?"

"The new associate position at Belles and Beaux." Lainie paused. "Wait, I thought Trip said you recommended me."

Bambi didn't remember discussing Lainie in connection with the position at Belles and Beaux. She did remember Trip saying something about wanting to hire someone new, a woman. She also remembered talking to him about Lainie. But she had never put the two together. Apparently, he had. "Not in so many words," she said. "But I'm glad something I said helped. And I'm sure that Trip and Mr. Whitley were very impressed by you."

"Well, whatever you did, thanks." Lainie gave her a quick hug. "And not to brag, but I did kill it." She laughed. "Come on. One drink to celebrate? We can have Jodi pour us some champagne cocktails and drink them in Joe's office."

Bambi was still flabbergasted, but she knew that she was incredibly tired and had a big day the next day. "I don't know. Won't Joe mind us taking over his office?"

"No, honey. I saw him on my way in and told him the news about the new job. He suggested it himself—said we should toast my new job and your success at the conference."

"It's not success yet . . ." Bambi demurred.

"It will be, I promise. Come on. One drink."

Bambi figured that an hour spent in the company of two of her favorite people might be just the thing to get her into the appropriate mood for the conference. Plus, the champagne might make her drowsy so it would be easier to fall asleep without lying awake thinking about Trip Whitley. "Okay, I'm in. Thanks."

Lainie smiled and stood up. "No problem. I'm going to go talk to Jodi and get the drinks. I'll meet you in Joe's office. He said he wanted to wish you good luck in private."

"He's sweet. I'll see you in there." Bambi decided that she would try to catch some of Lainie's optimism and energy. "We are headed to the top of the world, aren't we?"

"You bet." Lainie turned around and left. Bambi pulled on her Uggs and headed toward Joe's office.

When she got there, the door was closed. That was uncharacteristic of Joe, especially during working hours. But he did know she was coming and had even invited her. So she rapped softly and went inside. The office and walls had been cleared, and on the wall opposite her as she entered were dozens of pieces of white printer paper tacked up in a collage. Each one of them said something, and she began to read a few.

"TRUTH: I weigh 188 pounds."

"TRUTH: I cheated off of Amy Black's science test in fourth grade."

"TRUTH: I make $75,000 per year, but I have a trust fund from my grandfather totaling over $5 million."

"TRUTH: I hated *The Handmaid's Tale*."

"TRUTH: I will never admit to liking *Little Women* better than *The Catcher in the Rye*, even if I did reread them and change my mind.

"TRUTH: I have slept with 17 women, not counting you."

"TRUTH: I used to love Connie Bradford."

In the middle of dozens more truths was one red paper with white writing. It read: "TRUTH: I love you." Around this piece were dozens of black and white pictures from what had to be Jack's camera. They showed Trip and Bambi skating at the Frog Pond, mingling at the Pops gala, toasting pints of beer at Kinsale, laughing at Beacon, and kissing in the street. Bambi blinked against the flood of tears.

She tore her eyes away from the pictures when she heard someone come in behind her. It was Trip. He looked as handsome as ever in jeans and a gray sweater.

"What is this?" she asked.

"I couldn't let you go," Trip said. He shrugged. "I don't know why I didn't tell you about what happened with Connie at Clink. It was stupid. You don't deserve lies. You deserve the truth."

He walked toward her. He gestured at the wall. "Some of these I'm not proud of. Some of them I wish weren't true, but you deserve to know everything. So here it is: everything that I can think of that I've lied about in my past. Going into the future, there won't be a need for this," he said as he gestured again at the wall, "because there won't be anything you don't know."

"Trip," Bambi started. "I need another truth from you."

"Anything."

Bambi nibbled her bottom lip. She wasn't sure she really wanted to know the answer to this one. "Lainie told me about the job."

"Isn't it great?" Trip asked. "Dad fell in love with her." He paused. "Wait, was I supposed to tell you? Because if so, I didn't realize it, not really."

"No, no." Bambi touched his chest to stop him. She took a breath. "Did she get the job because of me? Because you wanted me back?"

Trip studied her quizzically. "No. I mean sort of. You mentioned how great she was and I thought we might have a position open, so I brought her in to talk about it. You were right—she's smart and thoughtful and innovative. Dad thought the same, so we brought her on."

"Oh good," Bambi sighed.

"But wait. I'm not finished. You interrupted me in the middle of my grand speech. Can I finish?"

Bambi nodded and Trip took her hand. She could only stare at their joined fingers.

"This is not just about truths and lies. This is about what we have together and why it's worth fighting for. You and I make a great team. I noticed it for real for the first time that night at the museum. You pulled in lots of clients for Belles and Beaux, probably more than I could have on my own. So you adapt to my world and you make it that much better." Trip took his free hand and placed it on her cheek. "Bambi, look at me. I can't imagine living without that kind of partner now that I know what it's like. I can be a partner to you, too. I love hearing you talk about your work, and I will be a sounding board to you for the rest of your life."

"And I've been thinking. You can't always be doing work based on The Booby Trap. So maybe Belles and Beaux could help with your next topic? I don't know—sociological research on the dating scene?" He paused. "That's stupid."

"It's not stupid," Bambi whispered.

"Whatever. I'm just saying I can be your partner. Together,

we can accomplish anything. I can be your biggest cheering section after you give an amazing presentation in a few days." He took his hand from hers, reached into his pocket, and pulled out some papers. He handed them to her and she opened them to reveal the confirmation numbers and flight details for two first-class trips to London the next day. "Please let me go with you."

Bambi looked at the papers in her hand, then at Trip. She had come up with reason after reason that they shouldn't be together. Now, she recognized those reasons as excuses. She was scared. But Trip offered her the chance at true partnership, all wrapped up in the happily ever after she read about in those romance novels hidden underneath her bed. There was only one answer.

"Yes." She kissed him. "Come to London with me."

"Thank God." He picked her up in his arms and kissed her again.

Even though Bambi had the urge to either melt into Trip or to explode from sheer happiness and relief, she heard the knock on the door.

"Can we come in?" Joe asked. He stood in the door with Lainie, who was carrying the tray of promised champagne cocktails.

"Of course," Bambi said. She turned around and leaned against Trip's back.

"Looks like we have a lot to toast to, Joe," Lainie said with a wink.

"We sure do," he said. He passed around the glasses. "To my girls, who finally found what they were looking for."

Everyone raised a glass and toasted. Bambi looked at Trip and thought about how right Joe was. Trip had arrived in her life as an unwelcome distraction and had become a big part of her small world. She turned to him.

"I think I love you."

"No lies," he said. "I think I love you, too."

EPILOGUE

Bambi stood at the edge of the glass capsule, looking at London, which was laid out at her feet. The sky had begun to turn colors with the approaching evening, and they had made it about a quarter of the way up the circle on the London Eye. The giant Ferris wheel offered spectacular views of the city, and she and Trip had a pod all to themselves.

"Get on over here," she called to Trip. "I can see St. Paul's." Trip sat on the small bench in the middle of the capsule. He hadn't risen since they had gotten on board. Bambi crossed over to him, wrinkling her brow. "Are you feeling all right?"

Trip was taking even breaths, in through his nose, out through his mouth. "I might have one more truth for you."

"What's that?" she asked, sitting down next to him.

"I'm afraid of heights."

"Silly boy. Why did you think we should do this?" she asked, putting her arm around him and his head on her shoulder.

He looked up. "Because I wanted you to feel like you had London at your feet. Which you do. Bambi, your presentation was amazing."

"You're a goof. But thanks. I thought it went pretty well. Despite your unnecessarily loud applause at the end."

"I told you I would be your cheering section," Trip said. Bambi noticed that he smiled for the first time since they had started moving. "Besides, 'pretty well' doesn't even describe it. Martha Cheever practically salivated over you once it was over."

"True. And I did speak to someone from *Sociology Today* who wants to publish my article once it's finished."

"You didn't tell me about that!" Trip said.

"Well, it's not certain. She hasn't even seen my completed article. Mostly because I haven't finished it. Or even started it for that matter."

"She will love it, I know." He kissed her, and Bambi forgot for a minute all about the amazing view that surrounded them. Then, he pulled away. "Come on. I can't let you miss this view." He picked up a glass of champagne that the London Eye staff had provided and handed it to her.

Bambi extended her free hand to Trip. "Come on. Who knows how far we can see when we look together?"

ACKNOWLEDGMENTS

Obviously, with a first-time novel, there are lots of people to thank.

First, my family. Granny, Debbie, Jan, Rachel, Tim, Jackson, Abigail, and Justin read through countless drafts and inspired me when I thought that I could write only drivel. They gave this book, and me, the opportunity to grow.

Second, my team at Pixel Entertainment. Jan and Kristy made the dream a reality and gave me a much-needed dose of confidence whenever I needed it. See you back at HQ, Mamas.

Third, Matt and Anna. Without them, an 8-week novel-writing course, and my competitive spirit, this story may never have escaped from my head. Did I win?

Fourth, my editors. Any holes you see or mistakes I've made are completely mine, not theirs. In fact, they probably tried to fix it, and I probably dug in my heels. Many thanks to my professional editors: Jaimee, Feifei, and Susan. And thanks to my friends, who plowed through vigorously and valiantly: Jess, Julie K., Mary Jordan, Scott, and Julie F.

Finally, I would like to thank Lauren Willig and the women of the website *Smart Bitches, Trashy Books*. They help remind everyone that smart girls read romances, too! I only hope that this book makes the grade.

ENDNOTE

Emerson, Ralph Waldo. "Address to the Inhabitants of Concord at the Consecration of Sleepy Hollow Cemetery, September 29, 1855." *The Later Lectures of Ralph Waldo Emerson, 1843–1871.* Vol. 2. Ed. Ronald A. Bosco and Joel Myerson. Athens, GA: University of Georgia Press, 2001.

Dear Readers,

Thank you for taking this journey with me into the world of *The Booby Trap*. I've been addicted to romance novels ever since I first read *Silver Springs* by Carolyn Lampman as a young teenager. Embarrassingly, it got in the hands of my younger cousin, a voracious reader and kid who wanted to be "grown up" like me. But my initiation into romance novels has led to many happy hours of reading.

One thing I love in my novels—romance or not—is a smart, savvy, sassy heroine. I tried to create Bambi to be one of those women. Did I succeed? You're the judge.

I hope you enjoyed *The Booby Trap*. If you did, I encourage you to follow me at www.annebrowningwalker.com. You can stay tuned as I begin writing my second novel, tentatively titled *The Getaway Car*. In it, a 3000-mile road trip brings a broken woman back into contact with a college flame, who seems as wild as ever. With an open road, a steamy history, and a newfound chemistry, there are as many possibilities as there are miles to go before they reach the West Coast . . . and the rest of their lives.

Thanks!
Anne